About the author

Martin Morton lives mostly in the Adriatic on a boat.

Visit Martin Morton at www.martinmorton.co.uk

Lion and Giant
Book 6 of The Claudia Series

Martin Morton

Lion and Giant

Chimera

Lion and Giant

The Claudia Series Book 6

Other titles in the series:

The Water's Edge;

The Water's Depth;

Careless Hours;

The Mist in the Valleys;

Catch Me.

Introduction

Hi, and welcome.

I very much hope you will enjoy the unfolding story.

Lion and Giant is about a particular phase in our characters' lives, yet is a complete story in itself.

For the new readers, however, I thought an introduction might be helpful.

Claudia Brodie and Peter Dickinson have settled together and successfully restructured his complex, global business after his divorce, from which he had escaped with far less damage than he had, at one time, feared.

The divorce process, and the break-up of Claudia's intense affair with Jack Stephens, had been complicated by the clandestine interference of Rod Henderson through his shadowy Networks organisation.

As part of the restructuring, Alphonse Newman, Peter's property group head, is planning a huge Asian expansion into luxury resorts in partnership with the Senlin Group, owned by the Shen family. Peter had initially been sceptical of the plan but had been won round by pressure from his Funds Group, of which the Senlin Group is a major client, and by the more considered and independent views of Will Uprichard, his finance head.

Isobel Allen, an old friend of Will's who had also worked on a project in Peter's house, has been invited, on Peter's recommendation to Alphonse, to submit designs for the hotel projects.

She will be your principal guide through the story.

Lion and Giant is about how the expansion unfolds.

I hope you find it absorbing and entertaining,
Martin

1

"Isobel, it's Alphonse Newman."

"Good morning. I'm glad you called. Tell me, do we know each other well enough for me to tell you straight that I'm not happy with you?"

"I would like to think so. Do you want to go ahead and tell me why?"

"I've seen the magazine shoot on that new resort property of yours."

"Morkuda?"

"That's the one. Do you want to guess why I'm unhappy?"

"Because the décor in the villas is too close to your proposals?"

I don't flabbergast easily, but then, I'm more used to people squirming on issues like this. It's quite common, of course, and they'll tell you that they've observed contractual obligations and paid a fee for your designs — but they squirm because they know the understanding is always that the designer should implement the scheme. Especially here, where the finished article looks so splendid in a glossy magazine and I get no credit whatsoever. And now I have this smooth bastard explaining to me exactly why I'm unhappy.

"You're not even going to try to deny it!"

"Would you feel any better if I did?"

Actually, I probably wouldn't, I prefer to be very straight with people. "No, so are you ringing to apologise?"

"I would if I felt it necessary, but I'm calling to talk business."

I'm busy, but I don't turn things away lightly; nevertheless, I'm not looking for new ways to supply brilliant designs to copycats who implement on the cheap. I didn't expect it. I'd done a bedroom and bathroom project for his boss in Barnes a couple of years ago and I couldn't have had a more charming, decisive and punctilious client. For a man to spend that much money and take that much trouble for his beloved, well, I didn't abandon my cynicism about the ways of men, but I was able to suspend it for the duration.

Punctilious is important to me: I want to get every detail right, always, and I love working with people to whom it's also important; and I had this man, with his multi-billion-dollar empire to attend to, spending hours with me on every aspect of the project. I don't want to meet the woman; she could only disappoint.

And I thought this Alphonse might be the same as his boss — and the project was much bigger, a resort hotel and forty-eight villas in Malaysia! He was exactly as smooth and charming as his boss, even more deliciously handsome — and younger! I almost wanted my gaydar to be faulty — there was certainly something ambiguous about him — but project first! I submitted designs that met their target budget — but I insisted they should allow a significant contingency on a project like this; we argued about that as well as the timings. Finally — well, quite soon to be fair — I heard that they'd chosen someone else: OK, that can happen — but then to steal my fucking designs! More or less.

"Are you prepared to have a conversation?"

I'd been slow responding, I'd obviously been letting too many thoughts go through my head, "I'd like to be sure I'd have a chance of implementing this time, or you won't get the quality you say you're striving for — and I'd like to get my name in the glossies. I'm a working girl, publicity matters."

"I really am sorry you feel bad about Morkuda, it was down to time scales in the end. I just didn't feel confident you could guarantee to meet the deadline on such a remote project. We obviously thought your designs superior, but I think you'd have needed more time to meet our cost targets. I should also say the discussion we had on your contingency budget counted against you. As it was, we came in under target."

The bastard had made some fair points, "So why do you think I could meet timing and cost on anything new? Are we less remote this time?"

"No, we're still talking Asia; but we're rolling out, initially, to five new locations throughout the region.

The other seven will follow, but they're not so run down. They'll be OK for a couple of years under the new managers. But these five are urgent, although I do want them done perfectly. I want the designs to belong to a family, but each location will have its own distinctive features. It's the overall design schemes I'm looking for and the local interpretations of each one. I'd still implement locally, the team is well-connected out there, but there are two reasons why I'd like you to work with us on this."

"You weren't convinced before that I could combine urgent and perfect."

"That's still a discussion we need to have. But perfect is priority."

"Good! Anyway, go on." Obviously, this is interesting, but I'm still feeling sore about the spread in the glossies — more about the theft of ideas, though, than about publicity.

"First, your designs were obviously superior. You caught the right balance: there's what the premium traveller wants in terms of luxury and features, but she or he also wants it sympathetic to the environment of the locale. They want to feel they're somewhere at least distinctive, but ideally unique. I have to compliment you on that, you hadn't had a site visit, but you did do very well. Our clients want to feel they're somewhere distinctively different, with indigenous features and atmosphere, but they don't want to compromise at all on their comforts — or even on their luxuries."

"I could have done better still with a trip to the region." That was true, but I'd rather opened the door for the rejoinder.

"I would have happily funded that but…"

"I know, I know, that would have made the timing worse. What's the second point?"

"Well, the local people did well — and I'm not denying they copied a lot but, contractually, we had bought your designs — now we have to move further afield and I want someone independent who can conceive the overview but then give appropriate local interpretations. I think your sensitivity, coupled with your outstanding talent, would enable you to do both. Can we talk about it?"

"We can certainly talk about it. Will you come to the studio?"

"I have all the plans and layouts in my office; it's easier to talk there, when do you have some time?"

"Friday afternoon?"

"Perfect."

"I'll see you at four, then," I say. Excellent. I like serious people, not people whose weekends start at lunchtime. Look, I'm intrigued, and I have loads of questions — and maybe he has too. I do very little work out of the country — or out of London for that matter; the big houses in the country usually arise after a London commission.

But I put a lot of work into the hotel project, it was a new area for me and, OK, it would have helped to travel there, but I spent lots of evening and weekend time doing all the research I could. That's why I was so pissed off seeing 'my' designs, unattributed, in the magazine.

He doesn't have the class of his boss.

OK, time for a little intrigue here. I loved the bedroom project — and I'm still hoping they'll want the whole of that house done — but when I asked if I could see the whole house to get a sense of what I would be integrating into, I was given a very 'interesting' tour by my host. He has these wonderful blue eyes, and he'd looked straight at me and said, 'I'm guessing you're broad-minded enough to cope with the cellar's unusual uses.' I knew what he meant immediately. I felt almost disappointed that I'd never made it to any events there in my past. He was very matter-of-fact about it but said it didn't get used much these days.

Hmm, I'm not getting used much these days!

There was another strange aspect of the project. It was set up by a contact, a German-sounding guy, called Andreas, I think, so I didn't meet Peter until I got to the house. I realised immediately who it must be, but I didn't want to embarrass Will by revealing that connection.

Ah, Will! He's married now. He did tell me, bless him. But it shook me. I'd looked after him when Merle left him — and helped him, I think, when she wrote to him a year later and he was wavering. So, I saw him every one or two months and we were very good together. Not a real match, of course, we're both a bit toppy for that, but I loved being with him. He was probably the most straightforward man I've met. Not like Alphonse the snake, trying to tell me it was my fault because of timings. Will would never have done that, it was so easy to have this honest, open relationship with him.

I should be careful here; when I say relationship in this context, I mean arrangement. We had similar kinks. When I called him straightforward just now, I meant that he was, or became, entirely comfortable with his kinks — a lot of people never do — and I like to feel I educated him. Well, I certainly did that, but I'd given up on relationships. I just liked being with like-minded people. And he was free too, after Merle, and reluctant to re-engage in anything serious. He knew a few girls in Brussels, where he lived mostly, and I assumed he had a few adventures on his travels. But maybe I'm projecting there. He was very serious about work. Thinking back, very little really distracted him.

So, when he said he was getting close to someone, I was surprised. But I'd always told him that might happen. And that I would understand.

I just didn't think it would.

And I didn't!

I was brave. I don't think he ever knew how much it hurt. But I always allow myself to take things at face value. It's up to you to be honest with me, and I'll take you at your word.

But I hadn't been honest with him. I'd told him it wouldn't matter.

I think I may even have believed that but, really, I wasn't being honest with myself. That's what I've had to come to terms with.

Then finding out she was my age...

Yes, that did make it worse.

I haven't contacted him. Obviously, I'm less self-aware than I thought, but I still have class.

It would have been wrong... I'm fairly sure.

Enough of my reveries! I've introduced you to Alphonse, and Will, and Peter Dickinson. Oh, and Merle. I need to say more about them.

Let's get her out of the way first. She was married to Michael, who was Will's boss at the time, and Will and she 'fell in love'. They actually did, I only put the parenthesis there because the way you interpret that phrase is so dependent on your own experiences. But they did, and they were actually in love — however you looked at it and they were also quite well-suited. He is a top, as I've said, which I'd helped him discover, and she was a classic bottom, with all the manipulative skills and self-centredness that bottoms bring to everything.

It might have worked, but there was a massive financial scandal that her husband had perpetrated and Will had uncovered. There were all sorts of threats and Merle, with typical selfish cowardice, just ran away. She's regretted it bitterly since, but the poor man was devastated.

Will, I mean, of course. Michael found an escape route. I still see him occasionally. I top him, but he's less fun these days.

I don't mind you being intrigued by my sexuality, but we've no need to spend time on it here, we have time later. I should use this opportunity to tell you more about Peter D and Will.

Peter rescued Will, through a connection in his empire that Will had been working with — that was where the scandal started when Michael tried to exploit something Will was doing for them. So, Will ended up, broken-hearted, in Brussels, enjoying the occasional solace of visits from me.

So, through Will, I'd had a little history of Peter, right up to the time of his expensive divorce, but it was about then that Will met this other woman, Martha. I'm sure we'll talk more about her later, damn it!

But I was naturally very intrigued to get the summons, once I'd realised who it was. Will had always spoken so highly of him, and the feeling must obviously be mutual, since Will's career seems to have progressed stratospherically in that organisation. And it's a huge organisation: there's a funds division, they were the guys who engaged Will, originally; there's a property division, this is Alphonse, who's now expanding that division into resorts, hence my involvement; and there's a group of manufacturing and consultancy units that seems to be run by this woman, Claudia, who now sleeps in one of the world's most desirable bedrooms. (You're not going to get false modesty from me; don't go looking for it!)

Anyway, I'm not surprised my boy has done well. Will is just about the brightest and most balanced man I've ever met. Yes, I've missed him.

I wonder if I'll get a chance to meet him.

2

Bringing in Isobel hadn't been a condition Peter had placed on the project, but Alphonse felt he was being given a definite steer.

Peter was resigned to the resort programme now and one of the few real elements of enthusiasm he'd shown, at that first stage, was on the villa designs that Isobel had submitted. They were the best, undoubtedly, but she was pushing to exceed the budget he'd given her — 'I'm being honest with you, and you've been in property long enough to know that's rare' — and her timings didn't fit. Morkuda, their second site, would be truly new and they wanted themselves established quickly.

She was an interesting woman. Peter evidently thought so. Alphonse never questioned his devotion to Claudia — which caused problems because of Alphonse's own feelings — but he felt certain Peter would have enjoyed Isobel's company at the parties in the old days. Although, if Alphonse's intuition was correct, they wouldn't have been play partners directly. Peter's tastes were quite narrow, it seemed to Alphonse, and he liked to take people on as projects. He rather felt that Isobel might do that too.

She wasn't one for him, anyway, so there would be no complicating chemistry on the project. But he enjoyed dealing with her, she had a frank manner that was unusual among her peers, and she had grasped the brief quickly and delivered the submission on time; it had been her implementation timescale that hadn't met his needs.

He doubted whether the other London-based designer would have even met the timetable, although he was claiming to be able to do so. Somehow Isobel had more credibility. He'd also resented the less than subtle come-on from the man, combined with a hint that this should be a 'wavelength thing between us' — oh please, he'd thought stylish always; camp never!

Not that Alphonse was averse to business and pleasure mixing but, when that happened, business came emphatically first.

He'd gathered an impression that Isobel might look at life the same way. Peter's appreciation of her work seemed to imply that he'd enjoyed dealing with her and, to be fair, so had Alphonse and he was glad she'd accepted the invitation. Her reaction hadn't been unexpected, but his conscience was fairly clear — and the next stage would be a far bigger project. The deal had been done; the chain had been bought. He smiled to himself, he'd pushed the bank down from two point five to two point three billion. Within that, he was buying the extra sites that the bank had acquired at fire-sale prices two years before when the family selling the chain was struggling with cash-flow. Armed with exact numbers and dark hints of making information more widely available, he was able to renegotiate them down to three hundred million for the greenfield sites — they were still almost trebling their money.

He'd been delighted with the deal. He'd got them down to two for the chain initially by offering five hundred for the extra sites. So, a chain of twelve properties being marketed for three billion — four initially, but there had been no interest then — was acquired for two point three, including six extra undeveloped locations, all superb. Excellent, he even had enough funds now to move on his Whitsundays project — although he mistrusted his own emotional commitment to that venture. He loved the place too much, probably, never a good basis for a decision.

That also might be pushing things too far with Peter, who seemed to have settled down now. He just wasn't sure that Claudia was perfectly content, and their awkwardness now with each other told him that she was managing her feelings for him about as well as he was managing his feelings for her. There was an implicit understanding that Peter would be relaxed if the two of them resurrected their old arrangement of occasional meetings, but they also shared an unspoken awareness that feelings would run too deep and not be easily concealed.

Isobel arrived at four, with a cheery smile; he appeared to have been forgiven. And was she just a little smarter than last time? More effort being made? Of course, but that was a common practice among the clients, designers and architects he dealt with. At least with her he had the impression that she understood how much effort went into seeming so perfectly casual. But that was the part of the morning he always enjoyed; thinking of appointments, locations, weather, and clients — and challenging himself to find the one outfit for the day. Occasionally a lunchtime change was necessary — standards must never slip — but he always caught himself smiling in the mirror as his last act before leaving the apartment, almost mocking himself. But, yes, it was important — and it was what he was!

The Chelsea office was lightly used, but a necessary extravagance. Hayley kept the admin together but was seldom there. He trusted her completely and the informal arrangement they'd developed enabled her to deal with two young children. She attempted to overlap with his rare office days, but he was surprised to see her still there at four on a Friday. "Thank you for staying, but there is really no need."

She had smiled, "He tells me he likes to come home early on Fridays to play with them, so they're looked after," then she chuckled, "but I dread what I have to go back to. I do want to keep abreast here, though, it's the biggest thing we've ever done. Do you mind if I sit in?"

"I'd be delighted, thank you. It will get more and more complex." She was very good at managing projects and, with operations increasingly global, it

meant her hours could be easily flexible. He'd brought
her from his old firm when Peter asked him to set up the
property operation. She'd been savvy enough from the
start to understand him and hadn't gone through the
embarrassing infatuation phase that affected most of her
team. He was always surprised that any new starter's
colleagues would let them discover his orientation for
themselves. It was cruel, and it happened less after
Hayley had joined, so she was an obvious choice to ask
to join him — and that worked out well with her
marriage and family plans; he could offer flexibility no
normal business would. She'd more than repaid him
with hours and commitment, in addition to expertise,
humour and charm.

"Isobel, this is Hayley. She runs the business."

They shook hands warmly, "I've had most of the
stuff from you, haven't I?"

Hayley smiled, "Yes, there is only me here in this
office. And I know it may be a touchy subject, but can I
say how impressed I was with your designs on the
Morkuda project."

Alphonse hadn't really briefed her but, as was usual
with Hayley's instincts, it did seem to dispel any
residual tensions. Isobel smiled, "Well, let's hope I have
more success this time. Are these they?"

She was looking at models of hotel buildings and
villas on the large table in the room behind the small
reception area.

"Yes, they're the architects' initial schemes and the maps of the locations are all around the wall. Shall I take a deep breath and start?"

"And shall I organise drinks while he's doing that?"

"Wonderful. Earl Grey?"

"Of course. You too?" Alphonse nodded and when Hayley stepped out, he began to take Isobel through the whole plan.

He loved discussions on the subject, it became more real each time. The two steps already: the takeover at Teluk and the project at Morkuda had been great thrills but here he would be creating his whole Psamathe chain — and although Peter hadn't been wholly wrong in attributing his initial motivation as being competitive, of wanting to outdo his old lover's family — the project now had its own life and it was becoming his central obsession. He'd picked his architects as much for their enthusiasm as for their reputation and he wanted Isobel to be similarly infected. He had the sense she might be, she'd put a lot into the initial design, presumably because it was so new and different for her; and, although he hadn't doubted her motivation, it was a useful measure of her intense interest that she'd come today without him having to apply too much charm.

So, here she was, listening intently, asking lots of questions, better informed on the geography than he'd expected: "No, not been there much, but Hayley had sent me the locations and I checked them out." She hadn't added 'of course', that would have been crass, but it was implied — and inferred. He thought she was showing signs of catching the disease, as well as showing the professionalism he'd expected.

"Have you been out there much?"

"A lot in the last three years. I'm not going to say that the travel is easy, but the evening's first cocktail, looking at the sun setting on the water — most of the terraces face west — makes even the most hideous journey seem worthwhile."

"And you, Hayley?"

Hayley laughed, "I think I've been promised a family vacation when the first new one opens," she looked to Alphonse.

"Most definitely, here in front of a witness." Isobel smiled. "But look, it's six. I think we might go on talking a while." He turned to Isobel and was delighted to see her nodding vigorously, "I don't think we should trust him with bath-time, do you?"

Hayley laughed, "Thank you, but I didn't want to miss this. It seems to move on every time." She turned to Isobel, "I'd better get going. It's been lovely meeting you; I do hope you come on board… Oops, I'm not supposed to say that, am I?"

But she was. It was one of the little tricks she and Alphonse employed in their assessments of people. And they both wanted Isobel working on this.

When Hayley had left, Alphonse said, "I'm sensing a curiosity which might keep you here a while yet." He looked at her expectantly, she nodded again, "Do you have plans for the evening or could we let this roll on into dinner?"

"I think you're trying to enthuse me, Mister Newman, and I should reserve my position until I'm clearer about the deal." He smiled at her, it usually worked. "But thank you, I am sufficiently intrigued."

"Wonderful. Let me see what I can book and then we can get back to it."

***

He managed to get a late table at Marcus', ideal for a quiet discussion — and it would help her to feel flattered, without seeming, for her, he assumed, overly extravagant.

She'd nodded to his champagne question as they sat down, but she started with a question of her own before it arrived, "Can you help me on a personal point?"

"If I can, certainly."

"I didn't mention it to Peter, but I knew one of his people quite well a few years ago…"

Alphonse smiled, "You know I'm going to ask why you couldn't mention it to Peter."

"I wasn't assessing you as an insensitive man," she smiled, "just pleasantly forthright, I knew you'd ask. I like that. Anyway, it was Will Uprichard; is he still with you?"

Alphonse was quickly making assessments — assumptions, if he was honest with himself. "Very much

28

so, he's our finance head. He's the man who releases the money for me; he's based in New York now." He couldn't tell from her face what she was thinking — or feeling. "I wouldn't expect you to meet him, but you'll obviously get publicity in the Dickinson organisation if you take this on. Is there something embarrassing I should understand."

"Oh no; it's just, well, I knew him well for a time but we've rather lost contact since he got married. She's a banker, isn't she? I didn't want to be a ghost reappearing."

"Martha is a banker, yes, very senior." This was a time to avoid fatuous clichés, there had obviously been a serious relationship of sorts and it would intrigue him to understand it better — but that could come later perhaps, if the project got underway with Isobel and, as they raised their champagne glasses, his conviction was growing that it would.

3

"I'm impressed young man. When you wrote twelve, I assumed you meant your time. Are you always in the office by seven?"

"Usually, but it's so lovely to hear you. I was intrigued by your email, and a bit thrilled. I think it's a fantastic project but that's just between you and me. Officially, I'm the custodian of Peter Dickinson's best interests, and I remain at all times neutral, cautious and sceptical. You remember who he is."

"Of course I do. I did a project for him, in fact, in Barnes, but I didn't want to make any embarrassing connections and you were just heading towards married bliss. I suppose that's still going bloody well, is it?"

Will laughed, "It's wonderful, thank you."

"You realise I hate her… don't worry, I'm thrilled for you, just jealous, that's all."

"I don't need to remind you how you'd sworn off relationships, and… my God, it's seven in the morning and I'm in the office, this isn't a conversation about that, is it?"

"No, no, it's just like I wrote, I wanted to let you know I might be working with Alphonse. I didn't want you to get surprised by that. I've told him I knew you;

30

well, I sort of hinted we were quite close. I think he will have read between the lines."

"Oh, he will surely have read between the lines."

"He is gay, isn't he? I'm sorry, I've no right to ask Well, there's lots that intrigue me about him and the project, but I'm not going to try to bully you into being unprofessional or, better still, indiscreet. Ha, as if I could."

"Well, I'm thrilled you've made contact. I've been feeling a little ashamed, I should have been in touch."

"Don't be silly, my boy, you might have got my hopes up. Don't worry, but I would like a longer chat sometime and, I'll admit, I would like your perspective on this project however unfair it is to ask for that."

"You're right to see it that way, I'm afraid. But I'm sure you'll get everything you want from Alphonse; I admire him immensely — oops! You won't mention that to him, will you?"

"Ha, of course not, but thank you for the comment. I'm feeling inclined to trust him, he's been very frank and straightforward, I think, but it's good to have that confirmed."

"You're very welcome — and you're right on the other thing, to a degree, but I think he does have a more interesting life than that. Not one for you, though, I wouldn't have thought. Anyway, can we agree to keep in touch now? I just don't feel that gossipy at seven."
"I'd love to. Email me when it would suit you."

***

Ah, I love him. He was sweet when he told me about this woman he'd fallen for. I don't think I reacted very well. And that meant I couldn't ask that much about her, but I'm going to assume, if she's happy with Will, that she has some specific tastes. I wonder if he'll tell me when we chat.

His great love, Merle, is still unhappy, still not divorced, still not living with her husband. Still working for me sometimes, but I've obviously kept her away from these projects.

She's not looking quite like she used to, now — she was a gloriously beautiful woman. I wonder how Will is — my God, early thirties, he must be fabulous now; he sounded wonderful. I'll make him talk more soon.

4

"Good morning, Isobel, it's Alphonse again."

"Gosh, I'd only just posted my thank-you note this morning." She was plainly joking, "I enjoyed dinner very much, seriously, thank you."

"I had a wonderful time too, so thank you, and I'm calling hoping I can book you for something next week."

"Weeell, I hope you won't think me overly sensitive, but do we have timing for agreeing a contract this time? I assume it's about Project Psamathe — am I pronouncing that right?"

"Absolutely, silent p, Samath. She was the goddess of the sea-shore."

"You don't want my views on the name, do you?"

"I suspect I could have those for free, without a contract." She laughed. "Hayley is getting something to you by Friday. I'm around over the weekend if you need to discuss any of it."

"In a hurry?"

"I don't want to make it seem hasty, but I have two people in London next week who represent the family putting half of the money into this deal. I'd like to get you signed up so you can meet them. They've bought property here from us as part of the deal, and they're reviewing that. They've asked if I can also take them through the Project Psamathe, now that you've given it a name."

"It's your bloody stupid name."

"I think that was my free advice, wasn't it?"

She laughed again. He was beginning to enjoy her. People were seldom so open. She seemed entirely comfortable with herself, even though it sounded like her social diary was a little less full these days. She must have been pretty when she was younger — but the laughter lines she displayed so easily now, he found very appealing.

"You're welcome to it. Maybe I'll just call it The Project."

"Call it whatever you like, as long as you'll work on it."

"I shall read Hayley's paperwork extraordinarily carefully. The fact that she's even more charming than you are has made me very suspicious. But I can make myself available next week, I think, I'll need to check. You obviously have a date in mind?"

"Wednesday. I have them all day, I'll show them around the properties first, then get to my office around three, if you can manage it. I'm putting them in the Berkeley, so it's Marcus' for dinner again, I'm afraid."

"Alphonse, you're beginning to bore me!" He laughed with her. She paused, probably checking the diary, he thought. "Wednesday's good. Tell me something about them."

And he described the Hong Kong meeting, which was the only serious face-to-face time he'd had: Harry Li, the deal-maker, who affected a kin-relationship with the family with the money, but Alphonse had suspected it was, at best, distant; and Mei Tang, the project director, who'd seemed so fierce, but whose ideas had enabled them to structure the deal in a way that Peter, ultimately, had found acceptable.

It would be a business meeting but, Alphonse was smiling to himself, if personalities were a large room, these four characters would be far apart in its distant corners. But he should let the day unfold, he'd only spent time with Harry and Mei in a business conversation. He would be glad of Isobel's company at dinner, he thought.

She called him on Sunday morning, not too early, but had few comments on the contract, she seemed quite content with that. She talked more about Will. She'd called him and wanted to let Alphonse know. That was a fair point, but she began to ask more about his life now and it made it easy for him to confirm his earlier impression — her feelings had been quite strong. What Will's had been, he didn't know, but on the few occasions he'd seen him with Martha, they'd seemed very happy. It wasn't that Isobel was being too intrusive, but he'd merely begun to feel uncomfortable.

He would mention the phone call to Will when they next spoke.

***

When Alphonse brought his guests to the office on the Wednesday afternoon, Isobel was already there, chatting with Hayley in reception. She, at least, looked cheery. He'd had not such a good morning. The Chinese family's property investments were mainly centred in China and the US and consisted almost entirely of modern buildings. The air of tired dilapidation of the London properties had plainly disappointed them, although they'd had them surveyed and had been sent thick folders of pictures. There were many questions about the costs of renovation, all of which Alphonse had handled with his usual suave patience. But he became aware as they travelled around that he was being stretched and that drove him, as it usually did, to an exaggerated politeness that beguiled strangers. Hayley and others saw through it quickly. He'd texted a progress report to her at lunchtime and she'd evidently been able to forewarn Isobel, who welcomed the guests surprisingly effusively.

She commandeered the first hour, starting blithely with, "You poor things have had him all morning around our old city. Would you like to look at the future with me?"

Alphonse was slightly staggered, she worked from her laptop, projecting on to the big screen. She introduced herself and her business with photos from some of her projects, including a lavish blue bedroom that he guessed must be Peter's, and then moved on to schemes and sketches that she'd developed for Morkuda. He felt slightly embarrassed at that point by how closely they'd been copied. That could have led Harry and Mei to assume that she was the designer for that resort — well, in a way, he thought, she was, and it was no bad thing if they thought so. But then she came on to her first thoughts for the new places. She must have developed these in the past week and managed to talk, quite convincingly he thought, about particular detailing she would be aiming to integrate to make the resorts harmonise with their locations. And there were examples of furniture and design features that she maintained would be appropriate in Cambodia, Vietnam, Thailand, Indonesia and the Philippines. Alphonse had truly no idea how accurate or honest that was, but it was impressive showmanship.

He wanted to hug her, but he daren't risk any more than an appreciative nod.

The compliments rained down from Harry, "Oh, thank you so much Isobel, now I know why we want to work with this man — and especially with you. These will be splendid, wonderful."

Isobel beamed, "Thank you, Harry, I'm very excited by it, I get quite carried away — but

compliments are always welcome," and here Alphonse
was treated to an evil smile. He could only smirk and
nod. She would soon tire of making this point — he
hoped — and she had too much sense to actually
mention the compliment of plagiarism.

But Mei, as he'd expected, was harder to please, her
severity unbending. "May we discuss why you have
chosen these five as phase one, please?" Harry had
moved closer to Isobel and was looking at some of the
drawings and photos she'd brought with her. Alphonse
found their quiet whispers slightly distracting and he
knew he would get no respite from Mei. Even talking
louder didn't seem to encourage Harry and Isobel to pay
attention.

Why those five? They were, as he'd told Isobel, the
most urgent. He'd rather have rolled out in steps of
three, but Raymond, his CEO Resorts, saw no prospect
of these five making money and even good
management, which would help, would be quickly
demoralised. He was trying to make these points as
patiently as he could to Mei. It was a relatively easy
conclusion that he and Raymond had quickly reached
but any point he made was fiercely questioned by her:
couldn't you get better managers; couldn't you go
faster, our money is already available; should you go
slower then, if five at one time is so hard; are you sure
about cost control? And, inevitably, it seemed, pointing
out that Morkuda had come in under budget prompted a

'does that mean there is too much contingency in all these estimates?'

"May I come in on that one?" asked Isobel, taking a break from entertaining Harry — Alphonse was surprised that she'd also been paying attention to a conversation that was becoming a strain. "Between you and me, Mei, I suspect Alphonse just got lucky with Morkuda. In my experience, each major project encounters at least one disaster. Most clients are happier, though, with a rebate from a higher base than with a request to provide over-budget money. I think your point's a very good one, but my personal recommendation would be that you leave the money in, but you monitor progress closely. If there are no major problems, then expect some money back." Now she smiled, "Well, actually, you go in and demand it, girl!" That little speech had jarred with Alphonse, he felt sure that Mei would not have welcomed being spoken to like that but, there she was, smiling and nodding for the first time today.

***

When they had wrapped up and sent the guests to their hotel to get ready for dinner, Alphonse sat down with her in reception. "How come you got a smile out of her?"

"Oh, my poor dear man. She'd been trying so hard to get you to take her seriously but there you were, patiently paternal all afternoon. I think she thought she'd have to bite you to get a reaction. Don't let her worry you, though, she's gay, she won't come on to you."

Alphonse shook his head, slightly stunned, "I normally think I can spot that sort of thing."

She beamed at him, "Ah, there are still things I can teach you, maybe, even Harry might be a little interesting."

Alphonse looked at her with a puzzled frown.

"I think he might be more one for me as well, but at least you've introduced me to two potentially interesting people. Nevertheless," she enunciated slowly and loudly, "you and I are kindred spirits, I think. We always put work first!"

He smiled, "Work first! But I think we've earned a drink now, don't you?"

"Yes, I've just signed a big contract."

"Shouldn't I have signed it too?"

"Hayley did."

He laughed, "Let's go."

* * *

They weren't meeting until seven-thirty, so had almost an hour to themselves, "I'm going to bore you again by starting non-alcoholic, but may I order champagne for you."

"Go on, then, indiscretion is my trademark."

He smiled, "I don't think that claim is remotely fanciful — but, before we get carried away with anything outrageous, can I just say a big thank you for today and how thrilled I am you're with us on this. And, however you choose to interpret it, there were compliments in there."

"Oh, I'd already had the compliment of you stealing all my ideas on the first project, thank you," she smiled as he ordered the drinks, he could only smile back and hope that was the end of it — she'd signed now, for heaven's sake! "You're going to tell me more about this deal, aren't you?"

"Well, at the risk of boring you again, yes. The Shen family are Shanghai-based and immensely rich; rich enough to have moved out from their industrial base and created a family office, which manages all their investments outside the original conglomerate. It's now larger than the base business, and it focuses on funds and properties. They have a lot of money with GKD, that's Peter's fund group, and that's doing very well for them, but haven't been so successful with property, so they wanted to partner us on this. I met the old man and the two sons two years ago when we were making a big Asian push for new money and new partners. It was very successful for Tony, that's Tony King, the K of GKD, but, of course, with Peter there, it's easy to get people charmed," he paused, "as I think you've discovered."

"Oh, unquestionably, I ended up hating his wife, without even meeting her."

"I adore her, unfortunately," he regretted saying it, but thought that he and Isobel would be moving to quite a close relationship, a prospect that appealed to him, and a few personal insights would help that progress.

"I thought… sorry. Shut up, Isobel. I'm the last person who should query relationships."

"Yes, let's see… Will obviously means a lot to you, or did…"

"Still does, really," and she looked slightly rueful.

"You've tuned in to Mei — although I should have spotted that…"

"Hey, I'm not saying she interests me… but, well, maybe… a little… we'll see," and she was smiling as the drinks came.

"And Harry?"

"Just a little something; I think he might feel quite at home in Peter's cellar," now the smile was wicked.

"Where you, yourself…"

"Would feel entirely at home, yes. Not you so much, I don't think."

"Not so much, no, I tended to stay above ground at the parties, but that's a different story; we should get plenty of time during the project to talk more about that. We should focus on the Senlin group now. You're saying that even these two are interesting." She nodded. "Well, that won't be the only source of intrigue. The older son, who should take over everything, is gay and enjoys exactly as much love and respect from his father as you'd get from any right-thinking capitalist monster." She was smiling, he was relieved, it was meant to be irony, but it had come out too harshly "Look, I put that badly, it's only important because of the tensions it creates in what are now our partners."

"Not because number one son interests you."

"No, I'm being objective about this, but it will impact the project at some stage, if they all get involved."

"And who's principally interested? No, don't tell me. Number one son?"

"Drink your champagne, Isobel, work first, remember." But he'd probably given that away.

5

Well, I enjoyed that evening very much. I know he worried about my drinking, but I slowed down — work first! — he can be a little po-faced, but I do like him. It was the two Chinese, however, who interested me more — oh, don't get me wrong, whatever develops with Alphonse may be quite deep, that's a sense I have, but it will be a friendship only — but these two, in their different ways, were clearly a little taken with me. They both, separately and ever so discreetly, managed to slide me their business cards, without all this absurd Asian double-handed protocol, and said 'I hope we can keep in touch', or words to that effect. I, of course, would be happy playing with either — or both, if it came to it; that was just a cheeky little scene I was quietly imagining in my morning reverie today.

I could understand Mei's reaction to me quite easily; I know I do send out these waves, and it was a different woman who turned up for dinner, she is really quite pretty and didn't seem to mind appearing feminine. There was quite a lot of genteel hand-touching, too. Oh, yes, I admit it, I encouraged it. It was nice, and it was a sweet little kiss when we parted. But let's get the project underway, my dear, before we indulge ourselves.

But, in all my years of playing, I've found it more difficult to understand how men pick up the signals from me — my domme signals, I mean. But Harry plainly did and yes, I would be interested. He's youngish, OK, thirties, but this is my viewpoint nowadays. He's very well-groomed and fit-looking and... well, here I'm going to say something I shouldn't, as a responsible top, admit to... he inspired just that little frisson of contempt in me that I like to have if I'm going to treat my bottom to a real thrill. I think I could make him really enjoy a couple of hours, and he would inspire me to be quite imaginative — and decently cruel. Before you get too censorious, or accuse me of hypocrisy, you must remember that the bottom's experience is paramount and they all, to some degree, need that little bit of cruelty in their tops — and if it comes enriched with the sauce of authenticity, it can enhance the experience.

I will always prefer, if you're interested, a little cuddle time at the end of play, but I would never dream of attempting to impose that on a bottom who wanted a purer, more ascetic experience.

I think Harry would want a cuddle, and I'd be happy with that.

As a girl, of course, Mei will be a little more complex. I'm quite looking forward to investigating that. The passive-aggressive side she showed yesterday could indicate she might go either way, or even, and this would be stimulating, both ways. No, no, she is a lesbian, this speculation is about whether she tops or bottoms — and my preference is for people who like both. I'll tell you more about Will later, if it becomes relevant to the story.

Alphonse? I can easily imagine people being in love with him but, for playtimes, I prefer a little more spice.

But I am excited by it all. I've been busy enough, but everything has become a little humdrum here, both professionally and socially. But this! Well, I haven't worked through a weekend in years, but I did so want to make an impression yesterday.

And no, my dears, if the contract hadn't arrived on Friday, I wouldn't have lifted a finger.

Well, maybe that's not quite true, I'd probably have been researching. After all, I'm an Arbeitstier, as the Germans say, a work animal.

Work first! Jawohl, Herr Alphonse.

6

"Are you going to explain to me how you can possibly deal with Rod Henderson again?" It had been a tense breakfast and the topic had been hovering over them. Claudia had been hoping she would calm down and find a subtler way into the subject, but she could wait no longer.

"Technically and officially, my darling, this concerns funds and property and doesn't affect your group." She must have touched a nerve, he seldom appeared this pompous.

"Officially, my darling, I have board member oversight on all Peter Dickinson activities. Unofficially I can't believe you're doing this, and I can't believe you were going to slide it past me." Claudia couldn't remember feeling angrier — not since her life with Dave, her ex, and that felt like a lifetime ago. But Peter's preternatural calm still seemed almost undented.

He exhaled slowly, "Are we still going to the boat? Your guys are already there. If I promise to spend the journey trying to explain, will you calm down and get packed?"

She was still seething, "Only if you'll agree, in good faith, that you're prepared to reconsider."

"Of course I will, but what hurts about that," and now even the supremely placid Peter Dickinson finally looked a little tetchy, "is that I've never done anything in bad faith with you."

Now she stood up from the breakfast table and nudged him, "Bastard, that was a silly cliché of mine, now you've got me morally in the wrong. Cuddle! That's an order!"

He smiled, stood up and enveloped her, bear-like. It was a big body, and she loved it. "I do understand where you're coming from — and I really wasn't trying to slide it past you," he said.

"It was on your list for today?" and she looked up at him with a sceptical eye.

He smiled back, "It was," he protested, "well, for the weekend, anyway." Her look didn't change, "Maybe not the weekend, I'm hosting four young people, but we'd agreed a meeting on Wednesday, hadn't we, when Alphonse gets there? I might be able to make a better case when you've seen the whole picture."

"But you're committed to reconsidering?"

"I'm committed to reconsidering."

She thought that was probably genuine, he wasn't generally one for just mollifying the little woman. "Then I'll pack."

She still couldn't believe it, after all that had been said — and done. Henderson had, effectively, stolen twenty million dollars and Peter was considering using him again. It had been part of the settlement that he would retain Dickinson Enterprises, nominally, as a client but she was fairly sure that Peter hadn't even spoken to him in that time, but the brief email had popped up overnight, from RH: 'Will be interested to discuss Code PP soon, let me know when you want to talk'.

***

At least she'd broached the topic; it was now, officially, on their agenda, so she felt no need to pursue it on the trip. Hannes drove them to Farnborough for the chartered jet. She felt vicarious excitement for the guys. Peter had insisted, against her rather limp protests, that her children, Abbi and Jonah take their two friends on holiday via the same route: 'they'll miss out on real life'; 'six a.m. Gatwick is real life? I've not tried it, but I find it hard to imagine'. Her biggest concern had been whether Abbi would take Debbie or Jake. She'd tried to avoid giving an opinion, but from Abbi's knowing smile when she'd said 'oh, that's lovely darling' on hearing it would be Debbie, she knew her views were being considered.

She'd had time with them on the boat when it was new the previous summer. More accurately, Andreas had taken time with them, making mariners of them in the three weeks he'd had them. She was there for only one, their last week, when she'd been completely unnerved by Andreas standing beside her as the boat pulled away from the pontoon.

"Who's…?" she almost shrieked.

Andreas was looking supremely calm, "Jonah, of course," and he turned to Abbi, tidying the stern lines, and winked to her. "You wait till you see her docking us. They're both naturals." She got a modest smile from Abbi as she'd stared open-mouthed at her.

Her brain was still scrambled, this was a new six-million-pound boat, "Insurance?" — that came out almost hysterical, she knew.

"Confidence," smiled Andreas, with his adamantine German smugness. She almost loved him, but there was no-one she wanted to hit quite so often — if only he could be wrong just once.

Now he'd had four young ones for two days. She doubted whether her no-alcohol instruction was being rigidly observed but she trusted him to manage that carefully, and she knew how abstemious he was when in charge of the boat.

Now it was a new summer. They'd managed to use the boat in the spring as a base for some meetings, but Peter seemed genuinely to be distancing himself from the day-to-day. He still spent considerable time on what he called his studies, and almost half of his time on the telephone. It was her workload that had reduced the most, but she kept abreast of all that Tania was doing with the group, never intervening unless asked, speaking more often to Lavinia, who had more time and was office-based. She'd almost begun to forget that Lavinia was with Jack now. She was more troubled by the prospect of Alphonse's arrival. He'd be spending the night under the same roof for the first time in a year.

She looked at Peter, settling calmly into his seat after the inevitably ungainly entry. He turned to her, "I hated doing it, you know."

"I know. I'm sure the two of you will convince me on Wednesday."

He laughed, "I don't know about that. I haven't told Alphonse yet, only you see all of the emails."

"I thought we all had access."

"No, we have a board address, for all six of us, but we have another one, with the extra dot in the address, and that's just for you and me."

"I never noticed. You never said."

"There was no need before."

"And the address with the two extra dots?" Now she could tease him.

"Ah, the line for all my other ladies. Sadly, underutilised these last two years."

She felt calmer now, but keeping Alphonse out of the loop initially, especially when it involved 'that man' — she always thought of him in parenthesis — made it even more disturbing.

But in a few days, they would put Alphonse in the picture. She wished she weren't quite so excited about him coming.

She was comfortable enough to leave the topic, but it was now troubling him. When the steward had cleared their lunch away, he began, "I know we'll talk more on

Wednesday, but I should say something. You're right to suppose that Rod is the last person I want to have dealings with but, quite apart from all my misgivings about the project…"

"Are you questioning that again?"

"No, I'm not, I just feel the need to take precautions. I met the Shen family at the big Asia gathering we had just over two years ago, Tony had invited them. The old man, Wengwei, is a tyrant. Whether his two sons, Lee and Lou I think Alphonse calls them, Liqiang and Liuwei if I remember correctly, could ever grow enough while under his influence, I seriously doubt — but things work differently there, I guess. The older son, Lee, however, is gay, I think, and seemed very attracted to Alphonse." Now he looked at her cautiously, as if trying to gauge her reaction, but she'd known Alphonse had begun an affair at that meeting. It just didn't sound to her like it had been Liqiang, but, knowing that, she was able to avoid reacting. "I think the old man is worried by that, he has to support number one son, but it means number two son gets spoiled and favoured — and he didn't seem like a strong character anyway — too much bar time and flirting with waitresses, so I'm worried and I didn't know where to turn."

"Will you insist on Rod adhering to your new ethical code?"

Now he looked out of the window, plainly struggling. But, turning back, he said, "Yes," quite decisively. Then seemed to be thinking again.

"If I am interpreting you correctly, sometimes he will just happen on information that is acquired unethically."

He took a deep breath, "It's the nature of that game. The problem is, I'd like to have someone who could say to me 'I have knowledge and you should not do this thing' but…" he sighed, "I can't trust him to do that." He reached across to hold her hand, "I'm sorry to raise a sensitive point. We never talk about it now, do we?"

"There's no need to, it's all past," and she squeezed his hand, then looked out of the window. It still hurt when she was forced to remember that Rod's information had destroyed her relationship with Jack, and Peter would guess that was what she was thinking of — but she silently repeated her mantra: 'it wouldn't have worked, it wouldn't have worked…' like prayers on rosary beads, until she was calm again.

"Will Alphonse be surprised?"

He scowled, "He shouldn't be. It depends on whether he saw my questions at the time as simply arising out of my reluctance to let him pursue the programme. But he should see the dangers."

"And what would make you not hire Henderson?"

He drew breath sharply, but then relaxed when he saw that she was asking calmly.

"I would need a lot of reassurance that there were smaller dangers than I'm currently seeing. And they're easy to underestimate; personally, I got on splendidly with Wengwei, he regarded me as almost an equal," he chuckled, "I think he would bring a sense of arrogant superiority to any dealings with his fellow man. There were a few like him over the two weeks but Alphonse, bless him, kept them apart. He made each one feel unique." Now he laughed, "I spent two weeks dreading I'd confuse my wengs with my wangs, but I'm told I escaped with an unblemished record. Tony relied on his outback chutzpah to get him out of one or two mistakes. He does that Aussie thing and people seem able to laugh it off, especially at night when it mostly happens. We Brits make them suspicious still."

She squeezed his hand again, "Thank you for talking about it. I'm sorry if I seemed hysterical."

Now she got his big, caring smile, "I was going to talk it through, honestly — and I do understand why you're so sensitive."

Yes, there were ghosts in those memories.

***

Andreas was waiting for them at Zadar airport. Locating the boat in Croatia had been his suggestion: 'the islands are more interesting for boating', but the advantages of being a ten-minute drive from the airport and being in a splendid, spacious marina with amazing vistas into the

Kornati Islands had more than won them over to the location. And she would far rather let the guys loose here, where there was little to do, than in Monte Carlo.

Luca and Ivana, the couple Andreas used as crew, were waiting to greet them. They'd been wonderful the year before and she was delighted he'd found a way to keep them. She smiled to herself, now Andreas was captaining a smaller boat, he didn't have space to accommodate his usual preferences in the crew quarters, it had to be a married couple for weeks like these. But she suspected Andreas did a little of his own entertaining in what he called his Maintenance Weeks.

Luca took the bags. "Abbi and Jonah?" she looked to Ivana.

She smiled, "Beach Club cabana, they not sure when you coming."

She smiled back, "They ignore Mum's WhatsApp messages! Never mind, I'll go and join them." She turned to Peter, "I assumed you'd want to get on with some work."

"If you don't mind. You have the full me this evening. Andreas is sending us into Zadar. He has a restaurant recommendation."

"That'll be Fosa, I think. We tried it last year. It was so good we went back two days later."

She changed quickly and was soon in a floaty wrap over a bikini. It was a short walk to the club, the wide low building forming a quarter-circle round the artificial bay. The cabanas were busy, she was finding it hard to pick the guys out until she saw Abbi waving to her. She walked out along the middle pontoon to the outer left cabana and hugged her daughter, then hugged Debbie, who was standing now, almost as hard.

"The boys?" Abbi pointed to the distant buoyed rope stretched across the bay's entrance.

"Swimming. I think that's them in the middle." The distant heads were indistinguishable, but one body started waving and two young men swam quickly towards them. She threw her wrap on to the large square cushion.

"I'm prepared to get wet for a cuddle, but I'm not sacrificing that."

She watched them approach rapidly. It must have been Dickie leading, he slowed at the last minute to let Jonah climb the ladder first and she hugged the cold, wet, and now amazingly tall, body. She was already warm enough in the hot sun to find it pleasant. Dickie, even taller and broader, was hanging back self-consciously. "You don't have to hug an old lady, Dickie, but a kiss won't go amiss." He smiled, leaned forward and she got a peck on the cheek.

"All non-alcoholic," said Abbi defiantly without even turning to the bottles and glasses on the table.

She smiled back, "That was the first thing I noticed."

"You see," said Abbi, with mock outrage, "a tyrant, a tyrant."

"So, Andreas is running a dry ship?"

Abbi faltered, Debbie volunteered, "Andreas gives us wine with dinner, Mrs Brodie, and beer for the boys."

"Guys," she looked at them all, "I'm going to make only one rule for this week," she paused, "I'm Claudia, or Mum!"

"OK, Mum," said Dickie instantly. They all laughed, and she slapped him playfully.
"Well, I'm going to get some sunshine and a mocktail and listen to what you've been doing."

***

They'd all been thrilled. Andreas had taught the friends to ride the rib and the jet-ski, the boat faced into the large inner bay across to Sukošan, so they had easy access to calm water for all the manoeuvres, but mostly they were thrilled by the boat. She sometimes had to remind herself, when she thought back to the huge Yvonne D in Miami, that Careless Hours, at eighty-eight feet, was a palace for almost anybody, even the children of wealthy parents, as these two happened to be. Claudia had struggled a little with the invitations. The guys had lovely circles of quite diverse friends, but she was worried about how extraordinary the boat might seem to some — and there were none who wouldn't be impressed, but she could see one or two having an attitude. She'd worried needlessly, Abbi and Jonah had completely understood.

She went for a short swim herself, she was warm and it got the travel out of her system, not that the travel was a hardship these days, but the freedom of floating just washed so much away, all the grime and cares. The boys left soon, 'the jet-ski's out, Mum, and we don't know when our next chance is'. So, she was left chatting to the girls until Abbi asked when dinner was.

"Thank goodness you said, we should probably go now, I'm afraid I'm losing my ten-minute turnaround career-girl skills," and she ushered the girls back to the boat to get ready and waited to get the bill settled, enjoying, for a few moments, the continuing cacophony of inconsequential chatter all around her and the quiet lapping of waves — and also, she thought, some seriously cool music insinuating itself not too obtrusively from well-placed speakers.

***

Nobody rushed in the morning but somehow Andreas had them casting off at exactly ten-thirty with Jonah at the helm, Abbi smugly protecting her docking seniority. Claudia looked nervously at Peter, who simply sat back and watched the girls tidy the lines. Luca stayed nearby for Debbie. Even Claudia realised it was a simple exit, straight out into the bay and turn right. In only half an hour they were under the bridge between Passman and Ugljan, the two large offshore islands, Jonah still on the helm, but Andreas discreetly close to him; it was a narrow passage with, fortunately, no boats coming in the opposite direction. Soon they were travelling serenely through Kornati's oddly lunar islands, separating the deep blue of the sea from the brilliant azure above.

They anchored in a bay on the first night, with the jet-ski heavily in demand between bouts of the young ones sunbathing — on different decks from Peter and her. Even he seemed to be able to relax on a Sunday.

They weighed anchor a little earlier the next day and headed for Hvar. She deduced from the rising hubbub amongst the youth that her hopes that Carpe Diem would close on Mondays, or that no tables would be available, were already dashed.

She cornered Andreas as breakfast was being cleared, "Carpe Diem was you, admit it!"

She got a shrug and a smile. Oh, well, the Tuesday trip to Split would be unlikely to trouble the younger ones, they would sleep all day.

Alphonse, on the early flight, was with them by eleven on the Wednesday, and joined them before lunch on the back deck while Andreas took the guys on the water taxi to show them Split. Abbi and Jonah, having visited the year before, retained enough enthusiasm to want to show it off to their friends.

"You could have hired a jet," said Peter when he sat down.

Alphonse smiled and shrugged, "I do try to avoid wanton extravagance — but I have got one for the return this evening. I didn't know how long we'd need."

"Aren't you staying?" It was OK to sound disappointed, she thought — polite, even.

"I'd love to, but there's so much going on."

"Extraordinary!" said Peter. They both looked at him, puzzled. "That would be the first time ever you've admitted to any stress or pressure," and he smiled, "so, let's get down to business, then…"

Alphonse reviewed his meetings with the Harry and Mei and spoke warmly of the help 'Peter's friend' had given.

"She's the lady that did our bedroom. Wonderful woman. You're using her on the whole project, then, I assume?"

"Yes, she flies out there next week to look at the three renovation sites before we have the big week in Morkuda with everyone there," he paused and closed his eyes, "OK, honest Injun, I'm dreading it, but I have to get this thing kicked off and get the links and networks established. We're reviewing every site during the week with the architects and Raymond's team, plus the designer of course, and the Senlin two — that's Harry and Mei; also, Liqiang wants to come," he grimaced slightly, but Claudia couldn't tell how authentic that was. "Oh, and Will's bringing someone he's going to put on the project. He wants him to meet everyone before he puts financial controls in place. I thought about tackling it piecemeal, but it seemed to make sense to kick it off by getting everyone together."

"It does sound horrendous," Claudia said.

Peter was thinking. They waited, knowing he wanted to speak. "I'll come back to the Liqiang question in a moment, it's not actually trivial and it relates to a topic we'll come on to later," he seemed to relax a little, "my darling and I have already had words about it — but it needs three of us to find a consensus. Happy?" he looked to Claudia.

She smiled, "Thank you," she said.

"But the bigger point, and the one that's obviously bothering you the most, is keeping this monster controlled. Are you still committed to doing the first five at the same time?"

Alphonse looked troubled, "It does feel like too much, but these five are so run-down, we'll bleed business if we don't act quickly," he took a deep breath, "I think I'll keep the week as it is for now and take a view when we've seen everything. Raymond will say it's easy, of course, but…"

"Can I offer some help?" Peter plainly had a thought.

"It's your money. Haven't you done enough?"

"It's because it's my money that I'm offering help."

"I could use something, I don't know what, what's on your mind?"

"Claudia should be there."

"What? Me?"

Alphonse looked pensive, "Is it the management of the process you're thinking of, or having an independent observer?"

Claudia felt alarmed for a number of reasons, wondering even if this was some sort of test Peter was putting her into.

"I was thinking both, actually, but, since you'll obviously run the process, her input there would be before the event in helping you get your thinking straight about how to run it. It's a pretty unique event, after all. You'll note I'm stopping short of telling you it's madness," and he chuckled, "but it's the independent observer, probably with an active role, where she could be of most help during that week, I think." There was silence round the table, "Shall we have lunch now and get back to it later? You can tell me more about your designer lady, she intrigued me."

Alphonse laughed, "Well, she does that to me, too, I'm very glad you pointed me towards her. And she has pictures of your bedroom in her highlights presentation."

"It is beautiful," said Claudia, reflecting that it was not quite full of the joy and laughter she'd been hoping for. "Oh, you can stay long enough for an early dinner, can't you? Abbi will want to show you off to her friend Debbie," then a thought occurred to her, "I bet that's why she didn't invite the boyfriend, little minx, she didn't want him here with you around," and the men chuckled, and she hoped they hadn't noted her pensiveness about the bedroom.

***

Ivana brought the coffee after lunch and when Peter said, "Shall we get back to business?" She realised once again that he'd used his tactic of letting a suggestion — her trip to Asia — firm into a proposal, and then into an assumption, without further debate. She was, for a number of reasons, keen on the idea but it had several dangers. "I have told you," he was looking at Alphonse, "how much that family worries me," he held up his hands when Alphonse threatened to speak, "not enough to stop the deal; it's signed; it's going ahead, OK?"

Alphonse relaxed visibly. She relaxed too, although she tried to conceal it.

"But there's an inherent instability in the set-up. You do see that, don't you?"

"You mentioned Liqiang. I understand, of course, it's not what these powerful families want, questionable succession. But Lee is actually a smart businessman."

"My dear chap, you're a smart businessman and you can be entirely what you are here in the West," his eyes narrowed as he looked at both of them, "and that isn't exactly just gay, is it?" but then he smiled, apparently with sincerity. "But you're not embedded in a rigidly Confucian society. Do you know…" Peter had made his point and now it could settle in their minds while he embarked on an aside, "One of Wengwei's peers, I forget which, but his English was good, said to me over dinner; 'the problem with you Christians' when we were discussing human rights, I think it was. I was stopped in my tracks, but it made me reflect that, for all our louche and luxurious lifestyles, we do relate everything to that Christian perspective, however free-thinking we consider we've become — even our guilt is Christian guilt." He paused. "Anyway, in a roundabout way that brings me to Henderson."

"Henderson?" Alphonse was unusually animated and looked quickly at Claudia. She shrugged, plainly it was genuinely new to Alphonse. "Are you planning to get him involved?"

Now Peter shrugged, "Well, I think deals, partnerships even, like this need to be approached in a spirit of mutuality, but, as an old friend once said to me: 'you do mean-armed mutuality' — I think he thought that a Mexican stand-off was more effective if both parties had a gun."

Claudia was a little mystified by the analogy, but Alphonse was nodding.

"I want two things, good people: I want a little more intelligence on the inherent instabilities in the Shen family — how's that likely to play out; and I want some poker chips if this game gets tough."

"Won't you undermine the relationship if they detect Henderson poking around?"

Her question was probably naïve, but Peter avoided condescension in replying, "With families like these we might lose more respect if they think we're not doing our homework. Now, I'd love to find someone different, but I don't have anyone as good, especially not in Asia, so it would have to be Henderson," he snorted slightly, then looked straight at Alphonse, "at least he understands the tensions created by having a gay son." He paused, "It hasn't made him a better man, unfortunately."

"I still think he's irredeemable," Claudia knew she sounded huffy, but was becoming resigned to the idea anyway.

Alphonse was some way from that, "Aren't you worried he'll just find another angle to attack you again?"

Peter breathed deeply and nodded, "Yes, but we do have a clause that staggered his twenty million over five years, he must do no identifiable harm, and there's still twelve million waiting for him."

"Is he going soft?" asked Claudia sceptically.

Peter chuckled, "Will persuaded him of the tax advantages. He can be very plausible, our William. Anyway, I don't like it, I understand the reactions around the table, but it's the only offer I've got. Do we want to sleep on it?"

"Ha, typical, then you just let your suggestion solidify into a plan again. Just like you did earlier over my trip to Asia."

"So, you're agreeing to go then?" and she knew she could read anything into that smile. He still puzzled her.

"If Alphonse thinks it will help. I also want to know what he feels about Henderson." She looked to him.

He was obviously disturbed, "It would be silly of me not to recognise the dangers, but I don't have a better suggestion at the moment."

Peter shrugged again, "I admit I'll lose sleep over it, but I'll lose more sleep without the radar he gives us. Look, think about it overnight, both of you, please, but let me know in the morning if I can brief him."

They relaxed and the conversation, after a few more business issues, became more gossipy.

"Oh, by the way, designer lady, Isobel, she knows Will."

"Really? She never said. Still, I don't suppose she would have made the connection. I suppose it depends on when she knew him."

"It was up to the time he got serious with Martha, apparently," he smiled at both of them, "but you two understand more about that. Our Will, imagine, a dark horse. She sounded quite regretful. Anyway, it's encouraged her to get in touch with him, apparently."

"What's she like then, this Isobel?"

"Sadie," said Peter, darkly. But he smiled when they looked at him, mystified. "I got Andreas to find out more about her when she was going to be in the house a lot — and she'd seemed quite titillated when I showed her the cellar, so I guessed there was an interesting back story. She's a player, is our Isobel, and she's called Sadie in some circles because of her special tastes."

"Sadism?" asked Claudia, a little shocked, "but Will…" now she knew she was blushing, and Peter chuckling didn't help. He was obviously remembering the night out they'd had with Martha in Tokyo and the club where he'd spanked them both.

"Nothing's as simple as we'd like it to be, is it? What wonderfully complex and stimulating creatures we are."

She was nodding, "I just hope… Will and Martha…"

"These things play out as they will in the end," he took a deep breath, "we just need to stick to our good old Christian principles," and he laughed.

She felt a little uneasy and couldn't quite laugh with him.

7

You know how it is when you're meeting someone, and you just don't recognise them. Thank God there were so many people in the arrivals' hall, I could pretend I hadn't seen her. But, to be honest, I'd picked out the pretty woman in the orange silk dress through the thick ranks of nameplate-wielding drivers almost as soon as I came through the gate. I hope I didn't look too shocked when she came smiling towards me.

I just realised in time as she moved to kiss me and was able to respond; but I'm sure my "You look absolutely gorgeous! How can you do that at whatever time it is?" was overly effusive. It still didn't match my reactions, though, she looked stunning, "Thank you so much for meeting me."

"And you look so elegant after that long flight," she turned and waved a finger at a driver, who rushed up to take my bags. This was Mei! Slightly imperious — and the qualified compliment — 'after that long flight'. But I felt like shit, I hadn't slept well. And don't mix me with free booze!

Saigon airport — OK, OK, Ho Chi Minh airport — looked like every other, my cultural appreciation programme wasn't starting yet. We'd agreed on two days in each location, Cambodia and Thailand yet to come. That would give me, I thought, enough time to have a detailed look at the resorts and think about what they needed — and, my God, from the pictures, they certainly needed something — and a little time to get out and about and scratch the surface of the cultures.

I could understand Alphonse's point about the resorts though; on the face of it, the buildings could be lived with. His surveyors had said they were sound, and the layouts were pleasing. The other two of the five, that would be week three, well, from the pictures I'd seen, they couldn't bulldoze them soon enough — and it would be obviously easier to work from the ground up. Well, I should be careful, I've met some peculiar architects. But here was Mei, holding my hand as we walked through the airport. You're right, hand in hand is a little strange, wherever you are culturally, and I'm committed to spending a week with her. She intrigues me, of course, but there are some things she and I need to get clear about straight away.

Ha, I thought of that point again later. I was dozing in the suite at the resort and she was walking towards me, completely naked — small, pretty breasts and a perfect Brazilian — having made me a green tea. She put it by the bed and climbed in with me again. The aircon meant that we needed the light duvet, and it was cool enough to encourage us to cuddle closely again.

She kissed me and smiled, "I know you have a broader range of interests than me, but I am thrilled they extend to letting this happen," and her hand smoothed down my side and on to my hip.

I'm sure I'll get used to the default accent being American when they speak English. At the moment, of course, I'm finding her enchanting, and she does kiss well. Yes, she had enjoyed my technique too, I'm an unselfish lover. I apologise if I'm being a little too subtle here, but I do expect a little imaginative interpretation. I want to be frank with you — but not coarse!

"We have plenty of time to discuss our range of interests," I was smiling at her, "I'm very happy they're broad enough to let us enjoy each other."

She snuggled in. There's no point in comparing; men and women, I mean, they're just different experiences, each thrilling in their own way. This could be a lovely week, as long as we can keep it in control. I wasn't certain yet. And I can get bored with people.

I know, you'd already guessed.

She was certainly making a fuss of me. I knew I'd intrigued her, but I hadn't known whether that was because she desired me, or because she wanted to be like me. I still don't know yet.

But I think she's savvy enough to understand that a forty-three-year-old, single woman-of-the-world isn't seeking to start an intercontinental lesbian perma-relationship. Well, I hope she is. In the meantime, refreshed from my shower and my little sleep, I may get some more enjoyment from this smooth, slim, taut body lying beside me and, from the way she's moving, that's on her mind too.

Excuse us.

8

"May I say it first? I'm as ambivalent about you coming to Morkuda as I think you are, but I can so use your help."

Claudia looked pointedly towards the open door. She presumed he had no secrets from Hayley, but this was an exceptionally delicate topic. He closed his eyes, mouthed 'sorry' and pulled the door to. "You're right, I'm ambivalent. It's even crossed my mind that he was setting it up as some sort of test," she said.

"Surely not!"

"Alphonse, you've known him for nearly twenty years, you know how devious and subtle he can be," she shrugged, "I do love him, but he's not easy. Look, I'll be frank, I do miss the times we used to have — and it means a lot to me that we still feel this way. You're probably my best friend. No, not probably, you are. I just know you're there. And I'll be really happy if we can get a little time with each other," now she gave a hollow laugh, "but I've no idea how we get through all this stuff in a week," she gesticulated to the models on the desks and the maps and drawings around the walls, "let alone manage any privacy."

"So, we're good, then, friends with no benefits?"
She nodded, and they laughed.

"But it sounds like you may have a love interest anyway…"

"Lee, you mean?" She nodded. "Oh, I hope not," he hesitated, then smiled, "don't get me wrong, he's a lovely man and has a flair for this stuff, so he has a genuine interest in the project… but I'm not so naïve as to ignore that he might be coming with an ulterior motive — but that would so screw the project up."

"Even more than sleeping with me?"

Now he laughed louder, "Yes, even more than sleeping with you. Shall we get serious now?"

"I think Peter taking on Henderson says we should. It makes my flesh creep, of course, but it can't have been easy for him. Do you think there are that many dangers with this project?"

He looked at her levelly, "I'm pretty sure Wengwei is a very astute businessman, but I think we'll be wise to assume he's also completely unscrupulous. Added to that, I've less against Henderson personally than the two of you have, so I'm rather in favour. OK?" She nodded, reluctantly. "Where do you want me to start? You've read a lot and been involved in the big decisions."

"I've read about nothing else but this project and resort businesses since our Wednesday discussion on the boat and, like you say, I felt quite informed anyway. Were you expecting Will to come, by the way?"

"No, but I'm pleased he is. I thought he might just send his man and before you make one of your intuitive connections, he told me he was coming before I told him Isobel would be there."

She smiled slyly at him and tilted her head, "Do you think she might have told him she was going?"

"No!" then he paused, "No, she can't have, I didn't confirm any dates until… Oh, God, is that something else to worry about?" He couldn't remember when he'd mentioned dates in conversations. Maybe they had spoken.

"I don't think so, but I've not met your Isobel" that wasn't really reassuring, "and I don't know why I'm enjoying your discomfort about these arrangements. It's a pain I'm now sharing. OK, what do you want to accomplish in your megaweek?"

Fortunately, Alphonse did have the facility of remaining calm and clear — and Hayley helped him get well-prepared, "Look, do you mind if I ask her in?"

"No, of course not, you know how good I think she is."

He went to the door, "Hayley, can you come in, please, we're just going to review these task lists you've prepared."

They each took a prepared A3 sheet with a number of headings: projects; resources; finance — each with sub-headings and lines pencilled between them. It looked chaotic but she'd seen Hayley use the technique before. If you put yourself in her hands, you ended up

with much clearer lists of tasks and responsibilities —
and it was fun. But she'd never been involved on
anything this complex — and neither, it quickly became
obvious, had Alphonse or Hayley.

It was an intense five hours but the tasks and
resources had become much clearer, but Hayley was
suddenly fidgety, "Oh, Hayley, I'm sorry, of course you
must go. It's been a massive step forward, thank you so
much."

"I'm sorry I have to rush. I'll put it into an agenda
proposal in the morning and get that to you by
lunchtime."

"I'm thrilled you've offered to do that," said
Claudia, "I know it looks like it should be possible, but
it's very daunting. But you've been amazing, now, get
along."

She smiled and was gone.

"Happy enough to buy me a drink?"

He stood up, moved towards her and held out his
hands, "I'd be thrilled to, but may I have one chaste
cuddle first?"

She stood and moved into his arms, "This is us
now, isn't it? Chaste embraces — and champagne, come
on!"

9

We slept in our own rooms, of course, although it had been a lovely afternoon by the pool, and we'd chatted for hours about families and jobs and travels — and a lot about the project — over dinner. She lingered at my door when we parted, and it was a tender goodnight kiss; I'm sure she would have stayed if I'd wanted. But we have a lot of time with each other on this trip; more than I've spent with anyone in years.

I'd kept the briefing for the itinerary simple. I'd asked her to organise, for each location, a tour that included a temple, a fortress, and a large formal garden — I thought that would give me the visual clues about the elements I should include in the designs. I'll use locally-sourced furniture as far as I can, but it needs to show links to the cultural heritage — and I think I'll have time later to get local designers to come up with signature pieces for the individual resorts. I'll get them to sign exclusivity contracts, of course, but I'll have no chance of enforcing them if the pieces are successful but, hey, I have to be philosophical, I don't want people looking at stuff and thinking 'that's shit, I wouldn't have it in my house', I want them to desire it. But I can come back in a few weeks, after I've researched who's good, and see who can do what for me for the resorts. If I come up with some good things, I know people who would love to import; but I won't get my hopes up, I'd need to find real artists and craftsmen.

My little plan for the tour worked well. It wasn't a leisurely day, but it wasn't hectic either and we were back at the resort by five. I'd thanked her profusely in the car on the return, she had put a lot of thought and effort into it: the temple had many emblems and icons I could work with, and the garden was glorious — indigenous vegetation finds its way into much of a culture's favourite designs. We got back to our rooms and I told her I had lots of photos but wanted to make some sketches while the sights were still fresh in my mind.

"I'd love to see how you do that," she said, with those lovely eyes shining.

I did get enough done before we got into the bath. Well, she watched me do three or four and then said, "They're amazing! You just capture things brilliantly. I don't know how you do that at all, let alone after a tiring day. I'll run a bath for you." Which was a lovely idea — but I did guess that I'd find her in it when I was ready — but I had a good dozen sketches by then: work first!

I like baths with men, I really do, but they're complicated; either that thing gets in the way and you have to do something with it — usually uncomfortably — or it doesn't get in the way and you wonder where it's gone — or they wonder and worry, and that's worse.

It's much more relaxing with a woman. OK, I think I actually started it: toe manipulation of the clitoris. She just smiled and relaxed. But quite soon it was mutual and the conversation stopped for a while, with just brief pauses to sip champagne.

I thought I was managing her quite well, easing the pressure when her breathing became heavy, but, after one big smile and a raised glass, I realised she was managing me equally well, if not better. So, we seemed to find a plateau; there was no rush, after all, we had the week ahead of us and my sense was that she could be quite adventurous.

"Do you try men sometimes?" I asked.

"Sometimes, not often; I'm seldom attracted." She thought for a moment. "I would with Alphonse," she smiled wickedly but her femme fatale persona failed her utterly as her would-be sophisticated sip of champagne went up her nose and she snorted. That had us both laughing hysterically.

When we'd calmed down, I said, "You know he is…"

"Yes, yes, I know he is mostly, but I think he's maybe a little like you, isn't he? You're straight mostly, but like to…" by now we'd settled again and her toe was doing its work. "Can I say dabble?"

"That's a good word." It was a good word. It helped me know she wasn't expecting to take this too seriously. "Yes, I dabble."

"What else do you do?"

I have to be prepared to be the educator. I am also interested in learning what her tastes are, but that can come later. "I like playtimes — mostly with men but quite often with women."

"Playtimes?"

I think she understood. She just didn't want to risk embarrassing herself. These arrangements usually start like that. Most people are far more coy than she is, and men are worse than women until they have some experience. "I have a range of toys, I always carry some with me, even just to pleasure myself, but I wouldn't trade any one of them for what your toe is doing now. So, playtimes are people pleasing each other in whatever ways and with whatever devices appeal to them."

She smiled and rubbed me more firmly, "Will you show me later?"

"Of course, but don't you have some of your own?"

Here she managed to look a little demure, "Just a little vibrator. More at home, of course."

I laughed, "Oh, I have a lot more at home, but enough here, I think. Should we go for a light dinner and give ourselves some time, later?"

"I think that's a wonderful idea. Should we go soon?" But she smiled and settled down further in the bath. It was a sweet gesture, neither of us wanted to rush out, but the promise of the later playtime was drawing us on.

With a man there's always time pressure from the standing penis, he's always worried about the spirit evaporating. That drives its own passion, of course, and I'm in favour of that mostly. But being able to manage more relaxed and pleasurable rhythms is delicious.
But yes, we lay on the bed and cuddled and touched — and neither of us could wait until after dinner before coming.

***

And that post-orgasmic clear-headedness gave me space to remember I was working — I've grown out of thinking that orgasms bestow the philosopher's infinite insight. I have a contract to do rooms, and that's what I'll do.

There is also a clause for consultancy on the communal areas, and I get to approve the architects' plans — I insisted and I got support from Hayley: 'it makes sense, Alphonse, it's all got to tie in' — he got the idea, but I think he was worried about handing me that much power and foresaw struggles ahead. That was a fair concern — but he'll learn to appreciate that I'm pragmatic before I'm philosophical — and I work before I fuck! But I just don't look forward to dealing with architects — but not as much as they don't look forward to dealing with me! I think, deep down, they know they're up themselves, the small ones just don't like having that pointed out, the big guys try to ignore me, with limited success! But these reception and dining areas will need some input — and the themes and style and colours must link harmoniously to the rooms, of course.

I was explaining this to Mei and, bless her, she seemed very switched on to the idea. She's obviously had her own architect encounters herself. They may like her even less than they like me. I like to think I lace my observations with humour; it's a skill I'm not sure she possesses.

I assume Alphonse and his man — he keeps referring to this Raymond — will sort out the cuisine here. Acceptable but uninspiring, is how I would describe it currently. The maître d' was helpful, he knew who we were and why we were there, of course, and he described the cuisine as Vietnamese International... quite, I know your taste buds are watering now! Work to be done, I think. But it was pleasant enough — and our pre-prandial stay on the bed meant that we didn't have to rush away but could linger over the jasmine tea. The place wasn't busy. I could tell why Alphonse was in a hurry.

***

I take a little box with me on holidays and long trips, although the latter are infrequent — and the box isn't so little. It intrigued Mei, of course. "I think I know what they all are," she said when she opened it — yes, it was she who opened it, that showed me she was curious; I had simply put it on the bed. "Or I can guess anyway," — she was holding up the vibrating U that you fit over the vulva; that can be wicked if you get a sensitive man to work with you while he's fucking you. I know, I know, it's a big if! "We'll try that later?" she was looking at me expectantly.

I smiled, "We'll try anything later."

Now I got a wicked sideways glance as she lifted the ropes. "And these?" she said slowly.

"Knots aren't really my strong suit, but I'm passable if you're into it."

"Oh, I'm very good with knots," she said, evilly. She was plainly pondering how much to say. "If I have men, it's what I like to do to them."

This was interesting, "Have you tried Harry?"

"Of course not," she said sharply.

"There's a story there you'll have to explain to me," I said, "but that can wait."

"But why do you say Harry?"

We were looking hard at each other now. I don't think Mei's receptors are as powerful as her transmitters. There is something mannish about her. "I got that little puppy dog look from Harry. I think he'd like to be put on a lead."

"Harry?" I couldn't tell whether it was just shock or incredulity. But it all helped build the picture I was forming of her.

"Does Harry just go chasing women?"

"Yes," she said, quickly and contemptuously, "and sometimes he pays," she spat out.

"I've paid," I said. She looked appropriately shocked. Look, I did it once, with a particular man on a friend's recommendation. It wasn't as startling as she'd said it would be, but I probably went in with the wrong attitude — it was more of a challenge I'd set myself, one of those 'do it before you're forty' things — or maybe it was more 'do it before you need to', or even 'do it because you should try it', I'm no longer clear. But it's a story that comes in handy for shocking people, usually men — most of them start wondering if anybody would ever pay them — I recommend it as a challenge, it does make them think harder about how they're satisfying you — even a fifty, placed as a joke on the bedside table, has them licking more lasciviously: but Mei seemed to be reacting strangely.

I know you're wondering: yes, one guy's sense of humour did extend to him taking the money. I should have left it at that, but I was younger then: my commitment to playtimes being for the bottom's pleasure was abandoned for the next evening I met him. My nickname, Sadie, originated in the stories that went round after that. Anyway, sorry, I'm digressing.

"I can't believe a woman like you would do that," said Mei, she was huddled up, cocoon-like, in the duvet, sitting on the bed.

"Oh, my poor little Mei," I said, putting my arms around her — she seemed reluctant to accept me, "it

was just something I wanted to try. I've tried most things at different times."

She seemed to consider that, and relaxed slowly, "Would you try Harry?"

That was a tricky question. Yes, I would, obviously, but circumstances are important — and feelings. "I get the sense that there's quite a tense relationship between you two. So, I want to be careful how I respond. I know we're being relaxed about what goes on between us..." I touched her chin to lift her face towards me. I waited for her to nod. She did, slowly. "He's a good-looking young man — and I think he wants to be taken in hand, if you understand me — and I think you do understand me, right?" I waited for her to nod again, she did. "And it's more in my mainstream, I must admit, dealing with naughty men." Now she smiled. "But you and I have something between us now and I'm not going to spoil that if any Harry adventure would upset you."

Now a cheeky, but slightly evil, glint had come into her eye, she smiled, "Thank you. You may have given me an idea."

"Of who to tie up?"

"Yes," she said, enthusiastic now, "do you think we could?"

"Woah, you've obviously given some thought to that. It's an interesting possibility. We have a few days to think about it. Right now, I need some rope training."

"Do you want me to tie you?"

"I usually top."

"I know, so do I."

"You haven't surprised me," and we laughed, "but, if you're skilled, maybe I could learn more." And we began a surreal hour of bondage tutorial, where she got me, finally, to master the basic column ties — I mean, I could do them, but now they were looking neat and symmetrical; important for a designer — then she tied me in a variety of positions I'd admired and envied at some parties I'd attended.

But, by now, we'd been moving around each other's naked bodies for too long. I wanted her again. And her eyes said the same to me.

"I want to tie you," I said.

"I want you to tie me. What will you do to me?"

I smiled and shook my head at her, "I don't know yet. I will try lots of things. As you know, all this is about the sub's pleasure. That's why I want to tie you, so I can explore you."

"How will you tie me?"

"Just a cross, wrists and ankles to the bed corners with my newly perfected ties. I want to leave you open to most things frontal."

"Thank you," she said quietly, "I don't…"

I chuckled gently, "I thought you wouldn't. I do, as it happens, so we'll talk about that later too."

"But not tonight." She really was nervous — lots of people are.

"No, not tonight. Let's see how expert you've made me with single column ties."

As a special guest in the hotel, I had a suite with a four-poster, which is always handy. I take long ropes with me but finding solutions when there are no easy tying posts is a real passion-killer. But tonight I had her quickly spread-eagled, with a pillow under the small of her back to improve access, of course. And she had seriously improved my rope skills.

She looked perfect — and irresistible. I lay beside her, cuddled her and kissed her. When I moved my hand slowly down over her belly — oh, it's lovely when it's so lean you can feel the muscles tense — her movements told me how excited she was and her pussy, when I got there, was drenched already.

The major advantage of making love to a woman is recovery time. It's wonderful to be kept on edge, but if you trigger an orgasm, the pleasure is almost uninterrupted. You slow down, of course, or you should do, as the giver but, as the recipient, you're very happy to be touched or licked continuously, just, for a time, with a lower intensity.

Now, with the best will in the world — and I'm not even thinking of apologising for that dreadful pun — the post-orgasmic limp cock is a fairly useless article. If you guys could attune yourselves to slow sensual pleasures, you'll find that the clitoris, see above, still enjoys your attention but, I understand, anthropologically it's a deeply atavistic thing for you, it's the jungle still: plunge him in; come; disengage and immediately look around for the waiting predators. But guys, the sabre-tooth tiger is no longer hiding behind the bush, ready to pounce; slow down and enjoy the sensual pleasures of post-orgasmic contentment.

In the meantime, girls have fun! Mei has very pretty labia; slightly dark, as have been the few Asian women I've played with, but delightfully neat with a prominent clit, which made my plan easier to implement. But first I was gorging on her, touching and tasting and slowly sliding just one finger in. Ooh, she was writhing and getting very noisy. I enjoyed that, and I was glad I'd got the ropes well-tensioned. The ties themselves were no threat to circulation, but her limbs were well extended, she still, however, had the freedom to wriggle her torso and it made it hard to keep the right tongue pressure on her clit — but, you have to accept, she's partly responsible for her own pleasure so, when I pulled back and left her untouched, she rapidly calmed down and gasped "Touch me again."

I went easier on her for a while — I have wonderful tongue skills — yes, of course I've been told, but my principal awareness comes from my own observations of people's reactions. I can keep a cock erect for half an hour just by the way I lick the underside of the head. Few of them, by the way, merit that much attention.

That's not hypocritical; I still believe firmly in the primacy of the sub's experience but, come on (oh no I feel another pun coming), the top has to come in the end — and ideally not by just wanking on his or her own. That's not a proper playtime.

But I am focused on Mei, truly, you're just benefitting from my multi-tasking skills. Mei is having a wonderful time, but it's about to get better.

She's been wriggling violently again, and then whimpering "Don't leave me," when I withdraw. But I'm only reaching into my box.

"I'm going nowhere, just getting toys."

"Which ones?" She looks worried.

I move up and kiss her mouth. She relaxes. "I'm not even going to offer a yellow to stop, you'll be fine. I just want to try things and see what you like." I kissed her again and smiled, "OK?"

She looked a little nervous, but nodded. Then she frowned when I took out the large pink vibrator, I was quite keen to find out how she felt about penetration — obviously not good. But when I moved to put it away, she said, "No, no, please, I would like you to try. Maybe it's nice with you." There's obviously some awkward history here.

I kissed her again and moved close to her. She seemed to relax. I don't want to take it too far. There has to be a little tension, she's tied up. When I'm tied up, I like to be a little on edge — just not quite knowing what the top will do next — and the good ones, even ones I've played with before, will always try to bring something new. So, I left the vibrator on the bed, reached into the box and took out the pink nipple clamps (the black are the heavy ones — I obviously prefer them). She immediately looked tense again, but these are really quite soft, so I kissed her again and then applied them carefully. She was still frowning but I left them and began to let the vibrator buzz on her clit; now I moved down, kneeling between her legs, I can control it better that way. It's one of my favourites — not particularly large, but it has two different vibration modes; you can use both at once, but my pussy gets a little confused by that. It also has a clit-tickler for when fully inserted — if only men came with those, but vibrating cock rings are good, if anyone's waiting for advice. But at this point I was barely inserting the tip and was touching her clit with my fingers. She'd stopped wriggling so much now and had her eyes closed with a big smile on her face. I thought a little more penetration now, let's see what turns her on. She was frowning again when I went deeper but her pussy was coming towards me. This is not rare; the body reacts differently to the mind — the aim is to bring them into harmony. The disconnect is the cause of many misunderstandings and bad experiences: you know — a wet pussy is not a licence to ignore a 'No!', so I was going carefully, and I eased off on her clit. I would fool no-one by touching and licking her hot pussy while pushing in more than she wanted, but her hips were definitely pushing for more, and when the tickler touched her, she began bucking violently: that was just the vibrator, the clamps, and me gently stroking her thighs and her belly. She was going to come, the ropes were getting pulled very tight but the knots held beautifully, and the low noise from her throat began to rise in pitch and intensity. It was a wonderful crescendo, not screaming, just a high note of ecstasy, one of the prettiest sounds I've ever heard. I pulled the clamps off quickly while she was still singing and that subsided into a sigh and she gasped, "Oh, wonderful, wonderful," as I pulled the vibrator from her.

Now, there's no rush to untie anybody; you should let them down slowly with kisses and touches — they must still know you are the top, and you are managing their pleasure — and you have to let their mind engage with the thought that they must now consider your pleasure. If you have pleased them as you should have done, they will want to pleasure you. And I had no doubt that Mei would want to pleasure me.

I let her relax and settle. I kissed her lips, "Are you ready?"

"Oh, I feel wonderful, and I am so ready." I untied her and rubbed her wrists and ankles, some chafing had been caused by the violence of her movements. "I loved the clamps. I liked the little bit of pain but the release, when you take them away, is fabulous." She was rubbing her wrists vigorously now, "Would you like me to tie you?"

"Shall we leave that until tomorrow? I always like to prepare a little when I'm topping. Maybe we should just cuddle now and I'll tell you what I like."

"OK, I'd like to study the box anyway and see what I'd like to try."

I narrowed my eyes when I smiled at her, "You do know it's for the bottom's pleasure, don't you?"

"Of course I do. You were wonderful with me just now. I don't like that much, normally, but you made me such a focus, it was gorgeous. Can I do that with you tomorrow?" She was smiling wickedly.

"Of course you can, it's my favourite vibrator, but now I'm just happy if you kiss and play with me."

The wicked smile hadn't gone, she fished the black clit clamp out of the box, she waved it at me, "I have tried these," she said. I admit, it's there for when I'm topping, it's quite severe — but I suppose I have to let her try...

Oh, was I glad I did! It's quite painful, but when she was licking me and touching me, oh, it was fire and ice perfection — I was even louder than she'd been, I'm sure, but the feeling when she took it off and carried on licking me was sublime — I came twice in ten minutes — amazing! And I was exhausted. I was very happy that she just wanted to cuddle and sleep.

She was gone in the morning. Just a note on the bedside table:

Thank you for such a wonderful and truly memorable night. I thought you'd earned a little space. I will see you at breakfast XXX

Sweet girl!

10

Alphonse finally arrived at Morkuda on the Sunday afternoon. How essential was the itinerary that had taken him to the Vietnam and Cambodia sites? That he'd learned nothing new, beyond the conspiratorial whisper from the Vietnam hotel manager that 'the two ladies seemed very close', told him that he'd achieved nothing beyond avoiding travelling with Claudia.

They'd had an edgy conversation about travel arrangements, each aware of the temptation they represented to each other — and they'd both been relieved, he felt, when he arbitrarily decided that a fresh appraisal of some of the resorts they would be discussing, would help the week. She had tried a tentative 'perhaps it would help if I saw them too', but in the ensuing silence, they both realised what they were confronting. Well, he knew he did, and his 'you need to be as refreshed as possible to help with this process', had her agreeing with almost embarrassing rapidity. She understood, too.

The car swept into the portico at the end of the short journey from the heliport. It was oddly poignant for him as they passed through the grounds, he realised with each trip here how much emotional investment he had made. This place, because it was the first new one, and not the conversion at Teluk, felt like a home to him and he recognised how much more vulnerable that made him. He loved the place.

Raymond was waiting with his usual beaming smile, "Hello boss, wonderful to have you back." Alphonse smiled and shook hands. Raymond was certainly the most important man for him in the whole project. OK, vast amounts of money were being ploughed in by, ultimately, Peter Dickinson and Shen Wengwei, but Raymond was the difference between success and failure.

"Is everyone here?" he asked.

"Oh, no, most of the China people arrive tonight. The ladies are here though."

"Which ladies?" Two, or three, wondered Alphonse.

"All three," said Raymond, with a disturbingly knowing smile, "I introduced them, they're having tea together." Hoteliers, even the less inquisitive ones — and there were few of those — had extraordinary opportunities for peering into people's lives, so Alphonse assumed he had no secrets from Raymond — and neither would the other guests, which might be helpful, particularly given Peter's probably justifiable concerns about their Chinese partners.

"I'd better go and say hello…"

"Yes, yes," said Raymond, waving to the porters, "we'll get your room set up. You still want that reception at seven? They won't all be here."

"Oh, we'll stick with that. It might be the only informal thing we do this week," he smiled ruefully; it was an ambitious week, and Raymond's half-smile and slow nod told him that he knew it too.

It felt peculiar stepping into this gathering of strangers — well, Isobel and Mei apparently strangers no longer. They were all talking animatedly, he'd given himself a moment to observe them from a distance: Isobel rather holding court, but the other two, even Mei, participating eagerly.

"All that's missing is a cauldron," he said as he joined them. They stood up quickly, clearly excited by his arrival. Isobel, despite having to move around the coffee table, embraced him first. Then Mei, after the handshake, clearly wanted the cheek-to-cheek greeting — and she was smiling, which seemed to add some weight to the Vietnam story. Claudia was almost reticent, but this was no time for hesitant half-measures, he wrapped his arms around her and kissed her cheek. She gave herself to it for only an instant, then sat down again quickly.

"Well," said Isobel, "I've finally met the woman I've been hating for two years — and she's perfectly lovely."

Alphonse smiled at Claudia, "I presume we're talking about the blue bedroom." Claudia nodded, Mei looked puzzled. "You won't remember," he said to her, "but early in Isobel's London presentation…"

"Ah, there was a blue bedroom, yes, I do remember. It was wonderful."

Claudia looked strangely bashful.

"Well, when a very wealthy man loves you very much, he engages London's best designer," and here Isobel beamed a smile at him and nodded, "gives her a semi-infinite budget, and tells her to design the most glorious bedroom she possibly can, then you end up with something fabulous. Unfortunately, that implants unsustainable attitudes for more humble work…"

"Like a half-billion-dollar building programme for resorts," said Mei, with a cheeky smile, supported by a "Hah! Gotcha, Monsieur Alphonse, don't tell me your budgets are small," from Isobel. Wow, he thought, these two were a team. He didn't know how surprised he was: he had no views on their relationship or what it might become, but he was disappointed he'd not had more insight into the possibility, at least.

Mei had raised a good point that had troubled him a little. He'd bought the package for two-point-three with the hope of financing the developments out of income, but with the programme moving ahead as quickly as he now wanted, he would need all of the two hundred million he'd saved. He would need her with Will and his project man to plan the cashflow more accurately over the five years it would all take.

When he asked about what they'd seen on their tour, he got an animated travelogue with even Mei contributing. For him, the most important element of their descriptions was the enthusiasm they clearly both had for the project. Claudia was quiet but asked the occasional question, just to show an interest, it seemed to him — but no questions were really needed to sustain the duo's momentum.

"I'm thrilled with what you're saying, and I'd love to hear more later," he was interrupting them, "but I'm afraid I'd better unpack and get ready for the reception; I can't be late for that. I'll see you all there in an hour?"

"Gosh, yes," said Claudia, unnecessarily, "I must go and change."

Alphonse tried to ignore Isobel's suspicious glance at each of them as they left, Claudia some way behind him. But she caught up with him when he reached his door. He let her in. She fell into his arms as the door closed and they stood, holding each other. After a while he said, "There are no secrets in hotels."

"No," she said, without moving, "I should think everyone knows about those two already. She wasn't what I'd expected when Peter told me about her."

"Have you talked to Will about her?"

She leaned back, obviously surprised, "Why Will? He was just a friend, I thought you meant."

"I think he was a special sort of friend, before Martha."

"But those two downstairs, what's that about then, what is she?"

"And you're in the bedroom of a gay man? Not everyone is simple, are they? Well, very few people are."

She cuddled into him again, "But we're friends."

"We've taken a pretty broad view of friendship in our time, haven't we?"

"Kiss me," and she moved her mouth up to his. It was tender and sensual but their bodies, responding equally, suddenly pulled away from each other.

"There isn't enough time to tempt ourselves, thank goodness," he said, "we both need to get ready. Where are you? Not on this floor I hope."

She was turning away, only leaning her shoulder on to his chest now. "No, I have a villa. Peter is probably coming at the end of the week. Did you know that?"

"There was talk of him and Wengwei both being here to catch the summary and have dinner with me on Friday."

"The week doesn't get any easier, does it?" and she snuggled back into his arms again. "I'm going, don't worry," and she looked up, kissed him briefly, and left.

He stood a while, staring at the door she'd left through. It was a strange desire he felt. Yes, he enjoyed her body, and she understood his well enough to make those rare times thrilling, but it was the hours they'd had lying naked in each other's arms, simply talking, that were his life's most precious moments. But then he smiled to himself, their bodies still obeyed their own desires when it came to it. But it was time to get ready.

11

Work first!

I'm just reminding myself. That was such an interesting evening but it's easy to get distracted by the non-work facets of it all.

Those two, for a start; my gorgeous Alphonse and that woman.

No, don't get me wrong. She's lovely and wow, imagine having the choice of those two men. Although I might do better if she casts off Dickinson. I gather he might be here at the end of the week. When that came out it had the architects looking at their schedules. I don't think they'll have a chance of a top table invitation, but it'll stop them sloping off early. You know my views on Friday afternoons. I'm quite old-fashioned, really.

I'm a little old-fashioned about proper preparation too, so Mei's in her own room this evening. She was quite a big girl about it, but she did take the pink vibrator and the clamp. I'm glad, I'd quite like her to open herself up to the idea of men, she could have a lot of fun, particularly with her toppy attitude — and she can learn from the master. You see, I'm going to admit there to the gender ambiguity of that word, but I really am very comfortable being described as a master of my art; even of design, too.

I should start with the architects; they're the least interesting, of course. There are three. Alphonse has split the five resorts across them; the Aussie and the Chinaman have two each, and the Malay, who did this place, has one — and Alphonse has all three of them in every day for each other's projects. It's a brave idea, I told him, but I saw that woman with them a lot throughout the evening, she even sat with them for the meal; well, between the Aussie and the Chinaman. The Malay sat with his friend Raymond, but he must be in pole position for the remaining seven, and the new ones beyond that — this place is beautiful. It could be a template for all of them, but I do understand why Alphonse wants to keep layouts and designs evolving as he moves forward. It's the most intriguing challenge for me, integrating traditional cultural motifs into leading-edge design. But I liked the Aussie, Luke, he's a big, charming guy who at least talked a good game about working with me — he just seemed a little straightforward to be truly interesting. The Chinaman, Yang Lijun, was obviously a little stand-offish but at least his English is quite good. And Bobby, Raymond's friend, seems like a gem; they are two peas in a pod, both smiley, both talk with Aussie accents, which I found very disconcerting at first — like Mei's American — but I got used to it through the evening. I asked Bobby if he minded others being involved after he'd done such a wonderful job here; he glowed and said, manfully enough, he didn't have the people yet to manage that much work — and he was looking forward to learning from the others anyway. That's the sort of thing I would say, and I wouldn't mean it either, but he managed the sincerity thing much better than I could have done. I almost believed him.

They each had assistants with them, of course. They'd probably grumped when Alphonse had limited their entourages to one each. I didn't spend much time with the juniors, two of which were women. That's progress! Women in architecture, I mean, not me ignoring assistants. And it got Mei interested. Is that why she agreed to a night on her own? She spent a lot of time with Bobby's girl. That thought's just occurred to me — that she might have contrived an assignation. Funny, isn't it? However free and liberal we are in our encounters and arrangements, the speculations about our play-partners and what they might be doing can always put the acid of a little jealousy in our stomachs. I didn't even like that woman following Alphonse out this afternoon, although she'd been in perfect hostess mode this evening, talking to everyone and being perfectly charming — which tells me that she's probably in his room now!

Ah, but! I should be careful with this speculation.

But, to tell truth, Mei and I had been getting a mite too close. I have had a wonderful week with her, and I'll tell you more when we have time, but even I could feel myself getting a little attached. Some diversions this week — for both of us — would be a good thing, I think.

I met Liqiang this evening, and he showed even more discretion around Alphonse than Claudia did. Now this is one charming man. Taller than me — not all of them are — and exquisite, I can say no less. He had a slim face and an attractive tan. He looked very chiselled, as if he worked out at least regularly, if not obsessively. Just a little jewellery, I like that, a discreet gold chain around his neck and a pinkie ring. Now that wasn't discreet, that had a large red stone in it. I couldn't resist asking; the stone had been in a necklace of his grandmother's that had always fascinated him as a child.

"Your grandmother!" I'd said and he smiled, realising instantly that I was computing how such objects could have been sequestered during the Mao time.

"Our country's history is a little more complex than the '49 Revolution — and not all party leaders practised the self-denial propounded in the propaganda" he'd said with a cute smile. I liked him. A lot. His English was perfect, the light accent — West Coast, I assume — is tolerable if the man is handsome. And he wanted to know about how I was approaching designs, tuning in completely to my temple and garden sources.

It was Harry who'd introduced us. That'll be him at the door now. I'd told him not before midnight. Work first!

12

"This week is probably going to be safe for us, after all," said Claudia, "are you happy about your not-so-secret admirer?"

Alphonse smiled as he poured his whisky, she was limiting herself to water, "Lee, you mean?"

"I suppose I could have meant the ladies. I assume Isobel is also interested, but I think she casts a wide net."

"But she has us down as an item anyway."

"Is she that astute?"

"Maybe, but she doesn't have to be. I've told her I adore you."

"Why did you..." she looked cross, but then stopped herself and her face softened, "I suppose that's quite sweet, really, but do I need to know more about her? Were you telling her that to fend her off?"

He laughed, "No, it wasn't that. I like her, and we were talking. I don't suppose she's your type."

She looked thoughtful, "I don't think I have a type, really," she hesitated, "We are talking just friends, aren't we? You know I'm not remotely the other way." He laughed, and nodded. "As long as they have some life, and some sincerity. But what about your type. Is it Lee?"

"You're my type, you know that."

"Ah, I'm getting Alphonse the Enigmatic now, aren't I?"

"Come on," he sat at one end of the sofa and opened his arm to invite her, "I like Lee. OK, I like him a lot, but a week like this is a terrible time to explore a possible relationship and, as our dear Peter said, there is a vulnerability about a family where the succession question is unclear."

She nestled into him, "Does that mean there's space in your bed for me tonight?"

"I love you. How could I possibly refuse?"

She looked up and kissed him, then stood up, "I am sorry. It's a very big week for you, and me and my needs are the last thing you have time for. I'll see you at breakfast."

He stood up and pulled her to him. "I was thinking earlier today, I'm never happier than when I'm lying next to you, talking and sleeping."

"Yes, but we don't need the third element of the trio complicating our lives this week, do we? Talking, sleeping and… Can we agree we will when we're next on our own? I just like to nurture that little hope."

"No, come with me now," and he took her hand and led her to the bedroom.

Their couplings had been too infrequent to fall into patterns or habits, but he knew that for her, too, the embrace was the core of the experience.

She wanted his arms around her and her skin against his, their kisses always light and tender, like their touches. But she was pulling him closer and all the little clues had been telling him that she needed him like this. He slid a hand down to her hip and across her belly. She moved to meet him.

"Do you mind?" she whispered and kissed him without waiting for a reply.

He smiled, "I love you and you're beautiful."

Theirs was the easiest lovemaking of any for him, the orgasm was not the central experience for either of them. Oh, she would come, they both fully recognised her needs as he let his fingers slide across her, even inside her a little, but lying together, looking into each other's eyes, knowing excitement could come when it chose but just enjoying that sense of floating together — which they would sustain long after the cries and spasms had passed — was what had them coming back to each other with their decent infrequency.

She was moving more quickly now, "No, no, stay," she cried as he attempted to ease his fingers away, still holding her close to him, and she was shaking and gasping quietly as she came.

They lay, still cuddling, as her breath slowed, then her hand moved on to his cock, "You don't have to," he said quietly.

She looked up at him and smiled, "I'm afraid I want to — and I've finally got around to adopting American morality. Blowjobs are OK. Now lie back and be quiet."

He chuckled, this was lovely with her, it never felt too serious, it was only joyous and, for all that these were infrequent events, she understood his body better than anyone. He ran his hand across her back as she went gently down on him, always the perfect pressure in her grip, always keeping him tingling on the brink with her lips and her tongue and then pushing to his limit by going so much deeper and yes, he desperately wanted to come.

"Make me come now, make me come now," he breathed, and felt her hand moving faster and her mouth gripping him tighter and he rose rapidly to that waiting state of bliss. She stayed there a long while, even as he grew softer, then she moved slowly up to kiss him, her usual wicked smile still beaming at him.

"Don't worry," she was licking her lips, "it's all gone tonight. None left for you. But you do get a kiss before I fall asleep," and it was long and tender, before she turned slowly away and wrapped herself in him.

***

She was gone when he woke. He supposed that was best, he had an hour now to think about the day and what he wanted out of it. He was almost tempted to ignore emails but thought he should check for anything urgent. He put the light on and smiled as he saw the two large red lips, drawn in lipstick, on the pillow beside him. Monday morning, only Asia awake, no expectations —

but a brief email from Will: he would be arriving this evening and yes, he had heard Isobel would be there and he was looking forward to catching up with her. He began to speculate on Will's motives for coming, his project finance man would have been enough — but then, with Peter and Wengwei coming Friday, and Lee already here — and two billion plus being dispensed! Yes, the head finance man should be here.

He was nevertheless intrigued about Will's relationships but, as dead straight as he always appeared, Alphonse already knew enough about Martha's history to know that Will's tastes must be more colourful than the impression he gave. How endlessly fascinating people were.

And he tried to stop thinking about Lee and to focus on how to manage the day.

13

Well, that was entertaining. I had guessed right about him, but I let him play the stud to start with. I could afford to do that, I was sure he'd be good for at least two rounds, and his rather hasty completion of round one rather opened a door for me.

"I am so sorry, Isobel, you are so sexy, I just couldn't wait to have you," and he hadn't even tried to make me come. Harry, Harry, I thought, yes, you're young and handsome — and cheap-charming; oh, you know the lines they think will work, but I suspect he's had too many visits to hookers and he's got very lazy. So, I'm not attracted by any more than the challenge of setting him and Mei up together. I do think it could make them both better lovers: she needs to loosen up a bit and his cock performs well and it's not a bad size, considering — come on, I'm not going down the pc road of insisting that all men are equal, some cultures — I'm trying to find an inoffensive word — are just more blessed. He has more stamina than most, though, he was recovering well when I began playing with him, and it seemed to thrill him when my domme began to take over.

"You're a dynamic lover, Harry," I was looking straight into his eyes as I was playing with him — and I had his full attention, his rapid recovery made it easy to offer him compliments, "and you have a lovely big cock." Even Harry was smart enough to spot that bullshit — but he was smiling, perhaps he did believe me — no, surely not. "But you haven't looked after Isobel, have you?" I guided his hand to my pussy, and I was fairly wet, to be honest, and I got a mock shame-face out of him. "You know what this means…" Of course he didn't yet, but he looked expectant as well as puzzled and shook his head. "Well, I expect some service from Mister Cock here and I don't want you spoiling it for us."

I leaned over to the cabinet drawer — hey, I'm happy about showing my arse off still — and I fetched one of the ropes; now the puzzlement and expectancy went up a notch.

"I have to make sure I can enjoy you, young man. I will be tying your hands above your head — and your body will be mine." He was still looking nervous, but a little intrigued by now. I must admit, from his reactions to me in London and here, I'd assumed he'd already been into this. What was incontestable was that he wanted to be.

"I am very much going to enjoy your cock and, I promise you, your cock is very much going to enjoy me. Give me your hands." By now he was starting to look eager and, with my newly-practised skills (we'd done

more last week after my first lesson), I soon had him lying back, looking very comfortable on the pillows I'd built up for him. For the man, this is wonderful, of course — well, it is when I'm the domme. I don't need to humiliate or inflict pain necessarily — of course, I enjoy that very much if it's what the sub requires — but I have a buzz out of being completely in control — and Harry's reborn cock also looks like it can provide me with plenty of entertainment. He will enjoy it immensely — but I will control when he comes.

Of course I'll make him come, what do you think I am, a sadist?

But that was the important bit — it'll be when I want him to. And, if I'm judging him correctly, he'll scour the world afterwards, trying to emulate the experience. He'll find it if he looks hard, I'm not unique — but I am rare.

He's finding that already while I'm sucking him. It's a very nice cock, but it's no great challenge, I will be able to do anything I want. But this first phase is just licking and sucking the head of it. If he could, I know he'd press my head down — and then he'd come quickly and have about twenty percent of the fun he is going to have tonight. And I would have zero percent of the fun I intend to have. This is why I became a domme, but you do have to be prepared to give a lot to get a lot.

But it is so worth it. This sweet cock is very nice, and he wouldn't be far off coming if I took him deep. But we're a long way off that yet, for all his panting and gasping — and just be patient, Harry, pleading 'let me come, let me come' is not going to speed anything up. In fact, I'm enjoying it just that little bit more — yes, I know this is about the sub's pleasure, but the sub doesn't always know best — seldom, actually, in my experience, unless they're quite sophisticated.

I think that will do for now. I leave him alone for a moment and I'm pleased to see him staying vertical. I make a great ceremony out of rolling the condom down his cock — finally my pussy can take her time. I straddle him and slide down slowly. He's certainly big enough, I wouldn't want to leave you with a false impression — and I'm big enough too, and wet, I'm not going to bring him off soon by just riding him. But this is very pleasant and my breasts, I can tell, are also exciting him. I let him nibble me. He's quite good. "You can bite me, Harry," I say — and he does — wow! Good boy. I won't offer them again quickly.

My hands are on his shoulders. I like looking at him. He's handsome, and a good age for a man, and, now he's breathing and moving more steadily, he's smiling very nicely.

I lean down and kiss him and he's surprisingly good at that. I put my breasts to his mouth again and tell him to suck big, and he's good at letting his tongue play with my nipples.

Unless you've tried this quite often, you wouldn't believe how much more nicely men make love when their hands are tied. I am thoroughly enjoying moving up and down on this cock — and his smile is getting bigger; they do feel so thrilled when you show them how long they can go.

"Do you like anal, Harry?" I'm suddenly feeling a little dirty. He looks faintly petrified, 'no, no' but there's a glint of curiosity — he's learning that I'm here to please him. "You be a good boy for me!" I clamber off briefly and retrieve the lube from the drawer, then sit on him again. I am still rigorously pursuing the sub's best interests; I am just helping him to interpret what they are. I lean forward and reach back to smear myself, using a couple of fingers to check I'm relaxed. This isn't just naughty, I do find it very pleasurable, especially when, like this, I'm fully in control.

I'm not expecting it to last long, I'll be too tight and, since he's obviously overcoming any inhibitions he had, I can tell by his smile, he would come quite quickly — but we must educate the boy — and I take him in one hand and ease myself slowly down on him — oh, and he is just the perfect size. I feel a tiny bit stretched, well, a good deal stretched when I push down more firmly. So, I sit up a little. I'm finding it, as usual, extraordinarily arousing and I can tell from his breathing now that he is too. I really think that might be all we can manage of that. I have planned a different orgasm for us both tonight. So I climb off, more hasty than elegant I'm afraid, and strip his condom from him and hold his cock again. I look in his eyes, "Harry, you're a lucky boy, I am going to make you come in my mouth." He smiles —

like a lucky boy. "But while I'm holding you and sucking you, I am going to be sitting on your face. I am ready to come, so this will not be difficult for you. But understand this," I grip him firmly, "if I don't come, you don't come, understand?"

"I understand," he says, nodding, "but I don't know why you're worrying. I want so much to eat your cunt."

Ooh, good boy, he's even used a trigger word for me. I turn around and dock myself gently on to his mouth. I don't know why I worried, he's actually very good. I also have the other benefit of him having his hands tied; I move to where I want to be. But his tongue is very good, and he lets his teeth do some nice nibbling. I get so carried away I almost forget his cock but it's still there, nice and shiny now, with its beady eye staring at me. I take him in my mouth. I am nearly ready. So is he now, I can tell, so I ease off a little and push my clit more firmly down on his tongue. Oh yes, oh yes, this was such a good idea. I'm sorry if some of my narrative has seemed to disparage cocks and their owners but the truth is, I love them, especially when I'm controlling them. And now I really am coming, I'm loving pushing down on his face and his tongue is doing wonders. This is it, I'm coming, now for the sauce on this main course of mine. I take him deep to trigger him — and he reliably responds — stay there Harry, stop gasping, you're still working — but I am well underway and so, quite quickly, is he. Oh, that long build up is so worthwhile. I have to swallow and let some blobs squirt me before I go back to finish him. Oh, what an excellent pupil. He really did very well.

I untie him and we cuddle for a little while. He even starts to doze a little. I shake him, "No, no, Harry, you've been very, very good, but let's not spoil the night." He feigns sleep, so I push harder, "If you want this again, Harry, it's my rules," and I get him moving.

He'll be glad when he gets to his room. And he'll be very glad in the morning.

Whether he'll be quite so glad if he comes back later in the week, I don't know, but I have an interesting threesome in my mind. But, it's all for the subs' pleasure! Not all, maybe, but primarily!

And it's 1.30 now. Big day tomorrow, work first!

14

Claudia had given a lot of thought to how the meeting should be run, and that meant she had to explain her role first. She was there, she told them, partly on behalf of Peter Dickinson. This was a major investment for Peter Dickinson Enterprises, hence the presence of four board members this week — Will would be arriving that evening. She saw Isobel smile at this point but suspected that she'd known that already — and she confirmed that Peter himself would arrive by Friday. She also told them that Shen Wengwei was expected — Lee confirmed with a nod. So, they had the authority, in that room, to fix the plans for all five resorts, and they would have them ratified on Friday evening.

She meant that to sound empowering, but she guessed they all knew that in any organisational form on the planet, in business or in government — or even, perhaps especially, in the military — the person at the top made the key calls; the good ones at least took advice and used it, the bad ones hid behind it. It meant that if anything got really difficult during the week, it would take Friday to resolve it — she presumed that was everyone's tacit assumption. She tried to hide her concern that Peter and Wengwei might find issues to disagree on, or might, anyway, find other reasons to slow the project down, or even truncate it.

So, she spent more time on the role she intended to play as moderator. She thanked the architects for the spirit of cooperation in which they'd approached the project — that was merely a fiction that needed to be preserved, only Bobby of the three had shown real commitment to the principle. She was fairly sure that Alphonse and Raymond were hoping he could grow his business resources fast enough to enable him to take on a bigger share of the next phase. But she'd been encouraging them, as she always did in situations like this, to stay open-minded. They should do that anyway, but she also knew how quickly people picked up on the nuances of closed minds. She was there primarily, she told them, to manage the process, which meant staying flexible and, above all, receptive, and to look for valuable contributions from all around the table.

There was a lot of wishful thinking in that, she knew, she doubted whether the architects' assistants would contribute much in the open forum; and whether Harry and Mei would be allowed to contribute without Lee's guidance was yet to be seen. Although Lee had impressed her; she found him not only charming, he'd also seemed to want to listen.

And when encouraging all to contribute, she avoided looking at Isobel. She had no shred of doubt that the lady would offer decisive opinions. She liked her, and thought of her as, potentially, a helpful catalyst.

She handed over to Alphonse and was immediately struck by how strange it was for her to see him in this situation. She'd been in many meetings of this size in her corporate positions, even running some of them herself. But it was always a manager, of some level, running them.

What was unique for her now was not just that it was Alphonse out front, a man she assumed to be unfamiliar with the process and practice of meetings like this, but that the topic was absolutely about his business. It was not some regional boss or product sector head; this was Alphonse and, for all the decisions about buying and selling properties and blocks of properties, this was a man trying to create something that mattered existentially to him. A sad thought struck her — this was becoming his child. She'd seen, in his proud glow as he'd walked towards them yesterday, how much he owned, even loved, this place, how much he personified the Psamathe idea — however silly some people thought the name — it was growing on her slowly, she had started as a sceptic. But she was worried for him.

Why?

She wanted desperately for him to succeed, hoped for him to succeed, and, within a few moments of him starting to speak, her worries disappeared like water through fingers. He was tall, dark, slim, handsome — eye-catching really — with a beautifully modulated voice and an understated but impressive articulacy —

no verbiage, and few flourishes, he let the location pictures and the initial resort sketches capture the imaginations, his brief descriptions all clarity and succinctness.

She soon became engrossed in his vision of the project, almost forgetting that her role was to manage process, not to approve content.

When he moved on to numbers, he was mercifully brief, referring people to the tables they had been given of projected timetables and budgets, set against income projections for each of the five developments: and he pointed out that any issues raised or concerns expressed would be dealt with, or at least considered, in the Finance meeting on Thursday afternoon.

There were questions, all put respectfully, and most were simply dealt with; some were deferred, usually financial questions, but there were two slightly more aggressive enquiries on project management put by Mei — she obviously didn't consider herself inhibited by Lee's presence. Alphonse dealt with the first one easily, but Claudia found herself jumping in on the second like a mother defending a child — it was as if competence were being questioned somehow. She pointed out that Dickinson was a forty-billion-dollar corporation that managed complex businesses. Alphonse, however, very politely, cut across her. What Claudia had said was absolutely true, there was lots of relevant experience, but this was, in some respects, a unique venture, so it was a very good point Mei had made. That meant he was very grateful, therefore, to have Mei's expertise on board and he felt sure this area was the one in which she would have the most impact.

Oh, Alphonse, you smooth, smooth bastard, Claudia thought; the woman was almost purring — and Isobel was looking on as proud as a mother hen. Obviously, things had gone on between the three of them, she speculated — or maybe four, Harry had sought out Isobel at breakfast, he'd run to her like a puppy when he'd seen her. He'd even tried to keep the chair beside him in the meeting empty — he, of course, had to position himself next to Lee at the far end. Isobel, however, wanted to be between the two architects — smart lady, those would be the levers she would have to pull. She probably had Bobby in her pocket, although it occurred to Claudia that Isobel might be overestimating his malleability. She'd learned in Asia that smiles and nods reflect politeness, and not agreement, and she'd had to be doubly careful to ask questions before she made assumptions. She didn't know how much time Isobel had spent in this culture and made a note to talk to her.

Then, when Alphonse had taken them through the week's agenda and presented the aims: timetables and budgets confirmed; design principles established; issues and conflicts highlighted, he divided them into two groups for a tour of the resort led by Raymond and Bobby.

She and Alphonse had agreed that they would each accompany a different group and listen out for the issues raised and comments made. Raymond took the architects; it would have been naïve to expect a free flow of information had Bobby taken them. That would be Alphonse's group. She went to Bobby, who had Lee, Mei and Harry with him, and Lily, his own assistant. If they'd had a firm view on whether Isobel would fit best, she was glad they hadn't attempted to express it. Isobel went with the architects.

Claudia had wanted to do the tour with Bobby, she wondered how it would differ from the tour Raymond had given on her first visit — and it was a completely different perspective. Bobby, if anything, was even more proud than Raymond of the whole resort, spending at least as much time on the problems they'd encountered and resolved as on the innovations that had pleased him. He remained at all times sunny, even when Mei's questions were phrased and posed not merely aggressively, but almost disrespectfully on occasions. The questions were all relevant, and clearly prompted from a knowledgeable perspective, but they were unnecessarily rude — not that rude is ever necessary, she found herself thinking. Lee almost overcompensated in the way he addressed Bobby, but made no effort to rein Mei in. Harry remained silent apart from a few whispered Chinese asides to Lee.

She was almost shocked, however, when a smiling Mei thanked Bobby effusively on their return to the meeting room — "Thank you for being so informative, that was extremely helpful, I was very impressed." Lee caught Claudia's eye and smiled, as if to say 'she's not all bad'. It made her think of other countries and other cultures where people interacted simply differently, and what felt sometimes like disrespect was accepted as frankness. She still thought Germans were rude, though, and she smiled to herself as that thought went unavoidably through her head. But it was wrong to make culture an excuse — Lee had remained at all times charming, even as he was asking astute and difficult questions.

They made their way to the dining room. The other party was taking longer. They had planned for long lunchbreaks to allow everyone to catch up with any urgent business arising elsewhere, although Claudia recognised that, with her main focus now being the growing group in America, she was not going to be troubled at this time of the Asian day. Lee casually flicked through his phone, presumably to reassure himself that there were no burning issues, and settled in the chair beside her. Harry sat, limpet-like, on the other side of him, which might rather restrict the conversation, she felt but, as they walked to the buffet, Lee asked her quietly, "Would you have time to take a walk with me before the afternoon session begins?"

"I'd be delighted to," she said. Good, they would lose Harry for a little while.

Mei had placed herself between Bobby, to Claudia's left on the table for six, and Lily, his assistant, and appeared to be chatting in a very friendly way. Claudia reminded herself, once again, not to draw conclusions too quickly. She so much wanted open minds for this meeting. She must at least show that herself.

Lunch was still the Bobby show, and he spoke about the room designs, admitting quite cheerfully that the local designer had stolen — he used the word — from the London designs, but that he was very happy that Isobel was on board for the whole project. She'd shown surprising sympathy, in his view, in incorporating the right cultural elements into her proposals and, less surprisingly, appreciating what the star-grade traveller would want. That was his nomenclature she assumed, but it seemed to describe the proposition accurately.

No-one had more than a single simple course, so lunch was over even before the other party returned. They had more than an hour before the meeting restarted. Lee had asked, "Shall we go?" and, as she rose, he turned to Harry and said, "I have some things to discuss with Claudia." It was, it seemed to her, unnecessary, but it stopped Harry attempting to follow.

When they were outside it was warm, and Claudia suggested they use her veranda and have some cold drinks brought to them.

Lee nodded, "Good idea."

She rang for service from the bell on the wall — good not to have to go inside — and, her villa being near the hotel building, the waiter was there quickly. She was relieved; the Dickinson villa especially should receive quick service, but she also sensed that Lee wanted some privacy to begin his conversation. He waited for the waiter to disappear, then evidently decided he could interrupt himself when the man returned.

"You weren't here at the big meeting two years ago, were you? I would certainly have remembered."

"No, I wasn't," she said, and smiled, a little charm was always welcome.

"I was keen on this project right from the start; my father, not so much."

"How did you persuade him?"

"Our property portfolio was underperforming, so we wanted to tie in with someone who managed better in that area. You see, it's not just western property that we don't understand, we're failing in Asia as well."

"But this isn't truly property. Peter Dickinson struggles with that. We separate them, when we look at them now, into property and resorts. Of course, there's a great imbalance at the moment, this is only our second venture but if this goes ahead as fast as Alphonse and you are planning, well, it won't be at parity with property in five years, but it will be comparable — for us, and for you too, I think."

"I wanted to ask you about Alphonse. You are quite close to him, I think, yes?"

This was a time to be careful, "Yes, of course; we're colleagues, but we generally focus on different areas. I normally focus on our group. I'm here really because I'm more used to managing processes like this."

"Oh, I can see that. I thought you opened the session superbly this morning — and the two of you seem to work very well as a team. That's why I thought you were closer than normal colleagues. Is there something in the chemistry?"

"It's possible, I suppose," she shrugged, "but you wanted to ask about him. Is it something you can't ask him yourself?"

"No, no, but it is delicate, and a little research is always useful in preparing an approach. I just had the sense I might have a helpful discussion with you. It's my impression that you try to see everyone's best interests, I got that out of our talk last night, and out of how you ran the meeting this morning."

She smiled, "I think I'm meant to be flattered by that, Lee, but I work for — and am the partner of — Peter Dickinson, so I am going to have a bias because of that, however closely we work together on this project. I also know far too little about you and your Senlin set-up to have any idea what your best interests are."

"I had the feeling, when we spoke yesterday evening, that you were very well-informed."

"Well, I do a little research too, and I have a great deal of your key data stored in my head — I can even quote the mission statement of your industrial group in China. But your family office keeps its information more secret, as most of those type of businesses do, so it would be very hard for me to guess what your best interests are in that sense."

He looked thoughtful and nodded.

"I know we're waiting for the waiter to come with our drinks before you talk more about your delicate matter, but you could perhaps tell me a little bit more about the family office while we have the opportunity. I'm led to believe it's now bigger than the base corporation and that its holdings are principally in funds and property, that's right, isn't it?" He nodded. "But, beyond that, I know very little. Are you more focused on family office and your brother on the core business? How do you manage it all?"

He looked rueful, "My father would tell you — maybe he will tell you when you meet him on Friday — that he is teaching us to run everything but our education is, at best, an osmotic process, we're just expected to absorb. But we couldn't run things the way he does anyway — we're not him."

His father's influence clearly weighed heavily on him, but he spent a few minutes talking about how the family office had been set up and where the major investments were placed — widely distributed, but with GKD as the holder of their largest placement, "And, in most years, the most successful, I have to say," he was smiling, "and with Tony King, the most fun to do business with. The downside there is that my father worries that he leads Lou, my younger brother, and Harry astray." Now he looked a little thoughtful, "I think that's why I'm expected to spend more time on family office, while he keeps Lou mostly pinned down in Shanghai."

"So, your father runs everything still?"

He breathed deeply, "Very much so, I'm afraid."

"But he's doing so very successfully still, isn't he?"

Now he smiled, "Very much so, I'm afraid," he repeated.

"And he's in very good health?" Now he laughed — and she supplied the words for him, "Very much so, I'm afraid," and they were laughing together when the waiter returned with the lemonade.

"So, are we discussing Alphonse, or Senlin?" she asked when the waiter had gone, "although I'm not sure I'm truly qualified to discuss either. But Alphonse is maybe simpler and more in my area. What's on your mind?" It can't be what Alphonse is, she thought, surely the two of you have tuned into each other — he certainly knows you're gay.

"I will understand if you are unwilling to comment, but I had the impression that our partnership proposal encountered some reluctance from Peter Dickinson." She said nothing, merely looked levelly at him. "Tony seemed to have some trouble negotiating the deal, more with him than with us. Is that fair?"

"Is that what Tony's told you?"

"Is it trouble for him if I tell you it is?"

"You seem to know Tony quite well," she wondered what he made of Tony.

He smiled, "Well enough, I think, to assess that he wouldn't care about trouble very much."

She laughed, remembering the conversations and phone calls they'd had trying to get Peter's agreement. "Well, I think you've assessed Tony very accurately. He usually doesn't give a toss."

"Give a toss? Is that a bit like," he paused, "give a foxtrot?" and they both laughed again.

"Exactly right," she said, "he's the original WTF. OK, the background to the discussions we had is that Peter manages his corporation with some clear guidelines; they're in place to ensure he always has adequate control. In that respect, he's probably like your father, I imagine."

Lee looked thoughtful again now, "Well, I think there are more differences than similarities, but I understand your point." Then he spoke openly and at some length about the company history and how his grandfather had started the original business, but how his father had been the force that drove rapid expansion and the investment, mostly abroad, in new sectors, managed by the family office — he became more guarded about how his father sustained his political links while continuing to push beyond his industrial base.

"Peter likes to push out into new areas, but resorts are a field where he felt that we were expanding too fast, and we weren't guaranteeing the level of control he always thinks is necessary. He's happy owning only forty percent of some of the smaller businesses in my group, but he won't enter a bigger venture where his fifty-one percent is threatened. Did your father struggle with only owning forty-nine on our joint project?"

"He did," Lee was nodding, "but the bigger embarrassment for him was how poorly our property businesses were doing overall. That's why I wanted to ask you about Alphonse."

"OK," she said as a picture slowly began to form for her.

"When we were worried the deal might not come together, I sensed that Alphonse might not be happy — and I will say straight away that I am not asking you to comment on that, it was just a view I had — and I wondered if there might be a way of turning a negative into a positive. Now this might sound presumptuous of me, but we saw this big opportunity in itself, the resort programme I mean, and the possibility of associating ourselves with someone who has far more success with property than we do. And I will confess to you, I thought, maybe naively, that if he became very unhappy with Dickinson and the limited scope it was offering him, that he might think of becoming more independent and managing our property portfolio."

"Did you talk to your father about that?"

He looked uncomfortable, "I did, but do you mind if we come back to that?"

"I'm OK with parking that, but I am still a little mystified about why we are having this conversation. Can you not speak to Alphonse? And what is the issue, now the project's going ahead."

"The issue is that, while we're very happy it's going ahead, we still have a weakness in property management."

"Ah, I see," she said slowly, wondering if she was being stupid or he was being too circumspect. Her first instinct was always to blame herself; it was a very deep-rooted response which she had trained herself to, well, not quite to mute, she thought, but at least occasionally to disregard. "I think perhaps you want a view from me not only on how Alphonse would respond, but how it would be seen by Dickinson."

He smiled and nodded, "Your reputation preceded you, so I was expecting that insight and that perfect summary. I'm sorry I was so clumsy about getting us to this point."

"You weren't clumsy at all, Lee, you're right in guessing it's a delicate topic. You do understand why, don't you?"

"I imagine it's because Peter Dickinson must have absolute trust that his interests are being safeguarded."

"That's exactly right. I've said, effectively, that he struggles with the resort project, but at least that's discrete and clearly visible. I don't know property well enough, but I can imagine there is more scope for, well, I don't want to seem rude, but… scope for misunderstandings, can I put it that way?"

"I understand, but if all the property activities were open and transparent, would that work, especially if Alphonse had the overview?" He seemed very earnest and sincere.

"And you would like me to… sound out Peter? Talk to Alphonse quietly? How would it work anyway, are Harry and Mei your principal property managers?"

"The head of property is an old friend of my father's. Those two, report to him, but he is…"

"An old friend of your father's," she was nodding and smiling, "it would be wrong of me to offer an opinion on a man I don't know, but one of my earliest experiences when I set up my own consultancy was to persuade someone that his old best friend had to be fired. Are you saying that should happen here?"

"Oh, that would never happen here," he said, but his smile was telling her something different, "no, Zhao Long Wei will retain his prestigious office in Shanghai, and his prestigious secretary and his prestigious title, all in Shanghai, but he would travel less and less, and speak less and less."

"And he would be happy with that?"

"He would be content. His position would be secure, his reputation preserved — and his daughter could continue her successful career."

"His daughter?"

"Zhao Mei Tang. You have not formed a good first impression, I don't think."

Claudia laughed, "I'm sorry that was so noticeable — and it was inappropriate. I was annoyed with myself..."

"May I ask why?" he looked quite concerned.

"I should do better, Lee. I've spent the last, what, eight years, travelling the world, so I, of all people, should understand that different people, never mind different cultures, must go about things in their own ways. I admit I found her style a surprise — it was more, forgive me if this is harsh, more abrasive than I'd expected — but she plainly knows her subject, and she does have a charm button to switch on when she needs to."

He smiled, "Yes, I think she will be a major asset, but it would help her immensely — and us, of course — if she were able to learn from Alphonse. She can learn nothing more from her father, I only hope she will be able to inherit his contacts — although they are less useful as our investments in these areas are principally outside of China."

"I get it, really I get it, but working that closely would be a thorny issue, and Alphonse would have to be very much in favour. Then Peter would want some very secure safeguards…" she paused, "Look, that's only my initial reaction. Please don't think it's an official Dickinson response."

"No, of course not, we're having an off-the-record, informal chat, and I'm very grateful."

"OK, so, off-the-record and informal, what did your father say?"

And Lee, who'd looked so secure and confident, was suddenly tense. "My father is, as we said…"

"Very successful and very healthy."

Lee nodded, but this charming and communicative man was struggling to express himself.

"Lee, let me make a wild guess." She would risk this, she felt comfortable broaching what was undoubtedly an awkward subject, but she'd grown braver over the years. "He has some old-fashioned attitudes?" Lee pursed his lips and nodded. "And while he admires Alphonse's business skills…" she waited, Lee was sat expectantly, "he's uncomfortable with Alphonse the man."

"I knew you would understand. He is, I'm afraid, still a child of the Revolution — attitudes, and the laws, have changed in the last twenty years, but my father hasn't."

"But that must also make life very difficult for you personally, doesn't it?"

He leaned back in his chair, let his head move to one side, but managed a warm smile, "It's getting a little better now, but it was almost fucking impossible for many years," he gave a small laugh, "and I must apologise for my language."

"Oh, Lee, my dear man, I really couldn't give a fuck about your language," and they both laughed loudly, "and I'm flattered, on behalf of Dickinson, that you see us that way, but you have broached a very difficult topic."

"But what are your thoughts on it?" he was asking earnestly.

"I don't think my thoughts are very relevant, what's much more important is what Alphonse and Peter think."

"I would still like to know your views."

"Why?" She could feel herself liking him and understood his predicament, but this was a difficult topic and her allegiance was decidedly with the Dickinson perspective.

"If you felt there was merit in the idea…"

"How would it benefit Dickinson?"

Now he was smiling again, "I do like how straightforward you can be, and how you come quickly to the key issues…"

"And you like my susceptibility to charming, handsome men who flatter me…" but she was smiling at him — that was warning enough to let him know this was still a serious business conversation. She recognised that he had only spoken a truth — it was an area she excelled in — but it was still unnecessary flattery.

"It would mean you could effectively manage a property portfolio around twice the size that you currently have, there would be more scope for trade-offs and larger investments, and you would have a better-informed Asian network than you currently enjoy. We would still retain the operational capability, but it would be under Alphonse's direction."

She was nodding, that was all a little plausible, but she doubted whether Peter would be enthusiastic — but Alphonse's attitude would be harder to predict, partly because of the question that had been buzzing louder and louder in her head.

"There is a dimension to this that we're not overtly recognising..." this was difficult, but she was worrying about what people dear to her might be exposed to.

"Go on," he said, and she could safely assume, she felt, that he understood the problem.

"Would you be happy, personally, working closely with Alphonse?" The puzzled look on his face looked less than sincere. Was he expecting her to make the point more explicitly? This was uncomfortable — and exasperating. "Lee, if this were a man and a woman managing a similar situation across business boundaries, we would worry about a relationship forming — and we would have a frank conversation with them."

He leaned back, closed his eyes, and began nodding — evidently relieved that she had spoken directly about the issue.

"But this is more difficult than that, can't you see?"

"Because of my father, you mean?"

"Yes. Even I can't be clear about whether the logic is all business, or whether it's emotional. Can you answer that with sufficient self-knowledge?"

He seemed to deflate, "I know you have a point. You are being very frank with me — and I don't think even you can guess what a relief it is to be able to talk openly about an issue like this…"

"I think it's me who's been talking openly. You've made me work hard to get us to this point," she was making a fair point, but she was teasing him a little.

"I'm sorry. You are right, but at least I can say to you now that there is a personal chemistry thing that's driving me to want to pull this all closer together."

She thought for a while — and he was waiting for her to speak next, "Lee, if there's something there that you and he want to pursue, why don't you just do that anyway? You don't need a business link."

"I wanted him two years ago, in Teluk, but he went off with someone else then."

She laughed, this was a weird conversation, but then she worried that she might have hurt his feelings. He didn't look too concerned, and she hoped she was masking her own deeper feelings. Lee was apparently expecting her to discuss the affections of the man who was, as they'd rediscovered the previous night, her lover. "That little affair in Teluk didn't last long though, did it? And it didn't compromise any business, I don't think. But he has honestly told me very little about it.

We're not as close as you seem to think we are." Now Lee was looking sceptical — that didn't matter, he really should decide for himself what he wanted, and not complicate her business — and her life — with his desires and ambitions. But she managed to move herself to his sofa and take his hand, "Why don't you first see if there's an emotional basis between you?"

"Because, if there is, it would block off the business opportunity, my father would see to that, yet that's the only area I work in that really interests me." He sighed heavily. "I don't feel I'm any further forward, apart from being deeply grateful that I've been able to have a conversation like this," and he leaned forward and kissed her gently on the cheek.

And I'm very grateful, she thought, as her own turbulent feelings began to trouble her more, to at least have been alerted. "Are we ready to face the afternoon now? This is where it might get interesting."

"Are you worried?"

"I'm glad we're starting with Bobby's project, but I'm still going to expect some tensions between architects and design, if I've understood Alphonse correctly, but the bigger issues will be between the two of you, on the one hand, and the architects on the other. We have those outline timetables and budgets, but I believe they are presenting challenges. That's where your young lady will be very useful, but I'm not expecting my role as moderator to be an easy one."

They laughed together, he stood and offered his hand, "Time to head back then."

15

As if the day hadn't been hard enough, Mei wanted to see me before dinner.

Don't get me wrong, the meeting made progress, I think, but the tensions were bound to arise. I could tell that on the tour before lunch; poor Raymond got bombarded with some very technical questions. It was as if both of the architects — even Luke, who'd made himself out to be so relaxed and friendly — were making points that were meant to sow doubts in Alphonse's mind about Bobby's credentials. Raymond's answers always seemed well-informed, but they'd given Luke and his Chinese counterpart plenty of ammunition to attack Bobby's project — the Thailand one that Mei and I had visited last Friday — and, therefore, to undermine the costings and time plans that Alphonse had proposed — and that they, of course, had originally agreed to in their submissions.

I thought Claudia wrapped it up very well; she isolated what the issues were and at least got consensus on what would have to be resolved — and she made us finish at five. I think she's expecting a few conversations to take place before dinner at seven.

And Will's expected here by nine! Yes, I am excited. Just about seeing him, honestly.

But in the middle of all that, Mei wanted to meet. It could have been about a number of things, of course.

Yes, I ended up spanking her. I expect you want to know why.

At one level, of course, that's nonsense. I ended up spanking her because she wanted to be spanked, but she had three excuses ready to try to induce me to be stern with her — I wasn't fundamentally opposed, you understand.

The easiest one, and the one I used, in fact, was about her spying on me and getting jealous about my time with Harry last night — it had been jealousy, of course, that made her want this contact with me.

Anyway, she has the room next to his and heard him go out just before midnight — I'll tell you why she was still awake a little later, that relates to excuse number two! But the idea that I might restrict or restrain myself is objectionable, nor would I impose those sorts of restrictions on her; we'd covered that ground on our tour last week, but the worst feature I found was the spying. I don't know if she exaggerated what she'd done in order that I would spank her harder. It didn't matter anyway. The point was, we'd found a cause, so she was over my lap, and I was quite fierce with the paddle. I also, and this pushed her past a boundary, quietly took the little plug and, after a quick dollop of lube, pushed it into her bottom. I don't recommend doing it that way

— overt, even ceremonial, and careful and slow is far preferable to furtive and quick, I believe — but she had been so prissy last week when I started playing more adventurously with her. It made me think her subs wouldn't get as much out of her topping them as they could or should do, she needed to loosen up.

I'll be more open here, I was already looking forward to a threesome with her and Harry; I think those two could be good if guided appropriately, and this was important preparation. I do enjoy choreographing people fucking, but I tend to make myself the star as well as the director.

Anyway, she was over my knee, naked, and I was mostly naked, so there was plenty of gentle and sensual skin contact and she quickly got over her outrage — calling me a hypocrite and a violator earned her another two very heavy ones — OTK, I can't wield a paddle any harder than I was doing — and I'd guessed she wouldn't call yellow; although I hadn't been so certain when I was pushing the plug in — I was telling her 'this is for being very naughty' while I was manipulating it. Anyway, as for almost everyone who gives themselves to the experience, she found it very pleasurable, I could tell from how she was soon moving and moaning. Of course, her commitment to 'never spy on you again' was undermined by the way she was beginning to enjoy her punishment, which was, by now, by no means a disincentive — but it's all in the game, of course, you do whatever it takes to get you there. And she came very easily when I touched her, still with the plug in.

She wanted to pleasure me afterwards — naturally, she will become a good top one day — but time was moving on. I wanted to meet Luke in the bar. I mistrust him after today's shenanigans, but in a different way from how I mistrust his counterpart, John — I think his name's Yang Lijun, or something like that, but he seems happy to be called John — but not happy with much else. Now if you tell me there's a racial element to my perception, I won't even begin to attempt to dissuade you. But please give me credit for some self-awareness, I know I'm starting with a particular attitude and I simply have to stop that becoming a problem. Prejudices are universal, they just have to be managed. I won't even pretend to be prepared to discuss that with you.

But Luke is my first target; John will be in my firing line tomorrow. Claudia thinks I'm taking Bobby for granted, that was a quiet aside, not in so many words, during the break this afternoon: 'it's easy to be fooled by all the nodding and smiling' — I felt a little patronised, to be honest, but I still admire her, she did well today; it was not easy.

But I'm rambling. I still have Mei across my lap. Her bum is a little flat to be pretty, if I'm honest, there will be those little Asian saddlebags if she's not careful, but her skin is flawless and we touch each other tenderly. She started to make a fuss about wanting to make me come, I tried not to show irritation and I've promised her an interesting midnight rendezvous tomorrow. I think she knows what's in my mind. And anyway, I've told her she can go and see her own little trollop later.

Yes! Now I've got you to her second possible punishment cause. Of course, it didn't work with me. I am genuinely liberal about who my play partners enjoy themselves with — but she'd teamed up with Bobby's assistant, Li Ling, I think, but we're to call her Lily. She's a pretty little Chinese girl — sorry, woman. She must surely have been distracted by Mei paying so much attention to Harry's comings and goings but that's their business. I'm fairly sure they'll end up together this evening, now that Mei knows I'm going to be busy. I think she thinks I'm going to fuck Will. I would, of course, but I love him enough to want him to be happily married. Look, of course I fuck people who remain happily married, but those playtimes are carefully considered arrangements, there is nothing clandestine about them. Of course, if he were to tell me that he and his beloved Martha (of course I know her name) have an open relationship, then I would be delighted to enjoy his body again — but he wouldn't be the Will I remember.

But it was her third 'reason to be spanked' that was probably the most intriguing — and disturbing, so I deliberately didn't follow it up. She'd been talking to John about my photos and sketches, i.e. about the raw material — my stimuli — and my initial ideas for the designs I want to use. She knew that would irritate me, I like to keep my methods secret and I only expose the designs I choose to expose. Letting an architect know how I work and what ideas I'm working on is dangerous, but it would also have been dangerous to let her know how cross I was. I think John had been pushing her for information. I need to talk to Alphonse. I don't want more designs stolen and it may indicate that John's way of working is less than constructive. I'm putting that very mildly, it's actually unethical, in my view. I am just not trusting this John at all; I'll find a way of tackling him tomorrow.

So, I was left with her spying on me as her naughty reason — and that sufficed to spank her really hard — and to introduce her to the new thrill of a little anal play We kissed very tenderly before she dressed to leave.

And when I got out of the shower, I was amused to see that the little plug had been borrowed.

16

Alphonse had agreed that he and Claudia would have a debrief at the end of the formal part of each day — and meeting in her villa felt curiously safer than in his suite, where the bed had already welcomed them.

"That wasn't quite the disaster it could have been," he said, as she let him in, "thank God you were there." He kissed her cheek lightly.

"Considering you've so seldom run a meeting like that, I thought you did astonishingly well."

"Well, I certainly don't want to make a habit of it. Did you get the sense of some collusion between the two architects? How naïve was I, thinking some element of competition might keep them in check, with the prospect of the other seven resorts, and then the greenfield six. It was like they'd decided there was enough work for the two of them and they'd better find ways of ramping up margins and contingencies. Poor Bobby, he was trying to be so constructive, but they'd clearly decided he wouldn't be able to manage more than one at a time, so he wouldn't be a threat. I'd love him to do more, but even Raymond's concerned about how much he can take on." She was busying herself; he wasn't sure she was listening. "What are you doing?"

"Fixing you the docking gin and tonic, now sit down and relax."

"A docking gin and tonic?"

"Yes, I've forgotten all the knots and names I learned when I was on a boat with Jack, but when you'd tied up or anchored, especially if it had been tricky, you sat down on the back deck with a big gin and tonic. I think we're back in port for the day now, and we've earned these."

"Well, I am going to be grateful, thank you. Oh, did you disappear at lunchtime for a chat with Lee, by the way?" They were the two missing from the other lunch table when his party had returned — it had been obvious on the tour from the way questions were asked and points were made that there would be difficulties in the afternoon — he'd wanted to alert her. The discussions and interrogations had made them late back. He'd been intrigued by her absence, but he almost cursed himself now for raising the topic — if she wanted to tell him something, she undoubtedly would; why pressure her?

"I was going to come on to that, do you want to cover off the meeting first?"

"I thought you'd summarised everything very accurately, I thought your list at the end was very comprehensive. I've told John I want to sit with him at dinner — I think he's aware I'm not happy. Could you do the same with Luke?"

"Ha, that'll be a pleasant evening for him. I heard Isobel pinning him down for a drink before dinner. She might be quite an asset, she doesn't take prisoners… or maybe…"

He found himself laughing loudly, rare for him. She looked a little shocked, then puzzled, and then it slowly seemed to dawn on her what the woman's tastes might run to. She blushed sweetly, "I cannot believe I just said that. Is that really what she's into?"

"I couldn't honestly say, but she was interested in Peter's cellar, and I'm guessing she's more top than bottom."

"Oh, you think that's why puppy dog Harry is running around after her? Those really aren't the distractions we need this week."

"I'm too much of a gentleman to remind you of a more than pleasant hour yesterday evening."

"I have no idea what you're talking about," she said, smiling, as she put his drink down. She sat beside him, leaned back and looked more relaxed, "I did have a dangerously wonderful time, thank you." Then she leaned forward with a more concerned look on her face, "We are going to be good now for the rest of the week, aren't we?"

It would be better if they could be, he thought. "'Fraid so." He took her hand, and looked into her eyes, "I think we should try to stay chaste, but it maybe that we need a cuddle time-out at some point."

She smiled again, "Only if we're desperate."

"Only if we're desperate."

"I like that idea, a cuddle time-out. Now I feel like I have a safety net." She sat up straighter, this was now her business-like pose, "We have the meeting day follow-up fixed: you find out more about John, and I buttonhole Luke. OK?" He nodded. "I'll come on to the Lee topic then, shall I?"

Part of him was dreading this, but he knew it was important. He'd almost avoided Lee that first time in Teluk, he'd read some danger signs — in himself, as much as in Lee — and he'd almost deliberately pitched himself into a different affair to enable him to stay distracted. There had been no point in feeling guilty about that, it had probably been best for everyone. But he'd found, in the increasing number of phone calls — always with a relevant business purpose, of course, he assured himself — a growing attraction to the man. Well, perhaps it was merely a growing recognition of the attraction that had been there from the beginning. Claudia seemed to recognise the problem — or problems. "Yes, please do. I can't keep ignoring it, can I?"

"Well, ignoring it may actually be your best course of action, nevertheless. But I think I have to put you in the picture, although these may be things you already know about."

"Is it something to do with me getting closer to the Senlin business?" Lee had often asked 'what would you do' questions.

"That's part of it…"

They didn't play games in conversations, but this topic would be bound to be more embarrassing to him, whatever was happening, "I've spoken to him a few times on the phone, but I'm puzzled about why he's chosen to speak to you."

"I didn't understand that either, but I should come straight to the point, shouldn't I?"

He felt relieved, "I'd be very grateful if you would."

"Putting it simply, he would like your help and direction on their property business and also," she hesitated, "this is a little bit more difficult to say, but I think he'd like to be closer to you, but he's worried that, if that happens, even the current deal is endangered, and there would be no prospect of his father allowing a closer business relationship, however poorly their property sector is performing. Does that all make sense to you?"

He smiled ruefully, "It makes perfect sense, he's hinted at it before," which was true, but probably understated how far the conversations had gone.

"Hinted at closer work on properties, or on a relationship? Or am I prying where I shouldn't?"

"Well, he's kind of dragged you into it, hasn't he? I was rather hoping it wouldn't come together like this."

"What are your feelings on it?"

"I feel I'm compromising my loyalty, in different ways, to Peter and to you."

She put her drink down, put her hands on his face and kissed him, "My darling, lovely man, I don't know how I've done it, but I have got into some strange relationship with you — and I love it, but we knew what it was." She dropped her hands to his, "Well, I didn't at first, but I knew from our time on the boat when you told me about Éric that what we would have would be a friendship — and I'd never want it to get in the way of you having a real relationship." Now, having looked so serious, she smiled, "But couldn't you find someone more convenient?"

"I haven't found anyone yet. We're just speculating."

"Alphonse," she had a sly look, then she clearly decided not to pursue it.

"I like the man; in different circumstances I might like to be closer, but there's too much at stake."

"Well, as far as you and I are concerned, I'm quite happy, as long as I don't have to abandon my time-out cuddles; but I would expect Peter to have serious objections from the business perspective, even about the current arrangement — and he would have anyway about a bigger business tie-in. And as for Shen Wengwei, there's nothing I've heard about the man that would let me think for a minute that he'd ignore it. Am I right?"

"Oh, I think you most certainly are." And it didn't feel, reviewing it here with Claudia, that there was any point in pursuing it. "How did you leave it with him?"

"We certainly didn't resolve anything, in fact he said he didn't feel any further forward. He was just glad to have had the chance to talk to someone about it. Purely selfishly, I hope it goes away, but my views are the least important. Shall we get ready for dinner?"

"Yes, I'll see you in the bar. Sorry it's got you involved."

"Oh, it doesn't seem that big compared to what you've helped me through. Anyway, good luck with John."

And he left to go back to his room. Nothing had changed, except that, once you've given something a name, and you've looked at it and talked about it, whatever it was seems to have changed — and become more real.

17

Before you even think of asking, no we didn't! But it was wonderful to see him again.

It's not just that he looks wonderful, it's three or four years now and he's the full, ripe fruit — all smooth and glossy; but the manner too, the gaucheness wholly gone. This is a serious man, a real presence; even Alphonse treated him with some deference.

Don't get me wrong here. I would see our Alphonse holding his own anywhere, but in the little time I allowed them with each other, there just seemed to be a little pecking order thing, no question who the silverback was.

And I didn't monopolise him, not early on. I couldn't have done. He progressed regally through all the gathering, introducing himself to all, including Raymond's maître d' — but there are just some people for whom the room waits, aren't there?

Yes, I'd made sure the seat next to me was empty and that the kitchen was alerted for our two late guests. He'd told me he was bringing his project head with him — a nice enough young man — brief first impression — I expect he'll have a pleasant week. Claudia, who was the other side of Luke at the table with me, seemed to contemplate my machinations with a wry smile — I suspect she's intrigued to learn more about Will's dark past. But that woman's past can't be quite so pristine, judging from the dungeon in the house she now inhabits — and she does have a, let's call it a close, relationship with Alphonse, which can't be straightforward.

I digress, I'm as excited as a girl, and it really is because I've seen my protégé duckling as a full-grown swan. And we had plenty of time to chat after dinner (not enough, but the week continues), but I need to update you first on my architect conversation.

Luke knows Tony King (I don't know Tony King) but he was at pains to point out that it hadn't helped him get the contract. Actually, it doesn't matter a jot whether I believe that, but when someone goes out of their way to make a point like that, you're suspicious, aren't you? But, since he'd volunteered that he thought there was a close connection between his counterpart, John, and the Senlin property division, I suppose he had to say something about his own links.

For the record, I had checked both of their websites to see what they'd done (of course I had, you'd have expected no less) and I was quite impressed by both — so neither company seemed out of place being engaged here.

As for Bobby, well, the quality of this place tells me that Bobby belongs in this group too. But he and Raymond got my strict mistress face when we'd talked earlier about the theft of my designs. They weren't quite so blasé as Alphonse had been — I got a little of the required squirming and they were so complimentary about my work, and so effusive about my participation in the next phase... well, I'm not stone; sincere flattery is not just acceptable, it's welcome.

But anyway, back to Luke. He's built a couple of resort projects in Australia — impressive — and had some developments in Indonesia, so I can understand why he's on board. I was, well, let's call me challenging in a couple of areas. I think he was expecting me to make the points I did about the importance of the designer and of involving her (I know, some of us are men) and responding to her at all stages. I got the usual platitudes, of course. He was expecting me to lead with that and he was ready for it, but at least he knows I'm on his case.

What caught him out was me asking him why he was such an arsehole with Raymond, and by implication Bobby, on the tour this morning. I didn't get an excuse out of him, of course, I didn't even get a response — I just got a patronising 'they were valid questions, I need to know what's expected'. I wouldn't believe anything he said anyway; he must have some reason, I assume, it's probably just tactics, but I don't need to know that. I just wanted to make sure that our working arrangement is as it should be, and that involves me having a lot of control, and he needs to be aware that I work on this from all angles: pre-empt to prevent, don't dither!

All that being said, I quite liked him, although he wouldn't be my type.

He was trying it on with Claudia at dinner, and he really thought she was lapping it up. Just a bit pathetic, I'm afraid, but about par for his gender. But she is smart, that's becoming more obvious. She didn't wink at me or anything when he was holding forth, but I knew exactly what she was thinking from how she was looking at him.

We were on coffee when He arrived. Well, I was on coffee, most were on their different teas. I was ready for him, I thought; I was going to remain poised and cool, no question, but I caught sight of him as soon as he came into the dining room — wow, he'd grown into everything I'd hoped he would — and he even had the audacious cool to come to me first! I got a huge hug from him, possibly embarrassingly long, but I coped, and then he immediately excused himself to say hello to everyone else.

It did me no harm with Luke when he realised that the head money man and I were — well, fuck it, let's say we're close, it's my word this evening; he can assume whatever he wants, but now he knows I have serious influence in all this activity. Well, I don't suppose I do unduly, Will's far too professional for that, but it won't hurt to let that arsehole think so.

Will just ordered a salad but, by the time it came, the others had headed off to the bar, or even back to their rooms. His project head was on the next table, still being briefed by Alphonse. Luke had tried to invite Claudia to the bar — I don't think so, my man — but I'm not going to be too dismissive of the male's blind optimism, it does afford us plenty of amusement. She was gracious, not dismissive — almost flirtatious, but subtly so — I really am beginning to admire her.

But we were alone in the restaurant by the time I was finishing my grappa (OK, my second), and we were in full flow and I didn't want to stop.

"Will, I'd hate this to sound pathetic, but could we talk a little longer... privately, I mean." Something flashed in his eyes before the smile began to spread. "You have turned into a beautiful man, but this is, I promise you, just a conversation about loose ends from things past — and a demonstration of the new professional basis of our relationship."

He rather cheekily looked as though he didn't really believe me but seemed confident enough in himself for it not to matter — threatened was the last thing he looked.

"Will you come along to my villa? I should check it out, and I need to see if I have any messages, but I would love to catch up on things we couldn't discuss in public. I've missed you." You see, in control, unafraid and simple — and he was giving me no complicating vibes — this is a very close friend, like the best of old lovers are.

***

"You never used to drink whisky," I said as he put the two glasses on the table in front of us. He'd had a brief look at his bedroom, I assumed they'd unpacked for him, and flicked through his phone — and sent one text message; to her I expect. One came back shortly afterwards, and he smiled as he read it — and then seemed free to lean back on the sofa and relax.

"Whisky is a terrible habit I've picked up from Martha," he smiled, "I was never going to become addicted to your grappa," — ah, good, we were comfortable talking memories. "I'm embarrassed about losing touch, I was thrilled to get your message, I should have contacted you."

"No, you shouldn't. I was the one who misled you; you owed me nothing."

He looked puzzled, "How so, misled?"

"I misled myself, Will. I never realised how much it meant to me." Now there was a hint of alarm on his face, "Please don't worry. Sometimes you just end up happy for someone — and now I can see you like this, I'm truly thrilled for you. I assume you've just been texting Martha." He smiled and looked relieved. "And I'm going to guess that you and she are a better match than you and I would ever have been," now he even chuckled, "but in spite of being old and wise and understanding perfectly clearly that you and I had no basis for a stable partnership, I'd still fallen in love with you." That made him look tense again, but I made a joke of it and pretended to sniff and sob, "but" — pause to

fake choke — "but I'm almost over it now," and we both managed to smile. "I can tell you're happy, and I'm thrilled for you." Look, that's true actually! "I'm also very proud of you. I was pretty certain you'd do well."

"And get through my bad patch?"

"Oh, you were always going to do that, but nobody believes that at the time, especially when things finish so dramatically and abruptly..." I didn't know if he'd be comfortable talking about Merle and the aftermath but, if he wanted to talk, this would be our only chance. "Has she ever been in touch again?"

"Yes, each September for three years after. You were there when the first letter came, remember?"

"Of course I remember, we were in Brussels."

He chuckled, "Ah, where you were picking up the pieces and putting me back together again. Have I thanked you enough?"

"Oh, Will, you showed your gratitude in many ways after that," now it was my turn to chuckle and, bless him, he smiled but didn't look in any way embarrassed. That's what made him so good and what had surprised me about him, he enjoyed things quite unselfconsciously, once we'd examined just how much pleasure can be had. It made me think of my two little fledglings this week, who have a lot more to learn about themselves. Will had given himself to his education — embraced it, even. "All I want to know now, is that you're with someone who suits you. Do you enjoy each other?" He smiled and nodded. "Thank you. I'm not

going to press for details, but you were becoming a wonderful top," now there was a hint of embarrassment in his smile. *"Yes, I thought so, and I'm thrilled for you both, she's a very lucky lady,"* I raised my glass, *"Cheers to you both. It would never have worked between us."*

Now he tried to be a little gallant, "But we had wonderful times."

"Oh, we certainly did but, be honest, neither of us were exclusive with each other," he smiled again, *"but I always thought you might end up monogamous. Have you been?"*

He seemed relieved to be able to answer the question, "Yes, since well before we were married. In theory we're not; we've agreed, in principle, that a little adventure wouldn't ruin everything, but we both know it might, so, in practice, we are."

"Damn!" I said, but he knew I was being mischievous, *"I wouldn't dream of trying to threaten you though."*

He looked a little serious, "You didn't have any such inhibitions when I was with Merle."

"I was enjoying myself — and protecting you."

He sipped his whisky, "I can see that now, but I was confused at the time."

I laughed, "Well, fortunately, it didn't stop you trying anything."

Now he laughed with me, "No, I had a very rich education, thank you. But how are you, now? Are you still committed to 'no relationships'?"

I thought about that, I hadn't done for a while, "I don't suppose I'd rule it out now, but I doubt whether I could make anything work. I'd try to impose too many constraints and restrictions…"

"Like being committed to also fucking other people?" he was laughing.

"I suppose so, yes, although I know a few couples who seem to make it work."

"Seem to?"

"Oh, I think they do. There just aren't that many of them."

"Do they keep you busy?"

"Not so much, I admit," I wouldn't say he'd touched a nerve. Well, he probably had, but I know he was asking because he was caring about me, and I couldn't give in to thoughts like that, because that's not something I want to worry him with. "But maybe I'm finding the right balance. At least work's become interesting. And your Mr Dickinson intrigues me, you must know the house in Barnes."

He smiled, "Actually, I don't, but I've heard about it. You're thinking of the cellar, I assume."

"Yes, and Claudia must know all about that. I wouldn't immediately have guessed that was her thing but…" He'd taken my hand; he knew I was rambling.

"I was asking about you. I want to know that you're OK, and the more you babble on, the more worried I get."

"I'm OK, Will, really I am. But it is so good to see you," and I leaned into him and let him put his arms around me. *I think I am OK, but I'm finding being with him unnerving. It is going to make me re-evaluate things. I've meant everything I've said to him — and everything I've told you, for that matter — but this has awoken some lovely memories, not just of some thrilling encounters, but of being able to help someone you loved — there, I've said it now. I don't think, at the time, when I was in Brussels every couple of months, or he was in London for a day or two, that I would have put it that way. Well, I would have laughed at the idea, but when he'd moved on, I realised it had meant more than I'd thought.*

But it still wouldn't have worked! We're both tops!

But I do love his arm being round me while my head is on his chest.

"Will?"

"Yes."

"If I promise to leave your cock alone, would Martha let me borrow your chest occasionally?"

He laughed, "One of the many things you taught me was that it's irresponsible to regard the cock as an autonomous organ, so, current situation notwithstanding, I think I need to regard the chest the same way. I come as a whole. I don't think that's particularly worthy or moral, it's just the way life works best for me."

He's probably doing more for me than he should, and maybe I'm lusting after his body now to make myself ignore the rather more difficult issues he has confronted me with. "I'm going to be a big brave girl now and leave you in peace, because I love you."

"I wish I felt more convinced that you were content."

I stretched up and kissed his lips, "Will, my darling, this is an utter thrill to be with you again, and maybe it will give me a jolt to think about how I live, but it's triggered some lovely memories, that's all — and maybe a little regret, but I really am content. Now let's have a thoroughly successful week, there's plenty of work to be done — and find the odd hour to talk to me if you can. OK?"

"Of course, OK."

"Good, then I'm happy."

We stood up, he kissed me and we moved to the door.

OK, so I'm going to my room to use Harry a little. Will's made me feel horny as well as soppy — and Harry will be fine with being used; he won't even notice. But I will need to be a little subtle, that's all preparation for a threesome tomorrow night.

Tonight, I'm just very glad that Will is obviously happy — and it's nice to have someone worrying a little about you.

18

Alphonse had found the dinner unsatisfactory. John's English was perfectly adequate, his firm wouldn't have been selected had it not been, but each time a topic became delicate, he would ask his assistant for a translation, however simply Alphonse had phrased the question.

The man's firm had worked hard on the submission and they had some relevant experience in hotels and resorts, more than the other Chinese companies. But now they'd been signed for the next phase, he was becoming more difficult to work with. There really was a good reason to talk to Lee about this later, he needed to know how committed the Shen family was to an architect who had been chosen from their shortlist. He suspected the bond was quite strong. They had retreated into pleasantries during the main course; John would be presenting his projects tomorrow, that would be the time for more effective scrutiny.

It had almost been a relief when Will had arrived with Douglas. Douglas had been through London two weeks before to be briefed on the full project — and to be approved by Alphonse as the man he would be happy to have working on it. It meant that, when John excused himself immediately on Will and Douglas's arrival, Alphonse could relax and simply bring Douglas up to date on how the week was going. He didn't talk about his concerns and they were finished by the time Douglas had eaten the salad he'd ordered. Alphonse quietly observed the animated conversation from the neighbouring table, Will and Isobel clearly had a lot of news to catch up on. It would be interesting to hear about that later. He wondered if that would form part of Raymond's information.

He'd been surprised when Raymond had offered him what he called 'an intelligence debrief'. Raymond was almost always smiling, but there was something particularly mischievous in how he'd broached this topic with a 'text me after dinner if you like' suggestion.

***

"What's this about, Raymond?" he asked as he gestured to him to take a seat when he'd let him into the suite.

The smile was there again when Raymond had sat down. "Hospitality is relatively new to you, boss, isn't it? You have grasped it so well that I sometimes forget."

Alphonse smiled, "Cut the bullshit, Ray, what's this about?" He'd started calling him Ray in an attempt to irritate him when he'd been unhappy about something, probably more to do with his own mood than with any mistake of Raymond's, but Raymond seemed to enjoy having been given a personal nickname, so Alphonse used it occasionally privately.

"You're a man of the world, boss, you know people don't spend all their time in their own rooms."

"Oh, shit! I keep telling people there are no secrets in hotels, but I always forget I might be a target, even in my own place."

"Oh, don't worry, I understand why you and Mrs Brodie have a lot to discuss, this is an important and difficult meeting, but there are other arrangements where the logic is less obvious."

"Do you enjoy this?" It had been so clear when he thought about it. He was cursing himself and almost feeling cross with Raymond, before he calmed down and realised the unavoidability and the comprehensiveness of information like that — and the usefulness of it, potentially.

"I'm entirely neutral about it," said Raymond, with a completely disingenuous smile, "but in fulfilling my security obligations, I sometimes come across information…"

Alphonse couldn't help smiling now, "Information that some people might find useful. OK, I have got it. Do I have to hear everything?"

"Of course not. You can hear nothing if you choose."

"Raymond, I admit to feeling naïve for not having thought through the full implications of this aspect of the business — not the security, we've spent a lot of time on that — but the other possibilities." His mind was flooded with potential consequences, most of which would be, ethically, at least dubious — but which might also be quite destructive, if anyone tried to employ the information unwisely — destructive for the individuals, but also for the resort's reputation. He shook his head, "You'd better tell me what you've got."

"Some of this might come under the heading of gossip, you do realise?"

"Of course I do, but it might be useful to know who's talking to whom."

"Well, the first thing I should say is that Yang Lijun and his assistant have a very strong commitment to working together on this project."

"Ray, I know, in different circumstances, it's fun to pretend to be coy about this but, please, just who's spending time with whom? Claudia and I, you've got that," and he tried to appear as neutral as possible, as if he were in no way embarrassed about Claudia spending hours in his room — and if Ray conjectured that there was more than work discussed, well, too late to worry about that now; but a repeat would be inadvisable. "You're telling me that John spends a lot of time with his assistant, what else?"

"Ms Allen had formed a strong bond with Zhao Mei Tang, I believe you'd heard about that," Alphonse nodded, then thought of her effusive greeting of Will, "but Mei Tang is not her only visitor..." Alphonse dreaded what was coming — but he'd not long left Will and Isobel in the restaurant.

"Go on,"

"Harry Li has also enjoyed her company."

Alphonse chuckled, "What a woman. If she's shortening her sleep time, she's not showing it during the day." He hesitated, "There's something else, isn't there? What aren't you telling me?"

"Shen Liqiang and Yang Lijun have spent a lot of telephone time with each other."

"You monitor that as well?" He was a shocked, "Ray, I don't want to run the KGB."

"We don't monitor, we can interrogate the phone system and, before you ask, we don't record calls. I'm just keeping an eye on how independent Shen Liqiang is — or is allowed to be. So, worth just checking for you but it's only telephone time, no content recorded."

"Thank God for that, we're looking ethically shady already."

"We could if you want us to."

"No!" he said sharply. "It's probably already too much. You could be accused of spying in order to help Bobby, he's known to be your friend. But I had been wondering how tight John was to the Shen organisation," and those concerns are one of the main reasons why a closer relationship with Lee would be such a bad idea for him. "OK, is that it on that topic?"

"For now, yes. You want me to keep an eye on it?"

"It sounds like you will anyway — so you can let me know if anything seems relevant to the project. I don't need to tell you that you can't do or say anything that favours Bobby. I know we'd both like his organisation to be bigger, but this place stretched him. He'd have to work hard to convince me he could manage two at the same time. All the same, you took a lot of flak for him on the tour today, I thought a number of the questions were rude, even from the assistants. Perhaps John spent last night agreeing with his assistant what they were going to ask today."

They smiled at one another, "I think you're up-to-date now, boss, on everything relevant to the project anyway."

"Oh, no," groaned Alphonse, "there's something else, isn't there?"

"Lily?"

"Is that Bobby's assistant? Not with Bobby?"

"No, no, Bobby's happily married…"

"It's not my experience that that stops anybody."

"His wife's in the hotel with him."

"And Lily?"

"Friendly with Mei Tang, but not relevant."

"Well, let's hope it's just lust or friendship, but I'm getting a little paranoid about who might be plotting what with whom."

***

After Raymond had gone, he mulled over who might be looking for what: the efforts to undermine Bobby today by both of the others probably wasn't collusion — they would both have sensed that Bobby was the man with the completed project and he'd had a chance to forge the relationship with Alphonse himself. They might think he was favourite to get the majority of the new work and possibly eliminate one of them from future consideration. But John and Lee and a long conversation? It was hard to fathom that. And as for Luke, he wondered what Claudia had got out of the evening. He could call her, it would be brief, but it was already late. He texted: *Awake? Time for a chat about Luke?*

She answered quickly: *You coming round?*

She was awake, he could call. "It's not the main purpose of the call, but I've just had Raymond here telling me who spends time with whom."

"Oh!" and he let the thought sink in before he continued.

"Raymond knows we have a lot to talk about, we're running the week."

"Yes, quite. But Raymond is also not stupid. Is there anything else I should know?"

"This was just a brief call to ask you how you got on with Luke."

"I'll spare you the saga of how he was hitting on me, shall I?"

"Please do," but it hadn't surprised Alphonse at all.

"Well, I gathered Isobel had been hard on him about how he'd attacked Raymond… that's not too strong a word, is it, attacked? You were there…"

"It was rude, certainly, but attacked is maybe a bit strong; all credit to her, though."

"Well, he dealt with that quite phlegmatically. I think he's just interested in the lion's share of the roll-out programme."

"You don't suspect collusion with John to freeze Bobby out?"

"Not collusion, no, I just think they both look down on him and want to divvy up the future projects between themselves, but maybe they see a danger of Bobby getting most of it."

That made sense to him. "And collusion between John and Lee?"

"What are you saying? That's not in Lee's interests, surely. What information have you got?"

"A long phone call, apparently. Anyway, just something to keep an eye on."

"Yes, but is Raymond spying?"

"That worried me, but he maintains it's just information he has anyway, CCTV records and phone record interrogation if he thinks anything's worth pursuing."

"Is he recording calls? Is he listening to us now?"

"He says not, and I believe him — or I'd have rung your mobile. We get guests here who need absolute discretion, so this is just between you and me."

"So, what else is there?"

"I would tell you anything and everything, but do you really want to know?"

There was a pause, "Well, you'll tell me if it becomes relevant, won't you?"

"Yes, like us not being able to visit each other's rooms without it being noticed?"

"If I need a cuddle, my good man, that's not going to stop me."

"I'm delighted to hear it. Goodnight, my love."

"Goodnight."

19

Alphonse got back to his room at the end of the second day's meeting glad of the 'docking G&T'. Even with the calming presence of Claudia — and Will for part of the time — it had been a febrile day.

They'd given the first hour to Isobel to talk design themes. She had chosen only a few photographs to illustrate her points; everyone was well acquainted with why the three resorts needed renovation, but her choice of shots dramatised the need. What everyone found striking were her photos of cultural icons and historical design elements that she'd found in temples and gardens, so she would find distinctive themes in each of the three countries she'd visited. She then produced sketches of how she would see them integrated into furniture and fabrics, and how they might provide grander elements in the architects' plans for the common areas, reception and dining rooms. Even Yang Lijun joined in the light applause when her presentation was finished.

Alphonse was thrilled. He'd admired her work before but now, having absorbed some of the scenery, the architecture and the culture of the places, she was going to be able to give each resort its own unique feel, he felt sure.

The problems she would encounter soon became apparent as Luke, and his assistant Joe, began to talk about their two projects. The tactics were what he was always used to from architects and developers: budgets challenged; embellishments recommended — always with a significant on-cost after the dramatic 'artist's impression' had inspired everyone.

But he had hoped that, with further phases in the pipeline, they might rein in their extravagant habits and lessen the customary strength of their implication that the client was a penny-pinching dullard with no imagination or courage. But Luke was like many others.

The reason he'd started with Bobby the previous day was that Bobby had already delivered Morkuda. They were in it and most were utterly impressed — and he'd come in under budget. But even Bobby had effectively promised not to repeat that mistake in his presentation, which made Alphonse realise that having Raymond close to the development had meant that everything stayed much more in control. But he had five projects to start up, and he couldn't clone Raymond. And if the architects weren't exactly colluding, their DNA was pushing them, nevertheless, to behave in similar ways.

Claudia's list of open issues had grown long, and there were too many points on it with the unhealthy asterisk, meaning critical or urgent. It was a list that couldn't be exposed to Peter and Wengwei.

And now someone was at the door! Oh, well, his mind was only turning circles.

It was Lee.

"I hope I'm not disturbing."

"No, no, not at all. I could do with some help disentangling today. It wasn't good. Please, sit down, can I get you a drink?"

"Yes please, what are you drinking?"

"It's what Claudia calls her docking G&T," Lee looked suitably puzzled, "when you come back into port and dock successfully, you award yourself one of these. OK?" Lee smiled and nodded. "But I'm feeling rather that I've bashed the boat, but we haven't sunk. I suppose that's what matters most."

"You think it was that bad? You know much more than I do about these things, but bringing seductive and expensive additions into play, that's quite a common trick, isn't it?"

Alphonse handed him his drink, smiled, and said, "Cheers, and thank you, I was getting rather frazzled and a dose of common sense is very welcome. You're absolutely right, of course."

"I'm sure Claudia would see it the same way. She seems a very wise woman."

He chuckled, "Wise enough to go for a massage before dinner. I thought it was a good idea, but I just needed some time to think things through."

"I'm sorry if I'm interrupting, but we are confronting the same issues."

We should be doing, thought Alphonse, and maybe this visit meant that he was being unnecessarily cautious about Lee, "We certainly are, I think. Will we get more of the same from Yang Lijun tomorrow?"

"That's what I wanted to talk to you about," and Lee paused. This could go either way, thought Alphonse. "There is that danger. I have seen Yang Lijun use similar tactics to Luke's, so today wasn't unexpected for me. I have tried to warn him against approaching it this way, but today went exactly as I feared it would, and I suspect we shall get something similar tomorrow."

"I would like to avoid confronting your father and Peter with a long list of issues. But at least we shan't have the architects with us, we'll have given them clear instructions by then." Lee was looking troubled. "Do you want to tell me why you look so worried?"

"Do I give that much away? What about me being an inscrutable oriental?"

At least that helped Alphonse smile and relax a little, "So what's my oriental being inscrutable about?"

"I'm afraid Yang Lijun is close to my father."

"Was he your choice, or your father's? Please don't get me wrong, I was happy we chose him, and the past work and the site plans all impressed me, but weren't you worried?" Alphonse was showing his usual patience.

"The other two architects you saw were also friends of my father's," he gave a shrug, "just not as good."

Alphonse had to chuckle, but he was still concerned, "Could we not have gone outside your father's group of friends?" but it was clear from Lee's face that he would have found that impossible. "Anyway, there's no point in talking about it as a lost cause, like I just said, the past work is impressive. We'll see how we get on tomorrow, holding him to his original commitments. It's up to you and me to say yes or no."

Lee was still looking troubled, "How much influence will Peter Dickinson have on your decision?"

"I've never known him not support me." Alphonse remembered the difficult discussions when he'd first proposed the project, and the relationship with the Shen family. They were stormy and emotional, but Peter had supported him in the end.

Lee looked slightly dejected, "I wish I could say the same about my father."

"You talked to Claudia yesterday about me helping with your property division. Were you hoping I would fight those battles?"

"Fight them for me, is that what you're asking?" He looked slightly shocked, and then hurt.

Alphonse reached out and squeezed his hand, "I wasn't, really I wasn't. I can't imagine what it must have been like with such a powerful and dynamic father. Mine was just lovely and let me do whatever I wanted."

Lee lifted Alphonse's hand and lightly kissed his fingers, "And let you form the friendships you wanted?"

Alphonse smiled, and gently pulled his hand away, "Well, I'm not going to pretend that coming out was easy. I told my mother first," he leaned back and smiled. "'Of course you are, darling' she said, in her lovely musical way, 'we would never have wanted a boring child', but they were a little disappointed, I could tell. They always welcomed my friends, though. It was embarrassing how full our house would get with couples escaping from disapproving homes. My mother thought it was fabulous, of course, all these stylish young men fawning all over her. My father tried his best and developed his grumpy persona — 'I wouldn't mind seeing a young woman occasionally, Alphonse, and I wish your friends would compromise on their drinks; does expensive wine have to be consumed in such volume?' — but he never made anyone feel unwelcome. And in the end a few young ladies did come, it was a fun house to be in and they found it safe, I think — although my father did like to flirt with them; he wasn't dangerous, of course, and he had a wonderful time in the end."

"You're describing an idyll…"

Now Alphonse put his hand on Lee's shoulder, "You and I should talk more later, but thank you for coming here now, and let's remember we are in control." Then he smiled, "Or we should be! We should go to dinner now."

They stood — and trembled for a moment on the edge of an embrace; but Alphonse was relieved, when Lee had gone, that they'd made no definite move towards each other.

20

I'm going to admit that there was a certain lack of openness in my preparation for this evening. Neither Mei nor Harry was given a full briefing, but at least I'd told Mei I wanted her to look at Harry differently and that, if she wanted, she could content herself with watching. Poor Harry, I'd merely told him that I would be inviting a friend and he could enjoy a threesome. I've no idea who he thought I'd bring — when a cock gets an idea in its head, its minder becomes surprisingly stupid, almost without exception. If you're reading manipulation into this and taking a higher moral position, I'm going to show you that everything (well, almost everything — I always, as you know, qualify it this way) is done for the sub. Although Mei, of course, is more top, I do expect her to get drawn in; I'd sensed something spicy in their somewhat spiky relationship that would make the evening very interesting.

But I'm getting ahead of myself. The day had started really well. I had the first hour of the main meeting, although I ended up running over. I put a lot into the selection of photos. We were there to talk renovation, but it was useful to dramatise why it was so necessary in the three sites we'd looked at. When I came on to the national cultures and histories and the continuing threads of icons and patterns embedded in these, everyone seemed genuinely interested. Look, I truly mean enthralled here, it was very gratifying, but I thought that, for the purposes of my narrative, I had better make a more modest-seeming claim, relying on your acquaintance with my tendency to understatement to acknowledge the more appropriate term.

Joking aside, I was thrilled with how they responded. I had married my selections to the guidance I'd taken in my preparations. I now have, in the London office, a shelf of large, glossy books on the art of Asia, and I had been very pleased to find the themes they illustrated present in much of what I'd explored last week. I felt confident in the authenticity of my designs and proposals. It's immensely stimulating to work in these new areas.

I even had the architects looking on admiringly — although we had ample opportunity later in the day to appreciate where problems were going to arise with those guys. Even lovely Bobby seemed to be going over to the dark side. I know how this works. They'll be proposing limiting budgets for the rooms — my budgets — before we get to the end of the week. I'll be looking to Will and Alphonse to stamp on that — grand entrances are fine, but the real 'wow' should come when you enter your room or villa.

I'm not sure how strong Alphonse will be; there were times as costs were challenged and additional ideas were proposed — and all the architects supported each other, of course — when he seemed to be looking for help from Lee's corner, but Lee stayed subdued. I couldn't work out whether he was in awe of Alphonse, or in fear of his architect, John. I'm not too worried, this is a major project and they'll end up doing as directed. They'll know, deep down, that they can't push it too far — and Alphonse will know that too — but I do understand, he wants to move this forward in a spirit of harmony. Great leaders are able to create this illusion, or at least sustain it for themselves. He may be a little too sensitive for his own good. At any rate, he seems more worried about the rest of the week than I am, or would be in his position.

I didn't monopolise Will at dinner. I'd told him I wouldn't when we were drinking at the bar beforehand. I got one of those smiles from him that told me he was grateful I wouldn't make a fuss — he would have had to deny me that anyway, I knew that. I do love that boy, still, and I think his eyes were also telling me that we could have a little more private time later — just friend's time, you understand, there was no flirting. Of course, the best tops are like that: clear, decisive, and a little cold.

I really wouldn't have embarrassed him anyway; he has other relationships to build — and I had to plan my own evening. I'd asked Mei to my room for a quiet drink at the end of the main session. I had to work quite hard, she does think of herself as having an antipathy to males in general, and to Harry in particular. I didn't like selling her on the idea of Harry as the trussed-up victim, I did have to come up with my po-faced reminder that a top's work is to provide pleasure for the sub.

Her telling me that 'subs like pain and cruelty, that's why they're subs' I found neither enlightened nor endearing. I wouldn't say I lost some affection for her in that moment, but it did remind me that she has much to learn if she wants to have successful relationships — or arrangements. In the end, however, she agreed that she'd wait for my text after dinner, by which time I expected to have Harry not just in a position of physical readiness — he would be tied up and stimulated — but also in a state of emotional and erotic anticipation. Yes, I knew I would be relying by then on his lower brain dominating his thinking — but that's not too arduous a precondition in that gender!

I told him to give me twenty minutes after dinner. I'd told Mei to stay with Lily at a different table from me; that would be another evening of frustration for Luke as he and Joe were hitting on them, but it would deflect any suspicion that Harry might have developed about who our third party was to be. We sat with Yang Lijun and Daiyu, his 'assistant' — why parenthesis? Because I'm guessing there's more than a work relationship there, but the woman does understand the business. I'm not saying that because she was so complimentary about my spot this morning, she was genuinely insightful and, apparently, keen to integrate the ideas. We'll see tomorrow if we get some references in their presentation.

They were polite enough to speak English most of the time and it was hard to tell how they truly interacted. I got more of a sense of deference from Harry to John when they conversed occasionally in Chinese — and Harry is the client, or the client's representative. I'll wait for the dazzling and innovative — and expensive — surprises from John in tomorrow's presentation — and see what support he gets from the Chinese contingent. But it was a very pleasant dinner.

John had enquired early on about how close I was to Will; he could hardly have avoided seeing Will greet me the previous evening. Obviously, I told him we've been close for years and that I'd done work for him in the past. All true, of course, but his little apartment's makeover all those years ago was the smallest project I'd ever undertaken since I started my own business. And as for profit, well, it was truly a labour of love. I just about recouped my costs, that's all.

***

Harry arrived at my door exactly twenty minutes after I left the table. Mei had watched me go and smiled. I'd barely had time to shower and put on the obvious underwear. I wouldn't say I was proud of it, but I make quite an impact when I check in the mirror, I modestly admit to myself, but you have to get into the mood, or you can feel very silly. It's funny, though, how you can seldom look too cheap for most men. I imagine Alphonse might see it differently but, of course, he would have a very different perspective.

I'd wrapped myself in the hotel's cotton robe to let him in. He could spend a few moments guessing what I was wearing — or whether I was naked, probably his preferred option. But I made him sit down when I'd kissed him, we were going to have a drink and talk first. It was still early, we had plenty of time tonight. I wanted him to talk about his previous experiences, we'd been too busy in our two late-night sessions and I hadn't wanted him staying beyond that brief post-orgasm cuddle.

My rope tricks hadn't been completely new to him, but he hadn't liked the experience he'd had before, whereas, in his two nights with me, that had been spectacular, he said. I was pleased about that, and a little relieved, because I wanted to spread-eagle him again tonight, as I had done on the second occasion.

What I'd also introduced him to — well, he said it was new for him, but denial is a man thing in this area, few of them like admitting they like anal play — but I'd slid a couple of well-lubed fingers into him while I was sucking his cock and got him very close to exploding — and he, like many of them, still stayed stiff when I'd stopped sucking. It's fun to watch their faces; they only really like showing you an erect cock, not a limp one, but they're embarrassed by how stiff they stay when it's just your fingers playing with their bum. At least Harry had the decency to admit that he'd liked it.

I also got him intrigued by the prospect of the 'guessing game'. This was clever of me, if I do say so myself, I wanted him to submit to spread-eagling and the blindfold. He was to guess whose mouth was on his cock, and there would be a punishment for every mistake. He got a little nervous at that but my seductive 'you know you want me to spank you again, Harry' had him nodding. I wasn't sure how I would choreograph that, or how he would feel when he discovered that it was Mei who was my friend.

I asked him about threesomes, but he'd only tried MMF. The things they get up to with their best friends! He'd also tried foursomes, of course, but at least he was relaxed enough with me now to admit that the boys had come quickly — Harry is still quite poor like that, that's why bondage under someone's control is so good for him — and then they'd enjoyed the lesbian scene. Yes, they'd been paying, of course. He was quite open about that, too. Part of me quite likes him, but that doesn't extinguish the little corner of quiet contempt in my mind. Of course he will enjoy the night, but I'm organising it more for Mei — and, to a lesser extent, for Harry's future partners.

So, I stand up now and my robe falls open. He's more of a pussy man but my boobs have his attention. I slap his hand as he reaches for them. "Harry," I say quite sharply, "I think you've had two wonderful nights under my guidance..."

He looks down, already the naughty boy, and mumbles, "The best, Isobel."

"Well, if you behave, tonight will take you to a new level, but you will remain under my control at all times, is that clear?"

"Of course," still mumbling, but his somewhat crestfallen pose changes as I kneel down in front of him and begin unzipping him. He's already a little stiff, sex conversations and the sight of my boobs will do that, but few things make a man stand up as quickly as the prospect of a blowjob — but you knew that, of course, and Harry is absolutely no different.

But I enjoy his cock, it's a nice size for everything and, properly manipulated, it's capable of great stamina. But after a few minutes of mounting excitement, I get that 'hands on the back of the head' thing from him. I pull back immediately, "This is why I tie you up, Harry. You really don't know how to enjoy yourself properly. You will have so much more fun if you look after your partner." His hands drop, and I resume. I do like sucking cock, by the way. And I am quite good (yet another example of me lapsing into understatement). He'll probably be stiffer for longer tonight than he has ever been in his life.

By the time I have him tied and blindfolded, I'm feeling randy myself and tell him, "My friend will be here soon, Harry, but my pussy needs a little of you first." We'll stay with that quaint nomenclature for a while, I'm not sure how Mei feels about 'cunt', she can be a little prissy. I roll a condom down him quickly and just pull the thong to one side as I straddle him. Oh, it's lovely, I've never found much virtue in self-denial. I relax into a rhythm that pleases me, and with him blind and bound, he can only focus on letting his cock entertain me. His hips begin to push a little more vigorously, but he can't make himself come just like this. Try it! Keep their hands out of the way and you can control them for ages. But it's time to text Mei, so I climb off, text quickly — ah, the advantages of blindfolds — take off the condom and resume sucking. He remains Stiffness Undiminished, bless him. I could hardly have chosen a better victim. I kneel between his legs, hold his cock, just licking its head, and admire his trim body — I really should stick to the under thirty-fives.

"Ah!" I say unavoidably — stupidly — at the ring at the door. "Don't move!" and even he, with a rope on each limb, laughs at this; we've created a good atmosphere.

Just as well, because I have to recover from the shock of opening the door to Mei — and Lily.

I put my fingers to my lips in what I assume to be a universal gesture, but they have obviously come briefed for silence.

"You're a very lucky boy, Harry, you have three of us to play the guessing game with." I'm frowning at

Mei, and she's looking puzzled at me, but I'm slowly imagining the new possibilities that have just opened up. Lily is clearly intrigued by the sight of the blindfolded and trussed man sustaining, unaided, a very healthy erection. But I know that will need some support soon, so I move to the side of the bed and begin stroking him. I gesture to the ladies to see if either wishes to join me and Lily is first. She goes to the other side, her hand replaces mine. She wanks him a little quicker and I bend down to take his cock in my mouth briefly. He is obviously very excited, but we're not letting him come for a while yet. Mei is standing back, apparently transfixed. I have no idea what she's thinking but silence is part of the scene.

Lily begins sucking his cock, but takes only the head into her mouth, copying me — good girl!

"That's Amy on your cock now, Harry." I had one name ready, I needed a second. Easy, "We'll let Annie give you a quick suck and after that, you'll have to guess who's next." Mei — my Annie — screws up her face, but Lily looks up and motions to her. Mei kneels down opposite her and they kiss briefly before she lowers her mouth onto him. I've moved to the bottom of the bed — enjoying the scene. He won't find it hard to guess who 'Annie' is unless she engages with a little more enthusiasm, but suddenly Lily puts her hand on the back of Mei's head and pushes. Lily laughs as Mei jerks up suddenly with a flash of anger in her eyes, but Lily moves swiftly around the bed to embrace her, leaving

me to deal with the now lonely cock. Mei softens quickly and they are soon kissing, then Harry says, "That's you again, Isobel, isn't it?" The two of them separate and laugh and I'm chuckling — we've effectively ignored him as we've focused only on his cock.

So, I kneel up straight and tell him, "Well done, Harry, right first time," but an idea has come into my head, prompted by watching the girls kiss, "now we're going to sit on you. We'll come back to the guessing game later. When the ladies have undressed," — and Lily follows my direction immediately and is soon naked, Mei follows soon enough while I take a condom out of the drawer, unwrap it and am about to roll it on him when Lily takes over — bless you, Harry, and your unwavering erection — and she straddles him as soon as she has it on him. Lily and I gesture to Mei to sit on his face, but she shakes her head. I'm not wasting the opportunity, so I quickly lose my thong and straddle him, facing Lily who's clearly enjoying the cock and is smiling at me. She leans toward me and we kiss, lightly but sensually, and when she pulls back, she turns to Mei and puckers her lips. Mei now kneels on the bed and kisses her. The two of them are clearly fond of each other and we can't engineer too many opportunities like this.

"Would you like my seat, Annie?" I ask her, "He's very good at licking pussy," — he really is, I'm a little reluctant to relinquish the spot but I do so when Mei nods tentatively to me. I sit on the chair nearby and

watch her lower herself. At first, she seems more interested in kissing Lily again but establishes quite quickly that Lily is a little preoccupied with the cock in her cunt. Harry, meantime, is obviously enjoying the new pussy and must be employing his best technique, because Mei is soon moaning. The girls are still embracing but both are now grinding their hips.

"Easy, ladies," I say, "you'll make him come if you're too energetic!" and Lily realises it's her duty to lift herself from him, his hips have been gyrating ever more wildly with hers. Somewhere from beneath Mei we can hear a muffled sound of disappointment, but she herself is looking particularly happy — it's not just me who thinks he's good. I remove the condom, hold his cock and then lick again and suck lightly on its head, then invite Lily to do the same. She has taken up station on the other side of him. She smiles at me, looks into my eyes and leans forward to kiss me before she bends down to tease his cock, copying my actions of licking and then sucking the head. I move around to stand behind her. She sits up and I can rest my head on her shoulder, I'm trying to trick him by where my voice is coming from. "Which one was me, Harry?"

I signal to Mei to lift herself for a moment to allow him to speak. She pokes her tongue at me and makes a childish face, which makes Lily and me both laugh. That makes it a little easier for him.

"Ah, I thought you were trying to trick me. You were the first one but you moved around before you…"

and the rest is drowned by Mei sitting back on his face. She isn't waiting any longer. She reaches out to us. I move back to my side and she takes a hand of each of us. Her grip is now almost painfully strong. Each of us puts a hand on her shoulder, it's a wonderful way of connecting, we can feel her orgasm coming. As she begins shrieking, I assume her voice is too distorted for Harry to recognise but I worry that when she leans forward, puts her head on Lily's shoulder and subsides into 'oh, oh, oh, oh' — that might sound like her normal voice. Still, it's not a sound Harry will have heard from her.

"I think I'll have some of that," says Lily in a funny voice, which makes me laugh, she helps Mei to dismount and then replaces her on Harry's dripping wet face.

His 'I think I may recognise…' is stopped by her pussy on his mouth. She reaches out as Mei had done and we hold her hands. Mei touches her shoulder, but I keep one hand free to be nice to Harry and restore his erection's full vigour. He's obviously enjoying Lily's pussy very much because he tries to wank himself off using my hand, so I ease my grip and focus on Lily who is now pushing firmly on to him and is beginning to come. She and Mei are looking into each other's eyes and smiling, until Lily's face begins to contort with her orgasm. I'm glad I have a secluded room, she's at least as noisy as Mei — and she goes on for longer — but I do find it thrilling to watch all the way through to the 'oh, oh, oh and slump' phase which finishes with her head on Mei's shoulder.

We stay for a while like that, with me carefully massaging his straining cock, just not allowing enough pressure to let him come, "Now, ladies, it's decision time. I think I can trust us to raise him again if I let him come now, but if you'd prefer me to come on his face while you keep him stiff, I'll do that; but if you let me sit on his cock, I don't think we can stop him."

"Sit on his cock," says Lily, and Mei nods — a wicked smile spreads on her face, I think I know what she's thinking.

I roll another condom on him while Lily is disengaging. I straddle him and lower myself slowly on him. It is a nice cock, but Lily realises I'll need a little help, so she slides her fingers on to my clit and then kisses me while I'm fucking him.

I don't think they planned it this way but, while I'm distracted, Mei pulls the blindfold off him and says, "Good evening, Harry," just as his orgasm is building. "What!" he screams, seeing who is with him. I'm cross, but his cock doesn't miss a beat, so I quickly see the funny side of it.

She's a minx, she puts her face next to his and says, "I don't think you can stop, Harry, can you? Even with me watching."

And she's right. He rolls his eyes. I begin to kiss Lily again and she continues her wonderful job on my clitoris. I start to come a fraction after he does but it's as good as simultaneous as makes no difference and we both seem to come for ages, while Lily remains attentive the entire time.

I would normally slump on him for a cuddle, but Mei is now beside me, embracing me. I climb slowly off and Lily deals with the condom. I tell her, "Thank you, I normally play with myself like that. It's lovely to have someone else pay you so much attention." And we girls are in a huddle over the forcibly prostrate man.

"Am I going to be freed?" he wails — we were effectively ignoring him.

"Of course you are, Harry, just not yet."

"But you said I could say yellow."

He's right, of course, but sometimes the top just knows best, "So, are you telling me you've had enough? You wish to leave?" And I knew he'd struggle with the question. I've had two late night sessions with him, not much more than an hour each time, and he's easily come twice. OK, so his cock is now small, limp and dribbling but it would soon recover... is starting to recover, in fact, as Lily starts to stroke him. "We like your little friend, Harry, but we can hardly keep him if you leave."

"But I'm not saying I want to leave. I just want to be untied," he sounds a little pathetic, which isn't helping his case at all. If he'd proposed something entertaining, we might have been interested, but, as it is, he's a good-looking young man with a nice, reliable cock — and I can make sure he has a lot more pleasure

this evening. But I must confess, it's Lily who's interesting me; I can't tell yet if she's top or bottom, or even if she's genuinely bi. But she is pretty — and plainly adventurous, now she's sucking his cock again, and after not very long she looks up at us and winks, Harry is half-way back again.

"I don't think your little friend wants to leave, Harry."

"I don't want him to leave. I don't want to leave. I just want to be untied."

Lily starts sucking him again. I say, "Harry, these two ladies are lesbians, I was hoping that you and I could show them that the male body is also one to be enjoyed but, left to yourself, you are not the world's most sensitive lover. You have twice come without pleasing me." The girls hiss a little theatrically, but Lily is soon back at work, and Harry is not far off fully recovered and, as most of you are aware, once a man's cock is stiff, there's almost nothing he won't do for you. "But, to your credit, you have shown that you have very good oral technique." The girls nod, Harry whines a little, Lily's mouth has not left his cock while she'd nodding and he's finding that extremely pleasant. "Now I, at the very least, wish to be pleasured that way a little later, and the ladies might well want repeats," — again more nodding from them and some whimpering from Harry. "It seems to me that you believe our Lily here has a pretty special technique too, am I right?"

She takes him a little deeper now, "Oh yes, she's wonderful."

"So, are you telling me you wish to get up and leave?" He's hesitating now. "After all, we have a range of dildos and we can amuse ourselves, so if you want to say yellow, you have only to repeat the word and we can have a very enjoyable threesome on our own. So, what's it to be?"

"I'll stay," he says after a pause, but he looks uncomfortable.

"I think we need to hear one more word, Harry, what is it? Are you asking to stay?"

"Yes please, may I stay?" he mumbles, and Mei looks smug.

"Good, but before we bring you off again, and we'll fellate you for that…" Mei doesn't look too happy, but Lily is still smiling, "I have some education and training to engage in." The girls look expectant, Harry is still dubious. "Now Mei here is not yet a fan of anal. I've tried to persuade her how she's missing out, but my little attempts so far have not won her over."

I turn to Lily, who's shown herself to be more adventurous. "I haven't really tried it. I can't really say I've wanted to."

"Oh, my dear, what you're missing! I just thought I'd show you how pleasurable it can be." Now I have them all looking puzzled as I go to the bedside drawer. I take out the small vibrator and start it buzzing. I take out the lube as well.

"No!" says Harry, looking mildly terrified.

"Come, come, Harry, it's only what you've had before," and Lily's mouth is on his cock again and a look of happy resignation spreads across his face. "You're doing wonderfully well, Lily," I say, as I position myself between his legs and smear lots of lube on the vibrator, "but you'll have to ease off when I push this in him, it can almost make him come on his own." So, she sits up and just keeps wanking him gently. Mei is studiously not touching him but seems intrigued by my preparations; I'm now smearing lube into his crack and pushing one finger in to tantalise him. "You can't credibly deny you're enjoying it, can you?"

He says nothing, so I push a second finger in, and he sighs deeply. That's enough of a signal for me. I go very carefully with the vibrator. I'd have preferred to have him tied in a different position, but this will do for tonight. I start to push quite deeply, and the girls are fascinated. Lily sustains the light touch and Harry is gasping with pleasure. "There, you see, ladies, applied properly, it's a very pleasant sensation."

Mei still looks sceptical, but Lily looks more open-minded. I ease the thing out, I've had an idea and I need Harry to stay stiff. "I'm going to suggest you try it, Lily," she's not saying no, "but I think we'll try it while you're sat on Harry's cock."

"Oh, yes," she says, "I've wondered what that would feel like."

I fetch another condom and wet wipe the vibrator. Harry is stiff again now with her constant attention, but he is, I hope, still a long way from coming. He's been very good like that the past two nights. Lily quickly straddles him as soon as it's securely on him and, if she's not bi, she makes a passable impression of liking men as she leans forward to kiss him and flatten her small boobs on to his chest.

Now this is a very shapely arse, not like Mei's flat one. I have to admit to being fond of this view; her cunt is playing with his cock, moving slowly up and down to keep him stiff, and her pretty little anus is now staring at me. I squirt lube into the crack above it and hear a soft 'ooh'; it always feels cold, I'm surprised if she's surprised — she'd volunteered too quickly, I thought, for this to be a real novelty — but the short-breathed 'oohing' continues even louder when I slide my finger into that beautiful little tight space. Tight, but it relaxes, as most do, fairly easily. Mei's might stay tight if we get her that far, she's still showing reluctance and a lack of curiosity, more concerned to kiss Lily herself, rather than let her kiss Harry.

But Lily is kissing them both in turn and wiggling her hips as I push two fingers in. I move them to put more pressure on Harry's cock and now the 'oohs' are louder — and coming from him. I'm amused, but it's not my job to make him come, I need to focus on Lily — and I'm having a wonderful time playing with her arse but it's time to see what more she can enjoy. I remove my fingers and start up the vibrator and hear her murmur 'mmm, yes please' in anticipation.

It's not large but she's panting quite sharply as I begin to push it in, but it's not many moments before she's pushing her arse back to greet it.

"Oh, that feels amazing," she gasps, "a little more please?" It's only two inches in, and this may actually be new for her. I push a little further and the 'oh, oh, oh's' are louder. She gives Mei a longer kiss and says, "Can Mei do that for me?"

Mei looks a little wary still, but she comes round to join me, just as I have a new idea. I move to accommodate her, and that means that, as I move, I can place my clit on Harry's knee — this is a considerable side-benefit. Mei is now a little amused by my smile and my gyrating hips, so she copies me on his other leg and accepts my invitation to hold the vibrator. I watch her carefully; I know she's not the most considerate top. She slaps Lily's arse hard a couple of times but Lily's response is enthusiastic, so that's obviously part of their routine. She would like to cane Harry, I suspect, but it's beyond my imagination to contrive that tonight. But she is pushing the vibrator further. I tell her to be careful, but Lily is still gasping 'it's wonderful, wonderful'. I dismount and leave them for a moment, Mei now transfixed by this new option. I go back to the drawer and pull out the strap-on. I show it to Lily who, at first, looks alarmed — it is a little bigger than the vibrator — but then begins to smile as I nod towards Mei. Mei is startled, but quickly engages with the idea. Harry has his eyes closed and is just moaning but seems in no immediate danger of coming — he's a good boy, Harry.

It's not easy to strap it on Mei because we seem to have found an unspoken agreement that she will continue pleasuring Lily while I attach it. Finally, we're ready, and I get a big smile from Mei as I turn the vibrator pad on in the strap-on and her clit is being stimulated. She pulls the vibrator out of Lily's arse and I squirt lots of lube there and on Mei's new cock — I'm pretty sure Mei would not have been considerate enough. She pushes rather too quickly past Lily's squeal as she sticks her cock in and I'm glad I've only brought the short one with me. Mei, I can tell, is getting very excited and I suspect she's going to fuck as wildly as any man. Lily's discomfort is short-lived, I stroke her and ask if she's OK and she nods vigorously.

Mei is now fucking like a stud and I'm worried she might push Harry over the edge but, bless him, he's soldiering on, in no immediate danger — unlike the ladies, who are beginning to scream. They are having a wonderful time, Mei being almost too savage, but Lily pushing back to take what she can and now they are both very loud together. I am finding this enormous fun to watch. I'll worry about my next climax later, although I could make myself come by touching myself as I watch them. Mei, having come, now leans forward to cuddle Lily, who is enjoying the most protracted orgasm I have ever seen. It becomes almost humorously long and Mei and I are chuckling at her before she is finished but finally, on her emotional down-slope, she notices us and joins in the laughter. "Oh, let me cuddle you," she says suddenly to Mei and they disengage from Harry and stand by the side of the bed, hugging each other and laughing as Mei's 'cock' prods Lily's belly.

Harry, having been abandoned, looks disconcerted, but with a 'don't you worry, my good man', I straddle him and begin to enjoy his cock while I think of what to do next. It would be too simple just to let him come like this — and Mei has to learn a lesson about topping...

I turn to the ladies, this is a lovely position from which to conduct a conversation, "Mei, my dear..." she stops kissing and turns to me, looking suspicious, "we have some responsibilities as tops..." Her look changes to sceptical now. "Harry has done wonderfully well to pleasure us, and he deserves a reward."

"Of course he does," says Lily, and nudges her to nod, she also puts her hand around the new cock, which is still buzzing, "and you should try this."

There's a look of disapproval on Mei's face but she's surrounded by expectation.

"It's a thrilling feeling," says Lily reassuringly, "and it felt seriously like you were enjoying yourself up my bum."

Mei chuckles, and has to agree.

"That's it then," says Lily, "I'm going to fuck you while you suck him off."

Harry's smile is a little too big, I suspect he might enjoy Mei's humiliation a little too much, so I reverse my decision to untie him now. I decide I'm going to sit on his face while he's being pleasured by Mei and I free myself from his cock and turn around to get my clit on his mouth — bless him, he starts moving his tongue immediately to please me. I smile to myself; ah, for all his faults... and I reach down to keep his cock hard while an enthusiastic Lily is unstrapping the cock off a less enthusiastic Mei, "Look," says Lily, "I'll suck him off if you won't and you'll just be left watching us... and I do seriously want to fuck you now, come on." That triggers Mei to fetch the wipes while Lily finishes the ties before smiling as she brandishes her new 'cock' at us, making all of us laugh.

We're quickly ready and I'm really enjoying Harry's mouth. I pull off the condom and throw it aside — hoping I find them all before the cleaners come — funny what goes through your mind during an orgy. Mei, having wiped Lily's cock, rather unnecessarily wipes Harry's and then, hesitatingly, takes over control from me and I'm amused to see Lily standing behind her, staring greedily at her target.

Or targets, because suddenly Lily says, "I'm going to fuck your cunt first, bitch!" I worry about how deadly serious she looks but she suddenly turns to me, smiles, and says, "She hates the word 'cunt'," and we're both laughing — I can even feel Harry chuckling beneath me. Lily thrusts into Mei, pushing her mouth forward on to

Harry's cock. This is how it should be. If we get this right, we can all come at once — that's not an aim of mine, by the way, just a potentially happy outcome — but I need to remind Lily of the clit vibrator.

"There's a switch underneath the cock," I say to her.

She finds it quickly and is fucking Mei even more vigorously now, "Oh, we so have to get one of these," then there's a dirty chuckle from her, "but meantime this bitch has to take it up the arse!"

I'm not sure Mei is too thrilled by that, but that's maybe just one more reason she's not engaging properly with Harry's cock. I need to remember I'm orchestrating this for everyone's pleasure. "Would you like me to deal with Harry while you enjoy Lily?" I ask.

A fleeting look of failure flits across her face, followed by a look of relief and a nod. The bed is large, Lily withdraws, and Mei moves to the foot. I'm holding Harry, wanking him gently; we can wait while I choreograph the ladies. "Plenty of lube, remember, Lily," she dutifully obeys, "and it's better to play with her first to help her relax."

"Oh, I surely want to try that," and there's an evil glint in her eye as she pushes the first finger in. Mei is not yet looking happy about it.

Harry's OK, I'm holding him nicely, he can wait; I have to make sure these two are good. Lily is working a second finger in and plainly enjoying the exploration — Mei not so much yet. "You should play with yourself, dear, I always do." She is momentarily reluctant but, as soon as her fingers are on her clit, she relaxes and begins to push back to take more of the fingers. Lily is happy, she's now pushing more fingers in and there's no reaction of discomfort from Mei. It looks like she's a natural.

I can leave them for a while and can start sucking Harry. I test how near he is by going a little deeper — yes, Harry, when I decide you're going to come, it won't take me long. Thus reassured, I can study the girls again. Lily is, at least, careful as she introduces the cock into Mei's arse, but Mei is quickly gasping and pushing back, and Lily responds by starting to thrust harder — and there are only squeals of joy coming from Mei. The two of them will be coming again in no time, I think. Now I can enjoy Harry and I push my clit down firmly on to his tongue. Oh, that's so good, particularly with this glorious little scene in front of me: the girls are starting to come; and that triggers me; and, fortunately for Harry, I do my most enthusiastic sucking when I'm on the verge — not my best, just my most enthusiastic — and I take him very deep. I'm coming now and so, very soon, is he. I pull back a little, just keeping its head in my mouth and, bless him, he's still coming while I'm subsiding. Oh, the poppet, we've kept him on edge for so long, he just can't stop. He's still spurting when I take my mouth off and Lily, ever game, apparently, leans over and puts her mouth on him. Mei, who's slumped flat now, raises her eyebrows in not-very-

serious disapproval, but she won't engage in the same way. Lily kneels up and moves to kiss me. It's a funny gesture, we're trading Harry's fluids, it's kind of sweetly intimate. When we stop, Mei at least has joined the party and is wanking the last few drops from him.

"You've done wonderfully well, Harry," I tell him as I lift my pussy off his face.

"Does that mean I can be freed now," he sighs plaintively — and the three of us find that extraordinarily funny.

21

Claudia thought back to the first time she'd met Will in Tokyo a few years before. He'd seemed slightly diffident then, which surprised her because Peter had spoken so highly of him — she was expecting a more obvious self-confidence. But when the bank discussions had started, and in Peter's group meetings, he'd shown a very clear command of all the issues and an ability to make complex problems seem simple. His rapid progress to become Peter's CFO seemed, in retrospect, preordained. She would acknowledge that Peter deferred to her in many business issues, but she knew there was no-one whose judgement he trusted, or whose knowledge he valued, like Will's.

She'd asked him to meet for breakfast in her villa. As the juices, coffee and buffet were being laid out for them, he caught her eye when she began talking business and moved her back on to the topic of difficult journeys. She took the hint and quickly said, "Thank you, we'll manage the rest ourselves," to the waiter, who seemed politely reluctant to relinquish his duties.

"Do you remember that old rogue Ozawa in Tokyo?" asked Will, "he would never say anything at all with staff in the room."

She chuckled lightly, "I'm not sure I've ever met a man with more to hide."

"Are you not forgetting someone?"

She thought for a moment, there was one name she'd tried to bury, "Oh, Henderson you mean?" Will nodded. "Has Peter briefed you?"

"Yes," said Will cautiously.

She smiled, "It's OK, Will, you probably knew before I did, even though that's not what he let me believe."

"No, I didn't. He told me you were struggling with the idea when he told me, but he wanted you and Alphonse to agree to it."

She felt like saying 'I believe you', but that could only have caused offence. Will was the only person she knew who had never even attempted to mislead. Peter could find clever circumlocutions, but Will always seemed absolutely straight. He was sensitive but never seemed to let tact become the enemy of truth.

"I can understand why you wouldn't want him around."

She eyed him carefully; the original source of her misgivings was not Henderson's role in the divorce — Will was managing the aftermath of that, so he was well-briefed. "Are you saying that because of the divorce thing and the twenty million he's managed to screw out of us?"

"I think it goes further back, doesn't it? Martha's told me about the Far East story. I know he's not to be trusted, but I think Peter's point is that the Shen family are… well, let's be polite and call them unknowns. The contracts seem very solid, we do have majority control and their interests should coincide with ours, but I think we're right to remain cautious, and we should find out more about them. How have you got on with them this week? It's your first contact, isn't it?"

"Yes, and I've had quite a long chat with Lee, the elder son. I think he's lovely and he seems fully committed. I've tried to get close to the Chinese architect, Yang Lijun, we call him John, and he seems happy with that, but he lets little out. I suspect he might be quite close to the family; he's certainly done other projects for them in China. The two others, Mei and Harry, are managing it for Senlin; Alphonse has had more to do with them — and they seem to find ways of spending time with Isobel." Now she smiled at him, "I think you owe me a brief history of that, young William, don't you? What is there between you?"

He smiled, "Old friends."

"There's more to it than that, isn't there?"

He smiled, "There is, but we haven't been in touch for years. I'll tell you all about it some other time, but it's a long story and we do have a lot to get through. Martha does know all about it."

"Why am I not one tiny bit surprised? It's your absolute straightforward openness that is one of your most marvellous traits. I am intrigued, but I can wait. But you do rate her?" His brow furrowed, that made her smile, "As a designer, I mean, I assume you know a bit about her professionally."

"She's excellent: imaginative and thorough — and doesn't suffer fools." He smiled at that. "I'm delighted she's with us — and anyway, she's done a project for you, hasn't she?"

"Yes, the blue bedroom, although Peter organised that himself; I never met her. But I think it's wonderful." She admired it and she tried to sound enthusiastic, but it had never quite grown to be the room it should have been, because she and Peter hadn't quite become the couple she had wanted them to become — and maybe not the couple he'd wanted them to become. "More importantly, the architects here at least seem to appreciate her, but I don't suppose that's going to stop tensions arising when interests conflict. I just don't want there to be too many of those when the big boys join us on Friday."

"Will you brief Peter before we get involved in the meeting."

"Of course, but we can't let him and Wengwei have discussions about anything substantial; disagreements would be very disruptive."

"Yes, it's an attractive project financially, but it wouldn't take too many delays or changes to alter that picture. In most other situations, you set up a competitive situation and you get businesses fighting to offer you the best deal, particularly with a pipeline of future contracts, but I'm already getting the sense that there's something tribal about the architects; they belong to each other in a way and there seems to be a level of collusion, or at least an implicit understanding between them."

"I know what you mean, I've felt that too, but if Lee and Alphonse stay firm, we should tidy up most of the issues tomorrow. But and I feel awkward asking you this, how do you think Peter sees it all now? Perhaps I should know him best…"

He smiled, "I understand why you're asking," yes, she thought, he knew Peter listened to him more than anyone, and those two would have the most honest discussions in their group, "and I think you're probably worrying more than you need to. He's made the decision, and it would take something dramatic to change his view."

"And you support that?"

He looked slightly surprised she'd asked, "Of course. We all agreed." She felt relieved, and probably looked it. "We have agreed a set of numbers, and Douglas is here to make sure everyone understands those and controls to them. There's always got to be scope for adjusting things, but, if we go outside those…"

"I know, I know, project economics…"

He touched her hand, "It's got to do as well as your group does, or we should put our money with you and Tania for future investment."

She laughed, "Well, she wouldn't refuse. But our tie-in with Senlin commits us to this doesn't it?" She knew it did, the money had been spent.

"It's hard to see how we could extract ourselves from it. We've bought into the idea for now."

"What about doing more with them?"

"Is this about them wanting Alphonse to help them on property?"

"Did he tell you about that?" He looked slightly surprised, but then smiled when he saw her shake her head, "Of course he did, I think only three of us know. I don't think Peter will like it..." she raised her eyebrows questioningly, hoping Will might see some positives in the idea.

"I can't imagine he will, but there's an argument that we might have more control over things if we pursue that, and we'd be more in control of the partnership."

"So, you'd support it?"

He laughed lightly, "Maybe I put that badly. I said there's an argument for it; it's not necessarily one I would support, though. We're already at a point where Senlin is our biggest commercial partnership and we don't know that much about them yet."

"So, you're against it?"

Now he laughed louder, "I'm going to sit decisively on the fence for the time being. I can see the attractions of managing a property portfolio twice the size of the one we have, but would we really be controlling it?

That's where I'd need to feel more comfortable and, as you know, our Master may see it differently."

"But he listens to you."

"He does, a bit, but I certainly haven't made up my mind on it. I've had one brief conversation with Alphonse, and not a lot of thinking time but," now he looked searchingly at her, "I get the sense that you're pulled different ways on it…"

She trusted him enough to be open with him, "I am. I get the economics of scale argument, and Alphonse obviously manages our portfolio better than they manage theirs, so there is logic — and I do support the principal protagonists, but…"

"Alphonse and Lee, you mean?" She nodded. He waited. She looked into his eyes for a long time, he wanted to say something more. "Are you worrying about their relationship?"

She smiled slowly, "You must be an unnerving man to live with."

He smiled in return, "You're obviously not the only person who thinks that. But now, we've broached that topic…" he looked expectantly at her, she nodded, "is there anything?"

"I don't know how it works, but I think there's some emotional recognition between them. And I don't know if that makes it a stronger tie-in…"

"Or a more vulnerable one?"

"Exactly… from their point of view…"

"Or from the point of view of those around them?"

"Like I said, Master William, unnerving to live with."

"So, also decisively on the fence?"

She nodded, "At this stage, yes."

"I'm with you then."

Nothing resolved, she thought, but it felt reassuring to have him looking at it in a similar way.

22

Alphonse couldn't remember an intrusion ever being so disruptive. The meeting had been going surprisingly well. John was making the expected points, mirroring Luke's concerns from the day before; the challenges — from Douglas on cost implications, and from Isobel on design integration — had been expected but had not seemed critical; Alphonse even felt that compromises should be reachable. Lou's entry was relatively quiet — a cheery wave to Alphonse and a 'don't mind me' request, but, when he pushed a chair in beside John, the atmosphere completely changed. Daiyu, giving the presentation, carried on calmly, as if she had expected the arrival. John simply turned, smiled and moved his chair to make space. Harry, as ever next to Lee, beamed a smile and waved a hand; Lou gestured back.

Claudia and Will looked towards Alphonse, but he did no more than raise an eyebrow to them. It seemed important to remain calm and act as if he'd expected this, but his own quick look towards Lee told him that this was a shock and a violent breach of any family protocol — and that Lee had been caught completely off guard. Lee evidently decided to follow Alphonse's course and say nothing, but he looked ashen.

Daiyu offered to summarise briefly for Lou, he raised his hands, palms towards her, "No, no, please, it's lunchtime soon, you can help me catch up then."

"I hate to seem impolite," — this was Will, speaking calmly — "but could we be introduced to our new guest?"

"This is my younger brother, Shen Liuwei," said Lee quickly, "I will brief him fully later. We should not allow his arrival to disturb what is proving to be a very productive meeting, I think."

Lou merely smiled, nodded and gestured to Daiyu to continue.

Alphonse remembered him well from Teluk and still thought of him as 'the boy', which is the name Tony had given him — it was affectionate, rather than dismissive, but Tony's summary, after a couple of nights in the bars in Teluk, was 'Lou drinks more than he thinks'.

Lou, physically, was like his father; short, stocky, bespectacled and round-faced, with something of his father's easy assertiveness. His gesture to Daiyu was made with the conviction of a man who expected his world to fall into place around him.

A few questions were still posed, but only by Isobel and Douglas, and the ensuing discussions, lively and reasonably good-humoured before, shrivelled away. It was still well before their scheduled lunch break when Alphonse was asking Claudia if she felt she'd captured the important points. She seemed to have remained self-possessed, but he assumed she felt as uncomfortable as he did. He hadn't even expected Lou to arrive with his father, their project shouldn't concern him, but here he was, as fat as a cuckoo in their midst.

"I'd like to thank you very much for an excellent presentation, Daiyu," Alphonse decided he should give Lee time to work out why his brother was here, and they should leave the timetable and project work discussions on the two John sites until the afternoon, as originally planned. "I think we should take a little time to catch up on other business and take an early lunch. We'll meet again, as planned, at two." The meeting broke up into small conversations as people tidied their laptops and papers. He leaned across to Lee and asked quietly, "Could we have a minute before you catch up with Lou?"

"Of course," said Lee, through tight lips. Alphonse tried to calm him with a look, feeling that a scene was best avoided. Lee seemed to relax a little, "Shall we?" and he pointed to the door to the terrace, then turned to his brother and said something fiercely, turning back to Alphonse to say, "I've told him you and I need two minutes."

He looked even more upset when they stood outside; he must have been showing self-control in there, thought Alphonse. "I honestly have no idea what this is about. I am very sorry, it's already disrupted things, hasn't it?"

"It has, I can't deny that; we were developing quite a promising atmosphere in there, I thought." Lee looked pensive now. "John didn't seem at all surprised to see him, though, didn't you think?"

"You may be very astute, my friend. I thought that too."

This wasn't a time to ask more questions. Alphonse was now guessing that the long phone call between Lee and John may have somehow contributed to this intervention, "Look, take your time if you have issues to discuss with your brother. If you trust me, I think I can manage the discussions on the detailed project plans this afternoon."

Lee put his hand on Alphonse's arm and looked straight at him, his eyes welling, "You may be the only one I can trust. Thank you for your understanding. I'll tell you as soon as I'm clear what the hell's going on."

"Thank you, that's all I want. I'll keep things going in the meantime. I'd be grateful, though, if you could confirm your father is still coming. Peter Dickinson will be setting out soon, I don't imagine he'll be pleased about travelling if your father's not here,"

"I perfectly understand," and he probably did, but this sudden arrival had deeply unsettled him.

Alphonse followed him in. Lou was with John, waiting for Lee, he assumed. Lou's sunny smile had left him, but Alphonse walked swiftly up to him, extending his hand, "Lou, it's marvellous to see you again, I'm so glad you could make it." Lou looked nonplussed, John managed a smirk, he understood the weapon of European politeness — which was now turned on him, "Can I thank you for this morning, John?" John nodded modestly, the smirk a rictus on his face, "I think Daiyu did a great job of highlighting the issues, but it didn't feel like there was anything insurmountable."

Whether John's, "No, I think you're right, nothing we can't solve," was anything more than a formality didn't matter to Alphonse in that moment. It was important to keep talking and not break communication channels. He felt he'd observed the necessary civility, and they would be free to talk later. It is always too easy, he thought, when offence has been given or taken, to allow talk to become impossible. Now he could go to Claudia and Will, waiting for him just outside the meeting room door. He put his arms around their shoulders, ushering them towards Claudia's villa, whispering, "Just a few minutes to ourselves in your place Claudia, please, but we must join whoever's in the dining room for lunch." No-one demurred.

As soon as they were in the door, Alphonse said, "What was your impression about who knew?"

"About him coming, you mean?" asked Claudia. Alphonse nodded, "Well, I think Lee was shocked, but John and Daiyu, not so much."

"I'd go along with that," said Will, when Alphonse looked toward him.

"What about Harry and Mei?"

Will and Claudia looked to each other. She began, "That's a little harder. It seemed to me that Harry was pleased to see him, but I wasn't looking at him when Lou came in. Mei looked a bit cross," then she smiled, "but that seems to be her default condition."

Will was shaking his head, "I'm afraid I was paying attention to the new arrival. He walked in, unannounced, to a meeting of people of whom he knew, say, fifty percent tops, and looked supremely at home. That's either arrogance, or showmanship of a high order..."

"Or ownership?" Claudia looked to Alphonse, plainly worried.

"Well, that would be really surprising, but I have to admit, it did cross my mind. My impression was that Harry was a little surprised, he looked embarrassed after his greeting when he realised it was a shock to Lee — and I'm pretty certain he was shocked. OK, I think we're seeing it similarly enough, we'd better just smooth back in there and disperse. I'll grab John, if I can; I imagine Lee won't have allowed him to stay in the brothers' meeting. Will," he hesitated a moment, "could you have a quiet word with Isobel? You should brief her and ask her to keep her ears open for anything her sources say."

"Her sources?" but Will was smiling slyly.

Alphonse smiled back, "She seems to make connections easily."

"Understood. A little intrigue should appeal to her, but I will emphasise how serious this is, potentially. That's how we're seeing it, isn't it?"

"'Fraid so," said Alphonse and turned to Claudia, "Could you talk to Raymond and ask him to be on the alert — and ask him what's happened on booking. Lou must have a room, when did that get booked?"

Now Claudia managed a small smile, "And you want the full room watch?" she turned to Will, "be careful who you visit, Raymond has eyes on you."
"I suppose Henderson should have taught us caution, if nothing else. OK, shall we go? The sooner we rejoin everyone, the better."

***

When they got to the dining area, Alphonse could not see John, but Daiyu was talking to Lily and Mei. He tried to look as untroubled as possible — it was a useful skill of his, "Daiyu, I wonder if I could have a moment, please."

"Of course," and she turned to the others, her excuses echoing Alphonse's. He moved them out of earshot, feeling a little uncomfortable that this was his first conversation with Daiyu on her own.

"That was excellent this morning, thank you very much, you made me quite hopeful that nothing's insurmountable."

"I'm very pleased," she said, "thank you, but you are looking for John, I think." He smiled, her expression had given nothing away, but then she smiled back, "The brothers have gone off together, John has just gone to his room, I'm sure he'll be here shortly." She looked at him with a quiet intensity, "This project is very important to us, you know that, don't you?"

That was said with surprising conviction, he thought, "I'd always thought so, yes, you'd both impressed me right from our first meeting, but I felt truly convinced when you were speaking this morning I have to admit, though, I'm struggling to understand the significance of Lou's arrival..."

She seemed to weigh up her response, then said slowly, "Yes... me too, perhaps John will tell us more soon."

"But you weren't surprised?" Here she deliberated even longer. He thought he could risk it — "I think you've just told me, haven't you?"

Now she smiled a little, "I have told you nothing, Monsieur Alphonse. Do we understand each other?"

"Perfectly ambiguously," — he smiled — "and thank you. Shall we go for lunch?"

"In our new spirit of understanding, shall we separate for that?"

He nodded slowly, unable to fathom her thoughts, but thinking that he might just have formed a useful alliance.

There was still no sign of John when he re-joined the main party. He went to Raymond and Claudia. "All under control, boss," said Raymond quietly and decisively, obviously not wanting any conversation overheard, and then, in barely a whisper, "not booked at all."

Alphonse was puzzled, Raymond smiled and clapped his arm, but looked at Claudia, "He is so brilliant about this business, I forget how some of the details are new to him. Some guests are like that. We deal with it." He shrugged, but it left open the question of whether arriving with no booking was mere arrogance or haste.

In the dining room, Will was at a table with Isobel, Mei and Lily. They could be left alone for a while, Alphonse thought.

Daiyu had joined Luke and Joe, his assistant, and Bobby.

It was some time before John and Harry came in and took a separate table by themselves. By then, Alphonse had finished eating and went over to join them. John looked a little awkward, "We were going to keep those seats for the brothers…"

"Of course, of course," said Alphonse as reassuringly as he could, "I've finished anyway. I just thought I'd check that you were comfortable about continuing this afternoon."

"Yes, naturally we'll continue, we need to be ready for Shen Wengwei and Mister Dickinson, of course."

"So, Shen Wengwei will be here?"

Harry moved to say something, Alphonse saw John's arm twitch, as if he was touching Harry to restrain him, "Yes, I'm sure he will, we have heard of no change to his plans. And Mister Dickinson?"

"Is beginning his journey now, but I'd wondered if Shen Liuwei's arrival meant there was a change in how the family would be running the project."

"I have heard of no change. I expect no change," he made a noise that may have been meant to be a laugh, "I have a full-time team in my office waiting for a green light on Friday. I sincerely hope we shall be ready to go full steam ahead."

"That is my expectation. So, we'll start at two, with or without the brothers."

"Oh, I'm sure you will have family Shen in the meeting."

"Thank you, John, I hope they're finished in time to get something to eat." He stood, bowed slightly, and said, "I'll see you gentlemen at two, then."

One thirty; it would be six thirty in London, not too early to call Peter. He went to his room. "I'm not surprised you called," said Peter, "I had a very strange message yesterday evening from Wengwei's PA, saying he was very much looking forward to meeting me again and wanting to know when I would be arriving. I couldn't make much sense of it, but I was going to ring you this morning to ask if anything was happening. So, something clearly is, what's up?"

Alphonse went through the morning's events.

"Is there anything else in the background?"

"Lee has been floating the idea of us taking overall control of the property sector for them. Their results are still poor, even in Asia. They think we have superior skills. We've told him we don't think that's in Dickinson's interests."

"We?"

"He first had the conversation with Claudia. I think he found it easier to broach the topic with her," Peter was silent for too long, "What's on your mind?"

"A number of things, but my most urgent concern is the management of this project…"

"May I congratulate you?"

"Why?"

"A lesser man than yourself, considering how we've got here, might have said 'this fucking project'!"

Peter guffawed; thank God, thought Alphonse, that had been a risk worth taking. "OK, true confession, that thought did go through my mind, but, back to business, do you think he's going to switch the brothers?"

"That was one of those ugly, back-of-the-mind thoughts that popped into my head. I squashed it…"

"Twenty years of my best training efforts have never diminished your optimistic nature: look for the dangers, my man! Would it be bad?" This was difficult, it took Alphonse a long time to respond, too long. "Have you got any feelings wrapped up in this?"

"No, only business ones, I assure you. I think Lee's very good and is very much on board with the vision — he's also up to speed. I have a sinking feeling about this change, if that's what it is."

"And it's nothing to do with feelings?"

Another long pause, but this time Peter waited. Alphonse began again, "They're in there somewhere, I admit, but they're not uppermost. I do feel very sorry and embarrassed for him though, he looked completely shocked. Much more than the architect."

"Yes, I'm not completely surprised. Henderson's finding a few things. I hope I'll know more by the time I get there. In the meantime, stay calm… I know you will. And thank you for calling."

"You'd have rung anyway, you said."

"Yes, better this way, though, isn't it? See you tomorrow evening," And he hung up.

23

I'm expecting Mei any minute. I could say I've asked her, but it was more telling her really, and I certainly told her to come alone. That wasn't difficult, the poor girl looked as troubled as most by the events of the day so far and wanted a quiet moment. But she must realise I'm expecting to be a recipient of information, not a donor. We have an hour or so before dinner.

Will was also, well, I was going to say troubled but, since the Merle time, he seems to regard every event as an opportunity to do something constructive, and he always seems calm and in control. All he said to me before lunch was that they'd been surprised by Lou's arrival and would be grateful for anything I picked up. We should rendezvous after dinner, he said. I know, I know, it's only business!

Lou's arrival had been surprising, and slightly dramatic. What was more surprising was his opening of the afternoon session with, 'My brother will join us shortly, he has some business to discuss with Shen Wengwei,' — not with 'our father', not with 'my dad', no, with Shen Wengwei. What was not so surprising, but ultimately more dramatic, was that Lee did not reappear. Not at all for the meeting, that was a shame.

He'd been quiet and always deferential to Alphonse, but he'd made a number of good points, always expressed himself clearly and politely. He'd questioned the architects closely, all of them, when they were making points he considered inappropriate. He was never arrogant, or high-handed, and always seemed sensitive to the aims of the project.

His brother, while not intervening as much, was a little boorish, and very inclined to support Daiyu and her boss. Now, they hadn't looked at all surprised when Lou arrived, and there were plenty of sidelong glances to the man who, I assume, has now become his new leader. Certainly, Harry was fawning over him even more than he had over Lee. I'm hoping Mei will have been able to find out something, but she was definitely disgruntled and gave the impression she'd been left out of the loop. I'm afraid I used a few of my old Will stories at lunch to distract her. He took it mostly in good part, although I don't think he welcomed me hinting that we'd been lovers. But I was fair to him — I'd introduced him by saying how happily married he was. It sounds bad when I put it like that; as if I was setting him up in some way as a challenge for them, but I'm sure I got the point across appropriately. It was a little later when he said, "I'm sure the ladies are getting bored of our history, Isobel."

I teased him — "I don't think so," I said.

But before I could summon support, he said, "Well, I am" — but in a nice way and it got a laugh out of them.

Then he began talking business again. But at least we'd got Mei out of her mood.

Apart from Lou's interventions, the afternoon went quite well. Daiyu did a good job, as she had done in the morning. She had a good grasp of the numbers and when Lou began to question how appreciative the modern traveller would be of some of the 'costly, lavish refinements', as he called them, she side-stepped politely, without conceding the point. Alphonse must have been desperate for Lee to return, even though he might have found it a struggle to respond calmly. What Lou refers to as lavish refinements are at the core of the proposition. I know that sounds like marketing-speak, but few people spend the money to come to places like this without a feeling of hard-won entitlement, and the right to be pampered and have their senses seduced. I know how I want people to feel in my rooms.

The spoiled offspring and other louche beneficiaries? I work better if I don't think of them as my targets.

It's nearing six now, I assume she's still engaged in conversations. That's confirmed when I open the door to her and she falls into my arms, sobbing, "He's gone already, he's been called back..." then, more bitterly, "It's all such bullshit!"

I cuddle her for a while until she's calm, then I tell her to sit down while I get her a drink, "Bubbles are the only thing for when you're blue," I say. She looks sceptical but I know I'm right — no, I don't always know when I'm right, OK? But I do know about now, and I do know about bubbles.

When I have the two glasses ready, I put them down, sit on the sofa beside her, and pull her towards me. She lets herself be embraced and kisses me lightly as we come together. We stay a few minutes like that, then I suggest we drink.

"Look," I say, when we've clinked and sipped, "I'll understand if there are things you can't tell me. I do like us being friends, but there is a business relationship we're safeguarding, and I don't expect to know everything you know." She nods slowly to me. My conscience is clear after that little speech, but I admit I'm hoping she'll say more, so I ask, "Did Harry know before you?"

"He says he didn't," she paused to reflect, "and I think I believe him."

"Who have you spoken to?"

"Shen Liuwei mostly. He asked to see Harry and me. He didn't say very much, he was mostly asking about the project — and about the people. He just told us that his father wanted Shen Liqiang to return to run the main business in Shanghai; and that his father is a very decisive person; and that it would be better to make the change quickly — to give Shen Liuwei the chance to get up to speed as soon as possible."

"And you think that's bullshit?"

"Of course it's bullshit. He doesn't like Liqiang's independence..." here she hesitated.

"Or that he's gay?"

"Of course," she said bitterly, "that generation is still terrible."

I cuddled her again, "We can make this work, can't we?"

She struggled away from me and sat up straight, "You can make this work, still, but Liuwei and Harry are friends. Liqiang liked me, and he knew I was good, now I'll be pushed into some little woman role in my father's office."

"Is that what he's said?"

"No, of course not. It will just happen. I won't get invited to meetings or hear anything important. It's such bullshit."

"I can't imagine those two bringing anything to the project. I thought Lee was very good, but I could see he relied on you. I don't think he ever really listened to Harry; and he was quick to stop or contradict him whenever he said anything. You have to stay."

"You tell them that, then. See if they listen."

"Oh," I smiled, "I can be a lot more subtle than that." Not now though, she was still in meeting clothes and her face was red-rimmed and snivelly, "You have about twenty minutes to shower, change and put a new face on for dinner."

"I was going to..." but she withered under the Isobel gaze. "May I have a cuddle first?"

"Of course, my darling," — she does have a sweet side, it's just well-hidden.

Well, it's all very unwelcome for a number of reasons I can see, and for many I'm sure I can't. It should make for an interesting dinner.

24

Alphonse offered the letter to the two of them. Claudia pointed to Will, who took it.

My dear Alphonse,

You will know by now that I have left. We are implementing a decision of Shen Wengwei's. My brother informed me after you and I spoke at lunchtime. I hope you will understand if I confine myself to a few simple facts. I cannot, at this time, give in to emotions; that will help no-one, least of all you.

My father insists that I return to Shanghai to run the 'main' business; in other words, the smaller part of our total operation. I spent time on the phone with him this afternoon. I cannot pretend it was a long conversation — or that he gave any indication of wanting to listen to counter-arguments.

I decided it would be best to leave immediately to enable the cleanest possible transition. The project is, in any event, best served by your continuing leadership of it. Frankly, I expect my brother to cause some disruption — he fails to grasp the vision, but you knew that — but he is not a strong enough character to withstand you.

I will tell you personally that I am unhappy about the role that Yang Lijun has played but I don't believe him to be acting against the project itself, although he may seek to expand his influence over it — that is my caution to you.

I believe the other ideas we discussed are still relevant, and I believe my father might be open-minded about them — he has little to lose. That would depend more on the attitude of yourself and Peter Dickinson.

I bitterly regret having to leave you like this. I have never enjoyed work so much, or enjoyed such wonderful company, as on this project together — and I am hoping you will find it appropriate to show this to Claudia, whom I respect enormously.

I wish you everything good for the project, even as I watch its evolution now from a distance, still hoping that our paths will cross again.

With fondest regards,

Your Lee.

Will exhaled, "Wow, but I guess that's what we were assuming," and handed the note on to Claudia. "What time did you tell Lou you'd meet him?"

"I said six o'clock."

Will nodded slowly, "Yes, I think it came across as an instruction, he seemed to see it that way. He's no master of the subtleties of our language, the way his brother was," now he smiled a little, "he's certainly less deferential — and he'll want his status respected."

"I was forgetting those Chinese projects in your early days." Alphonse was smiling — and grateful.

"It made me wary of generalisations, I'm just looking at brother Lou; and it's not obvious to me from the body language that your work's got any easier."

Claudia folded the letter and handed it to Alphonse, "Well, at the very least, we shall miss him."

"I get that," said Will, "I barely met him, but I could see he is an attractive man…" he hesitated, "and you both know I mean that in the broadest sense of the word."

They both laughed lightly.

"What problems does this give us now?" asked Claudia.

"I suppose I'll find out shortly," said Alphonse. "I'll try to assess how on board he is. Is this a problem Wengwei has with the project, or with his sons?"

"It looks a little like it's just one son," said Will cautiously.

"You can't rule out that he thinks Lou might benefit from some exposure to how we work," Claudia was trying to at least keep optimistic options open.

Alphonse felt more inclined towards Will's view, "I can't rule out the potential double whammy: if he has some homophobic motivation for treating Lee like this, what does that mean for the project?"

"Or Lee's ideas of you having a larger role?"

"I think we should discount that completely," said Will, "a partner who makes a move like this without consultation would be bad enough — but without even notification," he shrugged, "I can't see Peter buying that." He looked to Alphonse, "I'd struggle, too, you know that?"

Alphonse gave a hollow laugh, "Of course I do. I wasn't convinced anyway. I think this puts it beyond the pale. I think we're agreeing; we have to get the project in the best shape before our masters arrive. I don't want them confronted with open issues — choices, maybe, but only if we're comfortable with any alternatives presented."

"I agree," they both murmured, but Will continued, "although I'd be careful about even offering them any choices, why risk giving them a chance to disagree? I don't think Peter will want that. I wouldn't."

"Fair point," said Alphonse — and Will was the best interpreter of what Peter would want, in spite of Claudia's closeness to him. "OK, thank you both very much, it's time I got ready for The Boy," he smiled at them and held up his hands, "last time I use the expression, I promise."

***

Lou was at the bar with what looked like a large scotch, chatting to the barman.

"I'm not late, am I?" asked Alphonse, knowing he wasn't. They shook hands again after Lou slipped down off his stool.

"No, shall we go to the corner table?" he pointed to a quiet corner, "What would you like?"

Alphonse looked to the barman, "A glass of champagne, please," he turned back to Lou, "we should celebrate your arrival."

Lou looked at him sceptically and motioned to the corner again, saying, "He'll bring it," tersely.

They sat down, "It won't help either of us if you bullshit me like that. You don't want me here."

Alphonse tried not to look taken aback, and thought being direct might help, "I liked working with your brother, so it's not a change I welcome, I admit. But you're here now, these things happen, the project still has to go ahead, and it's still half a Senlin business."

Lou swigged his scotch — Alphonse could tell easily now, it smelt very peaty — and shrugged, "Forty-nine percent."

"Legally, yes, but your brother and I ran it as a joint venture — equal say."

Lou seemed to consider, but didn't look convinced, "So, he's told you he's gone?"

"He wrote me a note."

"Didn't say goodbye?" Lou was being surly — and was staring hard to see what response he was provoking.

"That was his goodbye, I assume. He thought a clean break would make for an easier transition."

"What will your Mister Dickinson think about it?"

"I can tell you now; he's surprised."

"You've talked to him already?"

Alphonse thought it strange that Lou could find that unusual, "Of course, a change of project co-head is a major development, although I wasn't sure of that when we spoke." He let that sink in, doubtful whether Lou accepted the status he was nominally being offered, "What else are you taking on? The whole family office?"

Another swig — that didn't augur well — "Just property and resorts. Funds will be looked after by Finance now. Family office still has my father as head. My brother should have understood that."

Maybe the story was more complex than Alphonse had assumed, "Is your brother head of Industry Group now, or is that still your father?"

"Still my father, of course. My brother might leave it all to him anyway, he doesn't like Industry Group."

"What do you want to do with this, Lou? Is it an appointment you're looking forward to?" The man seemed to be speaking frankly, but Alphonse wasn't sure who the edge of resentment was directed at; father or brother — the latter was more obvious, but even the more favoured younger son was hinting at problems in his relationship with his father.

"I don't know that much about it. This seems a very nice place and people are getting richer and taking more holidays, so I can see it makes sense."

"But what role do you want to play?"

Lou seemed to be struggling to find an answer. He emptied his glass and waved at the bar tender, who was on his way anyway with the champagne for Alphonse. "Another one of these," and he waved his glass.

Alphonse waited for the man to go, Lou was still thinking. "Well, it's probably too early for you to have got your thoughts together. When did you know you were taking over?"

"Last night."

"No hints beforehand?"

"You don't know my father, obviously."

"Obviously not, I've only been with him for the days in Teluk," Alphonse risked a smile, "he did seem a very decisive man."

"Is that what you would call a euphemism, or, no, wait, was that irony?"

Alphonse would have laughed if the question hadn't been posed with some bitterness. "It wasn't a euphemism," Lou was scowling, "but it may have been ironic." This was difficult, the man might be sensitive to being patronised. "It was a very good question, Lou. If you think I'm implying a man can be too decisive, maybe I was — but I'm not the man who's built one of the largest businesses in China. It's amazing what he's achieved, and if he hadn't bought in decisively to this idea…"

"More decisively than your Mister Dickinson?"

"Peter thought the idea was good, he was concerned about the controls with a partnership like this. But I was delighted your father agreed, it meant we could buy the whole chain and go much more quickly."

"But he took forty-nine percent. He doesn't even do that with the government. Your Mister Dickinson is a very persuasive man…" he looked up as his fresh scotch arrived, "or maybe it's Monsieur Alphonse who's a very persuasive man."

"Is that what's worrying you… or your father?"

Lou shook his head, took another swig, and said, "We're not worried."

"Good. But you've made a big change here, and I'd like to make sure we don't disrupt progress. I think we've been moving forward well but if there's a conflicting view, I'd like to understand it. Your brother and I had a good working relationship…"

"Yes," was said very sharply, with an almost accusing look in his eyes.

"We have to work closely on this, Lou."

"Maybe not as closely as you and my brother."

"I need to understand that better…"

Lou suddenly looked towards the bar, held up a hand, Harry was approaching but turned around sharply at whatever Lou had said so aggressively to him.

"Is there a view we were too close?"

More scotch — this needs to slow down, thought Alphonse — "Some people thought so, yes."

That can only have been Lijun; so be it, it was important not to get distracted — he could have seen a relationship he disapproved of, or he could have seen his business losing out to the other firms. It didn't matter. "Well, I found Lee's input very helpful, and we only moved forward when we both agreed. I hope it can work like that with us."

He finished the next glass, looked into Alphonse's eyes, and said, "Actually, I do too. Time for dinner?" and he seemed to relax — but he had left Alphonse on edge. Maybe that's what he'd been trying to do, it was too easy to underestimate the subtleties and perversities of people's minds — and it was hard to guess what might be prompted by the tense relationships Lou had with his family.

25

Harry wanted me to meet 'my new boss, and old friend' Shen Liuwei before dinner. The man gave Harry a disapproving look, I would guess he didn't want any ambiguity of status; he was boss a long way before he was friend. He'd looked arrogant enough in the meeting for me to think he might be fragile like that. But I got a big smile out of him when he moved to shake hands — he'd obviously been drinking already.

"I have heard a lot about you, Miss Allen, will you join our table for dinner?"

Alarm bells were going off — but Isobel stays in control, and very alert. I waved Mei across, this could be useful. "I'd be delighted to. I was going to sit with Mei, she should perhaps join us?"

"Of course, of course, delighted to have your company Mei Tang," and he smiled, but I caught something in Harry's face that suggested some plan of his was being disrupted. Oh, Harry, you are such a stupid boy.

At least the boys switched to beer with the meal, that slowed down the pace of inebriation, but it was enough to reduce their commitment to speaking English. I'd decided quite early that I would get no work insights out of the conversation: yes, Lou thought the project was important; yes, he was glad to be here; no, he hadn't expected it; and he'd heard about the wonderful work I'd done and wanted to see it in more detail. Since Harry was keeping up with the alcohol consumption, it was easy for Mei and I to communicate with glances, the disapproval as profound as it was subtle.

By the time the jasmine tea was served, we were as bored as those two were noisy and preposterous, but by now their conversation was almost exclusively in Chinese. But when I stood to leave, Harry switched back to English to make his charming request that I have a drink with them later. I told him honestly that I had a meeting at nine, but the thought had formed in my mind that there might be things to learn from an unguarded conversation. Me, exploit a drunken man? The very idea! (Yeah, right!). "I may see you later, if I'm through soon enough." I'm afraid what was on Harry's mind was disgustingly transparent, but this might present an opportunity not to be missed. Mei was looking thoroughly disapprovingly at me. She would just have to learn.

She followed me as I made my way to my room. I still had a while before Will was due. "I can't believe you might meet them, they're both drunk."

"Come on in for a few minutes, my darling," I said, "Let me try and explain something to you." She looked hesitant, even after we'd sat down. I took her hand,

"Look, it's your project too. Now, I'm very much enjoying our friendship; in addition, I'm finding I'm dealing with an old friend whom I still love a little; and I'm working on a project that interests me greatly with some new people I like very much. I think what's happened today might threaten that, so I'll use any means I can to find out more about what's going on. If that means listening to two drunks who mistakenly think they're going to fuck me, so be it."

Suddenly her look changed, she was concerned, "You aren't worried?"

I laughed, "Of drunks? Not in a million. The worst that can happen is that Harry finds out why I'm also called Sadie."

Now she looked puzzled, "Why are you called Sadie?"

"I obviously haven't spanked you hard enough." Enlightenment seemed to dawn, she giggled. "Good, you understand. If I need help later, I may call you. I assume you'll just be with Lily?" She nodded coyly. "I liked her very much, as you'll have gathered."

"She likes you too," said Mei, and I just caught a little squeak of jealousy in the way she said that.

"You two are very good together, you could have a lot of fun. One more reason why we have to keep this project going — and keep you on it full time." She looked a little reassured. We stood up, I put my arms around her and rested my forehead on hers, "Look, Harry's mostly useless on this project stuff; if Lou has

any judgement when he's sober, he'll realise that quickly, if he doesn't know already. He needs you to stay on the project, and me flouncing off all offended because Harry thinks he's setting up a gang bang with me to impress his buddy, that isn't going to help anyone. I'm in no danger, I promise you, but we might have some fun later."

"We?"

"I don't have anything specific in mind yet, but you never know what those two might be daft enough to be trapped into. And I might need help."

"Could Lily come too?"

"Certainly, if anything embarrassing materialises, but now I have a very important visitor."

"Ah, your Will, your old lover. Will you…"

I turned her round and slapped her bottom, "No, certainly not — but yes, I would if he would, happy now?" I slapped her again and she giggled.

Perfect timing, Will was at the door. "Hello Mei," he said when I let him in, "I'm not disturbing you, am I?"

"Oh, no," she said, smiling up at him and delaying her exit. It's not that he oozes charm, he doesn't, but there's something so wonderfully manly about him — that rock-like solidity that so few of them have these days. That's part of what made him such a wonderful top, I'd love to be over his knee again, yet I'm a top myself. It's only Mei's evident reaction that's making these thoughts dash through my head. We have some

serious business now, Will and I. Mei exits slowly. Will looks bemused as I close the door.

"Didn't you say she was gay?" he whispers.

I smile at him. "She is, don't worry. What I find endearing about you is how unaware you are of the effect you have on ladies of any persuasion."

"Well, I'm not completely unaware. Without your education, I doubt whether Martha and I would have got together."

"Ah, I'm the architect of my own downfall."

"Which brings us neatly on to architects."

"Can I get you a drink?"

"Just water, please."

"I've been on that all evening."

"Keeping an eye on the boys? Oops."

"Oops?"

"We've agreed not to refer to Shen Liuwei as The Boy. It was the moniker Tony gave him, as well as calling him the man who drinks more than he thinks."

"Well, he's certainly lived up to that tonight."

"Was it bad? It sounded noisy."

"It wasn't bad, well, maybe that's hard to say, they were speaking more Chinese by the end. But I think Mei would have told me if anything really stupid had been said. I may find out more later, they want me to have a drink with them."

"They'll be comatose by then, or dangerous, we don't want a diplomatic incident. Be careful… for yourself as much as anything."

"Sweet boy! It's the project I'm worried about, I can look after myself. And they'll be either comatose or talkatively vulnerable, not dangerous. Anyway, what have you got for me, any new background?"

"I didn't get a lot out of the evening. I mentioned architects; Claudia and I sat with John and Daiyu at dinner. Alphonse had picked up from Lee that we should worry about him, as if he might have had a role in the change we've just seen. He'd also had that hinted at by Daiyu..."

"That's interesting..."

"Why are you saying that?"

"John and Daiyu are having a relationship..."

"Do you know that or is that feminine intuition?"

I love him, but he can be a little slow, "William, it's almost the same thing," and I pretend to be indignant, "do you doubt me?"

He smiles, "No. Alphonse knew that from Raymond's observations. No secrets in hotels, and all that."

I feel a mite triumphant, "Ha, now the next bit is speculation, but it's intuitive speculation. He's married and staying that way; she's his bit on the side — very good at her job but worried her place in the firm comes under threat if she doesn't please him. So, what did you get out of them?"

"Not a lot. He's quite clever. He was trying to find out more about Peter while we were trying to grill him about Wengwei. At least we're sure he's coming, but

that's about all he gave away, which kind of confirmed our suspicions that he's somehow a link."

"So, I should target Daiyu tomorrow and see what else she lets out. I think she's pretty committed to the project, so it should be easy to connect. I'm guessing she's making her work indispensable, she'll be worried her body can be changed — she's right, that's what most men think." I get that sly smile of his, "Are you thinking that cocks are also replaceable?" He laughs and nods. "Without wishing to complicate your life in any way, young Master William, you're a perfect example of why they're not. I did have more fun with you than with anybody else, after all, a cock comes with attachments and they make a difference. But, apart from me talking to Daiyu tomorrow, what's next?" I'm not worried about my flattery going to his head — and he's not seeing me as threatening — damn! I jest, I have the boys to attend to, if they're still awake.

"I think we see how tomorrow goes — and what Wengwei's attitude is. It may be that Peter will be able to get out of him why the change has been made — but the important thing is to understand if they want the programme to go ahead with full momentum. It's hard to see why they would change their minds on that. I doubt whether we'll get anything useful out of Lou tomorrow. John is the one to watch when we try to pin down budgets, timetables and issues, especially if he does have a direct connection to Wengwei. That's our best working assumption."

"Right, now I have some Mata Hari work to do, but I'm going to demand one big cuddle before I despatch you — and you're to tell Martha that I insisted, because I know you'll tell her — and you can add that I'm insanely jealous!" He is standing up and smiling — and opening his arms.

He laughs as he cuddles me, "She will ask, you know. You were the second topic in our call earlier, which means you were her first thought."

My arms are around his waist, I hug him tightly, for a fleeting moment I'm attracted by the illusion of a monogamous lifestyle. But we're going to be fair to each other — and we're not going to kiss. I've got what I wanted — I could feel his cock stiffening. I pull away, "Be off with you, see you in the morning."

He's holding my hands, looking into my eyes, "You will be careful, won't you?"

"It's more than twenty years since I got caught out. You're my only vulnerability now, you horrible man. Now fuck off and ring that woman. And tell her you love her."

He laughs and is gone. I could have had him, you know — he's wonderful — but not perfect. But I'm the one dabbing my eyes now — and that would have been even worse if he'd stayed. Now to develop a plan.

***

When I get to the bar, the boys are the only ones from our party still there, sat at a table on the terrace. I scan to find them, the place is pleasantly busy — that's good, we want it to be a success, after all — and it's Harry who see me first. He calls, "Isobel, here!" and stands up unsteadily — the glasses look like they have scotch in them. He's managed to stand by the time I get to the table and I have to tolerate the hug; I stifle my distaste. I'm not sure about my plan, these two may be too drunk already. Lou is wise enough not to attempt to get up but looks happy enough to see me.

"Where's everybody else?" I ask lamely — I'd assumed they'd all gone to bed, or to rooms, anyway.

"Gone," slurs Harry, "no fun, no balance, all work. You have a drink now?"

Well, he's noticed I've been on water all evening, it's time to play the party animal, "I think I'll have a champagne. We should celebrate Lou's appointment, shouldn't we?"

"You're not worried?" asks Lou. He doesn't sound as bad as Harry, but I'm sure he started earlier.

"No, I think you'll see things coming together well. Should I be worried?" — but I smile as cheekily as I can, and I get a smile out of him while Harry, quite unnecessarily, steps towards the bar to order my champagne.

"Have you been working on this long?" asks Lou.

"I worked on this project two years ago," and I gesture all around me.

"You happy with it?"

I think we're just talking pleasantries, but he might as well have the story — this could be work. "Happy that they copied my designs? I was flattered and annoyed — and there are some things I would have changed. But when they asked me to do all the work for the next five, I was thrilled."

"What would you have changed?"

Harry stumbles back into his chair, but Lou seems a little more cogent than I was expecting, so I risk the teasing smile now, "I think they might come into the category of what you called lavish refinements."

He shrugged, "You want to show me what you mean?"

I'm not stupid, and neither is he, apparently, I'm guessing what's on his mind, but it will give me the ideal segué, "I'll enjoy my champagne first, but I'm happy to take you on a tour later."

"I'd very much like you to take me on a tour," he leers. I know, I know, how do they ever think those sorts of suggestive remarks help them? "You give commentary on my villa, maybe?"

"No," I'm looking stern now — in my best top way, I'm going to stay in control of this — "it will be easier to show you using my suite as an example." I get a smile from him — and Harry smiles at him — my God, he thinks his plan is working. I'm pretty sure mine is. My champagne comes, along with two more glasses of scotch — Harry must have insisted on speed. I catch the

waiter's commentaryless eye. He'll be one of Raymond's spies, I assume. I'm happy enough with the scotch coming, I want them dozy as well as drunk. I raise my glass to toast his arrival, but I can see from Lou's eyes that he's already almost there. I'd better not take too long.

***

When we get to my room, there's obviously no interest in discussing the lavish refinements. I have to push Lou away, He seems surprised, "Sorry, Harry says you are very sexy lady."

"I am a very sexy lady, but did Harry also tell you that I stay in control?"

Lou looks puzzled. Harry looks embarrassed. "In control?" says Lou, "What's in control?"

"You two sit down. There are things I should explain." Harry's look doesn't change, but Lou's face moves from puzzled to intrigued. "I'm getting you water, you've had too much of the other stuff!" Good, they're looking like schoolboys. I hope this plan works, I can imagine playing with Harry's body, but Lou is short, stocky and, unfortunately, not very handsome — and, as you'll have gathered, he has a charm deficit. But I have them, for the moment, where I want them.

"Wait there!" I say, as I put glasses in front of them, "I'm going to get comfortable." I know, but there's no cliché that doesn't work with these people. I

go to the bedroom and swap my dress for a wrap. It's actually less revealing, but that's not how their minds work. I go back and sit in the chair opposite them. Yes, they're intrigued.

"I suppose Harry's told you a little about our adventures…"

Lou nods sheepishly and Harry looks mortified — he really was thinking this might just move to action. I'm sure he's told only parts of the story, and I don't plan to tell it all, only what serves my purposes.

"Well, I can tell you, Lou, that your boy is quite a stud." Lou leans forward, and Harry starts to relax and smile, especially when Lou turns towards him and starts nodding. "But, as a lover, he does have a glaring weakness," now Harry looks shocked again, but I have hooked Lou's interest, "I'm afraid he's far too quick…" Lou punches the unhappy Harry's shoulder and laughs, "so we have to control him."

"No!" shouts Harry, suddenly very alert.

But I've piqued Lou's interest, "How you control him?" The drink and the tiredness are affecting his English now.

I ignore Harry's repeated 'no', go to the bedroom and return with the ropes. "Our Harry likes to be tied up, Lou, and then he's magnificent. He satisfied three ladies the other night, all taking turns to sit on his cock." Lou is looking entranced and even Harry, now his prowess is being vouched for, is not averse to the story. *"Of course, when a lady is sat on his cock, she can also be approached from behind."*

Lou turns to Harry, "You have other man with you? You no say."

"No, no," I say quickly, "I'm afraid we had only strap-ons. We needed a second man, really. But Harry was brilliant. If you stop his hands moving, he can stay stiff for hours."

Lou looks at his friend with admiration.

"But I made up my mind then — I like his body, but no sex without these," and I wave the ropes again.

"Aw, Harry, you have to."

"No, I can't!"

"Harry!" and this is said fiercely — as I thought it might be. Lou is boss, not friend, now.

"I think you should undress, Harry. I'd like to see that sweet cock again. Can you get stiff tonight, do you think, or have you drunk too much — or do you think Isobel can't make you huge again?" I pick up the ropes and saunter through to the bedroom. I hear a brief Chinese quarrel behind me. I spend the time attaching the ropes to the four posts, and by the time I've done that and put two pillows in the middle of the bed, they shuffle in, Harry in front, being pushed by Lou. I sit on the end of the bed. "This will take a minute or two, Lou, why don't you relax on the chaise."

Yes, the chaise is exactly what I recommended in my scheme and the bastards copied that too. They probably sourced it cheaper than I could have done, but it's quite good quality — of course I've checked!

I have Harry stand in front of me, he's still reluctant to undress himself, so I begin. I slide the jacket down, undo tie and shirt, and give an occasional rub to the front of his trousers. Yes, it's starting, and I help the process by standing, throwing my wrap to the side and let them admire my underwear — provocative, of course, this is a well-worked-out plan. Lou finds me sexy, of course, but he's looking more and more comfortable, lying back on the chaise. "Come on, Harry," I say, "I need your cock soon," and finally he gets active and throws shoes and pants to the side. I leave the socks — no, of course they look ridiculous, but I need him tied up before Lou falls asleep.

I push Harry back on the bed and take his cock in my mouth for a moment, purely in the interests of keeping Lou awake just a little longer. Harry, of course, puts a hand on my head. I'm angry, but there's no point in showing it — I'm in control after all. I tie his hands first, "You're a bad boy, Harry," I make myself sound cross — not difficult — and Lou chortles, "No more blowjob until you're tied," and I'm quite quick now, two weeks' practice has been useful. When he's immobile, I step off the bed and pick up my phone.

"What…"

"I'm just texting Lily, I think she'd like to join us. What do you think Lou?" But I get no answer — perfect!

"Oh, dear. Never mind, we'll wake him up when she

gets here." I play with Harry's cock a little, it won't hurt to keep the deception going a while longer — and I am going to need to make him come at some point — and he's stiff again, so that won't be a problem. I'm just finishing his other ankle when the girls walk in.

"What she doing here?" he asks savagely when he sees Mei — I'd given her my other keycard.

"Like I said, Harry, you make us all happy and we want to reward you. And, sadly, you're on your own; your friend Lou is not going to be much help, but you'll make sure we're happy, won't you?" Lily is a trouper, she's already wanking him and, even if he'd been processing thoughts of this being a set-up, all the blood is now being summoned to his lower brain. I lie on one side of him, stroking him, kissing his face. I draw the line at his lips as he turns towards me, but Lily takes one for the team — she has her mouth on his cock. She must be good, because he's coming soon, but she gets out of the way — most of it squirts on him, but I catch a little in the face and shout 'ugh' and then laugh with both the girls.

"What you do now? Untie me!"

"Harry, Harry, Harry," I say soothingly, "we know you'll be ready again quickly, just relax" — and I take over wanking duties — Mei is just looking on with a horrified fascination. Lily is now kissing his face — and even, quite tenderly, his lips. She gets it, he's drowsy, he'll be asleep very soon. I leave him to Lily and move to Lou. Mei looks puzzled when I take off his

belt and unzip him, "Just hold his shoulders," I say to her, "I don't want him falling off when I undress him." She's still looking puzzled. I look back to Lily, who's wearing a triumphant smile as she kneels beside the sleeping man. She comes over and helps Mei and it's quite easy to get the lower half of him naked. The cock, of course, is just a shrivelled little worm, but it comes vaguely to life with a little manipulation. As I thought, in that state of dreamy half-arousal, he almost helps us help him on to the bed. I'm saying 'shhh' to the girls but stopping them laughing is quite unnecessary. We soon have slumbering Lou lying semi-naked with his arm around the trussed and slumbering Harry. The final embellishment before we take the photos is to put Lou's hand on Harry's cock. We nearly corpse when it looks like they're actually doing something — don't lose control, girls, capture the moment. I pick up my wrap and usher them into my sitting area after I've taken some pictures myself.

"What are we going to do with those two?" asks Mei.

"I think we're going to leave them. When they wake up, Lou can untie Harry and they'll wonder exactly what's happened."

"But you?"

"I'll borrow your bed, I think. If Lily will let you share her room for one night," and there's an unnecessarily coy smile between them, "I'm pretty sure they'll have gone by the time I'm back in the morning.

*In the meantime, please — and this is very important —
don't do anything with the photos. We have more
control if we never use them, OK?"*

*I think they do understand. This has been a very
successful evening.*

*I look in on the boys briefly, grab some clean
clothes — enough to walk through the hotel in the
morning — and retrieve my stuff from the bathroom.*

26

Alphonse was at breakfast early, hoping to catch anyone with something to report, but nervous about how the day might proceed — and particularly concerned about how the evening meeting with Peter and Wengwei would go — Peter had told him to be ready for that. He'd never felt so uncomfortable about something so important. His vision for the project was clear, but the danger of disruption palpable.

Will arrived first — a reassuring presence — and asked for orange juice and coffee from the attentive waitress, politely saying 'that's fine' when she tried to explain the buffet again. "Did you get anything out of the evening?"

"Only that the Aussies are as puzzled as we are," and the two men laughed at themselves as they caught each other's eyes darting around the room to check no-one was listening to them. It was early, the room was nearly empty. "Luke thought highly of Lee, he told me, the spiky debates were only what I should have expected — but he thought Lee valued his work and he's concerned there might be a push now to move more resorts to the Chinese. Exactly what we'd thought."

"That doesn't mean it's the reason this has happened."

"Do you have another one?" Alphonse was genuinely perplexed. The reason didn't have to be wrong because it was obvious — but he wondered what Will might be seeing. He admired him too much to dismiss any point he raised — and Will had a philosopher's scorn for the merely plausible.

"I don't have an alternative explanation yet, but that one seems too blatant. I'd rather keep thinking about it. Today should tell us more, although what we'll get out of Lou today, I dread to think," Suddenly his face brightened, "Ah, here she is!" and Alphonse turned just as Isobel came up behind him. Both men stood; she smiled and nodded appreciatively, went on tiptoe and kissed each of them.

"My two favourite men in the entire world," she said, sitting in the chair Will was holding for her, "I was hoping I'd catch you by being early."

"You're all right?" Will asked her, looking very concerned. Alphonse was puzzled.

"Of course I'm all right," she laughed almost dismissively, "but I don't think I'll have helped today's process by letting Lou get so drunk."

"Oh, you can't blame yourself, he was well on the way when I had a drink with him before dinner." Alphonse just raised his eyebrows questioningly, hoping she would add more. But now Isobel was the one casting glances around the room.

"We had some fun with the boys last night…" it was a conspiratorial whisper.

"We?" asked Will.

"I needed Mei and Lily's help to stage the photos."

"Oh, God," groaned Alphonse, "tell me this isn't happening."

"Look, it should be nothing more than a mild embarrassment, but you never know, with some people's sensitivities, the pictures might be useful."

She quickly exposed her phone screen to Will, who struggled to stifle a laugh. Alphonse glimpsed it and groaned again — two slumbering men; a semi-naked Lou with his hand on a naked and trussed Harry's half-standing cock — and then looked very serious as she put her phone back into her bag. "I appreciate your efforts, really I do, but there are some massive downsides if that gets out, or gets used clumsily." Then he relaxed a little — there might also be some upsides if the threats were used judiciously, that was obviously why Isobel had gone to all this trouble. "Who else has these — and do the boys…"

"Not boys," said Will quickly.

Alphonse breathed in sharply, "No, not boys, I'm sorry," but then he shrugged, smiled, and nodded towards Isobel's bag, "well, not to be called boys, anyway, even if they behave like them."

"So, who else has these?" asked Will, "Did Mei and Lily both take pictures?"

"Of course," said Isobel, "but I've stressed how dangerous it would be to expose them. I think they're smart girls. You might want to have a word though, Alphonse, and stress how important that is — and thank them for their efforts."

"Of course, I will — a little beyond the call of duty, though."

Isobel shook her head, "I don't know. Maybe necessary. Mei's worried about being marginalised, even pushed out — but she's good." Alphonse nodded, "I know she's awkward, but she gets it with the project — more than you can say for Harry! Anyway…" she nodded to the door, where Daiyu had appeared.

"May I join you?" she asked, but the men were already standing, and Alphonse was moving a chair for her.

"Please…" said Alphonse, wondering where John would sit, then deciding this might be deliberate and they should be careful what was said. He'd felt a connection with Daiyu the day before, but people could go to unscrupulous lengths to get information or gain advantage — and part of him was amused by the photo he'd just seen; he'd been gaining advantage himself, maybe.

"Our new arrival was up late last night, I believe…" — was she fishing, he wondered.

"I had a drink with him and Harry after dinner," said Isobel — Alphonse dreaded what she might say but consoled himself that she was a savvy woman — "I don't think either of them will be very constructive today, I'm afraid. Had you met him before?"

"Yes," said Daiyu, "well, we've worked for the family before and I've met him a few times, but I haven't actually worked with Liuwei at all," and she grimaced slightly. She wasn't speaking with any apparent calculation.

"I only met him at our Teluk meeting two years ago," said Alphonse, and smiled at Daiyu, "I'm afraid he was a bit of a party animal then, so yesterday's happenings have left me feeling nervous."

"Are you talking about his appointment, or his behaviour?" she asked, quite straightforwardly.

Alphonse wondered how much to say; was Daiyu spying for John, or positioning herself more firmly in the project? "Well, I didn't mind the questions so much yesterday. I mean, complaining about lavish refinements might seem to be out of step with the aims of the programme, but," and here he risked a smile at both the women, "someone has to keep a check on the extravagances of designers and architects — and I'm so soft with you that I might welcome a bad cop to help me." Isobel's gasp of mock outrage seemed to help Daiyu relax. "But I met him at six, and I'm sure it wasn't his first large scotch he was drinking. I admit I was worried. He seemed committed to getting drunk. Is he like that normally, do you know?" Alphonse wondered what Daiyu might volunteer, but, if she was spying, that concern of his was not a bad message to feed back.

"I don't know him well enough," she said — that was an easy thing to say, he thought, it wasn't exactly trading information, it was no *quid pro quo*, "but I worried when I saw him drinking. It's a difficult day today," and a small, soft smile lit her face as she looked at Alphonse, "especially with someone who pretends to be a good cop putting all that unreasonable pressure on the poor designers and architects and their budgets and timetables."

Will smiled at that, but Isobel laughed. "She's sussed you, Alphonse!"

"You are much too charming, Daiyu, I'm not falling for it," but he found himself smiling broadly at her, "especially when I see the unspoken collusion in the secret society of architects. They move their cost projections up in lock step together. You've even got Bobby moving over to your side. He seems to feel that building this place under budget is now a stain on his reputation." It was a serious point that he was making jocularly, but he couldn't assess whether she was influential enough to help head off some of the issues that had arisen during the week — issues he didn't want to take into the following day's conversations.

"Well, anyone can come under budget if they steal designs and copy them on the cheap!" This was Isobel, but it didn't feel like he was being attacked — she was smiling. And, after last night, he couldn't question her commitment to the cause. "And you haven't yet recognised the costs of underlap between design and architecture. If we haven't started fighting yet — and we haven't really — that means there are areas that haven't been worked on — or costed."

He couldn't assess how serious she was being. Daiyu was also looking puzzled. "Do you have some specific concerns?"

"A few. But, if Daiyu has time before the meeting, we can at least identify the areas we should look at more closely. It's work we'd have to do as follow-up anyway, but you should give us time to look at it today if you want to present a complete picture tomorrow."

Alphonse wasn't truly alarmed, there would be many areas where follow-up was necessary — and there were significant contingencies to allow for areas not covered. So, it seemed to him that Isobel was working to a different agenda — maybe setting up time with Daiyu.

"Do you want me to give you an hour with just the architects this morning to talk about your interfaces?"

"That would be a very good idea," she said, and she smiled like a proud mother whose child had got a sum right, "Daiyu and I will sit down after breakfast and work out how we best organise that." She turned to Daiyu, who still looked perplexed, but nodded eagerly. He got a very light nod from Will, which seemed to indicate that he should leave Isobel to it.

"I'll see what you tell us, then," he said, "Are we going to get our food?"

"Yes," said Daiyu, "but maybe we should take a separate table and make a start?" She looked to Isobel, who nodded.

Well, he thought, they seem to be on a wavelength now, but he could not tune in to it at all. The women took their choices to a distant table and began an animated conversation. "What do you think that's about?" he asked Will when they sat down again.

Will was shaking his head, but smiling, "I have no idea, but it can't be more potentially disruptive than her efforts last night. You had better have a word with the ladies, you know. Speak of the devils…" Mei and Lily were walking in together and Will was up quickly, stepping towards them. "Ladies, would you care to join us?"

Alphonse could see them conferring, seeming a little wrapped up in each other, but their relationship, especially after last night, was too complex to contemplate. He signalled the waitress to make good the spaces where Isobel and Daiyu had been sitting. Will stood talking to them while the table was made ready again.

Alphonse hated rushing into the topic, but he felt it was best dealt with quickly, before anyone else appeared; so, as soon as they'd sat down and ordered tea and juices, he said, in what he hoped was a friendly manner, "Just a small point quickly, if I may." They looked at him expectantly, as if they knew what was coming — and they must have seen Isobel in the far corner, "I've seen a very amusing photo this morning," now they were smiling, almost giggling, "and I suppose it might come in very useful. But I just wanted to say…"

"That it must never be shown," said Lily, smiling more broadly now.

"Exactly," he said, relieved that they'd grasped that, "but I am very grateful for the help you gave Isobel. It can't have been easy manhandling that…"

Now they both giggled, "I'm sorry, Monsieur Alphonse," said Lily, "but that is such a funny word — manhandling," and the two of them laughed again while he and Will looked helplessly at each other.

"Anyway, ladies, if I may come on to more serious work," he wasn't saying it harshly, but they quickly put on serious faces. "For you, Lily, we're planning to use an hour this morning to make sure we're leaving no gaps between architecture and design. That's what Isobel and Daiyu are planning now."

"Should I join them?" asked Lily.

"I wouldn't think so. They're just planning the session, the hour itself should give you and Bobby time. I'm just keen we resolve as much as possible before we present to the big guys, tomorrow." He was also keen to give Isobel space in case she had a more complex agenda than the one she'd described.

"OK," and she nodded, seeming content.

"Mei, my next point concerns you more specifically. May I talk while Lily's here?"

"Please, that's fine," which rather confirmed for him the status of their relationship.

"Yesterday's change has injected some uncertainties for us. I just wanted to say, from my point of view, I think you bring a great deal to the project — and Lee thought very highly of you — so I will certainly be resisting any changes in your status that anyone proposes. I'm assuming you want to continue full-time on it?"

"Oh, definitely," she beamed a smile and nodded vigorously, "and thank you very much." Lily squeezed her shoulder.

"I don't know what I can promise. I didn't have the impression that Lou was very clear about the role he is expected to play. But I definitely want you staying with us," he smiled at her, "I hope, however, that I won't need to use the photo to ensure that," and the ladies tittered in their sweet Asian way. "I'm sorry, I'm keeping you from breakfast."

27

*Daiyu is a smart lady. I'd guessed that at the start of the
week and everything's impressed me since. John's let
her do most of the presenting about his two projects —
and we're all glad when he does. His English isn't as
good as hers, and she makes her points much more
clearly.*

*We did spend a while talking about making my
efforts tie into theirs and how we'd best set up the
discussion in the larger meeting, but I obviously wanted
to dig a little deeper. "How long have you been with
John?"*

*"I joined Lijun's business seven years ago," she
said, narrowing her eyes at me — her English good
enough to spot the trap in my question.*

"You work very closely with him now, don't you?"

*She looked a little frosty, "My English is not so
good, but I think you're making an assumption about
the extent of our relationship."*

*OK, she'd caught me — but I was trying to be fairly
obvious, there was no point in letting her think I was
trying to trick her — I smiled, "Guilty as charged, but
I'm also making an assumption that you're smarter than
he is — and I do mean about work. My sense is, from*

the way you describe the two resorts you're working on, that the key ideas are yours." I look at her expectantly.

"He is very good," she says — telling me implicitly that I'm right — "and we wouldn't get the work without him."

"Is that just his contacts? I can't believe it's his presentation, you're seriously superior there."

She nods gently. I know she's embarrassed, but she has enough pride not to want to belittle herself — and I'm a woman running my own business, that's probably intriguing her a little. "I think that's just because my English is better. In Chinese he is excellent — but he does have very good contacts, that's true."

I'm fairly sure she's agreeing with me, "So, he's an old friend of Shen Wengwei?"

Now she's looking uncomfortable. "I don't know Shen Wengwei at all well, but I do know that he is a businessman."

This is interesting, but I don't have time to get too philosophical about it, "But doesn't it help them in China to do business with their friends? People they can trust?"

She seems to ponder, "I know it sometimes looks like that — and I hear a lot about that in the West — but I'm not sure that Shen Wengwei is a man who would trust people — and no-one should ever trust him." She quickly began fiddling with her breakfast, as if she'd said something she regretted, but didn't know how to retract it.

I squeeze her hand, she seems shocked, but doesn't pull away, "Daiyu, I know we're not going to trust each other yet, and I realise I'm asking you awkward questions, but, if this goes ahead, we'll be working closely together, and maybe we'll build trust then. In the meantime, I just want to make sure we don't ruin things tomorrow. For all I know, the big guys might get cold feet and just decide to patch up the properties and take what they can out of them. I just like the idea of leaving fabulous hotel rooms all around Asia, rooms I will always want to visit myself, and I'm just trying to make sure that no-one fucks that up — and I think your wonderful English can cope with that smattering of Anglo-Saxon."

Now I have her laughing.

And you shouldn't be so cynical, I am that impassioned, you must be aware of that by now — I don't go manipulating the flaccid stumps of charmless men without a greater purpose. Still with me? Of course you are!

28

Claudia was woken by the bell, she wrapped herself in the cotton robe and let the waiter in. Sleeping until seven-thirty was a luxury, but it had been after three when she'd got to her own bed. So, Raymond's cameras would have caught her, but she could have been discussing work in Alphonse's suite — she had been, in fact, for the first ten minutes, and for brief intervals in between.

And the short sleeps in his arms were the most blissful memories — and they wouldn't happen again for a while now, with Peter arriving this evening. She thought again: almost the most blissful memories! As she moved to the table by the open door on to the veranda, she was very conscious of the aches and soreness in her body. Strange to reflect that she sometimes thought of him as passionless — and in that moment she remembered that the main reason she'd ordered breakfast for the villa was to give him space for the others in the main room — and avoid the danger of mooning around near him. She knew she could easily give herself away — there were too many sharp-eyed people. Even Will probably knew, and certainly Isobel had guessed.

There was a hopelessness to be savoured in her feelings for him. But she knew they weren't as unthreatening as she pretended. Peter probably knew — but she couldn't bear to admit that he might not mind — that would say something unwelcome about her relationship with him: that she was more detached than she thought she should be. If he wanted her tonight, she would make love to him in their now affectionate way, but she knew the paddle and toys would stay in the drawer — and now she felt a small pang of guilt about her subterfuge; if she'd left them in the suitcase, he would know, should he display any interest, that she had no inclination to play. Was it deception they practised with each other now? She had a sort of love for him, she knew, but it was a picture, not a sculpture; it didn't have facets. Not as his love for her seemed to. And his love seemed to give her the luxury of any freedom she wanted. It was almost as if he'd pushed her here to be with Alphonse, as if that were something he was happy to sanction.

But she knew that, should he play elsewhere, even though she had no right, she would be stabbed with jealousy — as she still was, to some degree, when she thought of Lavinia with Jack.

But Peter was a wonderful man, and there was much in him, and about him, to enjoy. And if Alphonse weren't there, she wouldn't go seeking something to replace him. What could there be? What she had with Alphonse was, in some ways, like the love for a child;

it didn't have to be given bounds; it would always be there; and you willed every good thing for it — these ever-evolving people on the cusp of their bigger lives — Abbi effectively already independent, and yet never more than semi-detached.

So, Alphonse was free to have his whole life away from her; she felt strangely more affected by his arrangements with women — there were a few, they always seemed to come to him — she didn't doubt his stories, she could easily imagine Breeana, Tony's wife, needing his company even more than she did herself. The men he chose, even the possible dawn of something with Lee, left her only worrying for him, hoping he would not be hurt again.

She knew she lacked the imagination to ponder how that might be. It was easier to think of the needs of the women. It was a need for her, perhaps sharpened by it being the last chance— who knew for how long. She'd gone to his room last night soon after dinner. She'd wanted his arms around her. She wanted to sleep naked beside him. Then, when she was there, it always happened as it always did; they would kiss and her hand would waken him and she would find all guilt melted because she was so sure she would be able to sit by herself at breakfast and not feel any agonies of longing or of frustrated and unachievable possession.

But last night had been unusual, maybe because of the impending separation, the horizonless denial of opportunity. But she'd found herself greedily eating him, wanting him so deep in her mouth but anxious for him to hold on and have her everywhere. She smiled to herself as she poured tea, she normally spoke little during lovemaking, but she'd warned him early last night, 'I want you everywhere, come when you like, where you like, but I want all my body to remember you in the morning' — and it seemed to unleash a new Alphonse. He'd smiled his usual slow smile, but then, in a flurry of movement, the animal had taken over. He's spun to sit on her chest, his knees pinning her arms. He'd fucked her mouth! She loved his cock, but normally she was on him, taking as much as she could — carefully; but now! It wasn't quite reckless, he stayed a little attentive as she was choking and gagging on him — and he was laughing at her, letting her catch her breath for a moment, and then fucking her mouth again for a while, threatening to come in the back of her throat, but pulling away just as she felt he might do.

"Turn over!" he said sharply, "You want everything, you get everything!"

It was completely new from him, but there was a different look in his eye — and she knew he'd guessed what she wanted. Her affectionate jibes about how tender and caring he always was seemed finally to have provoked a different approach in him. She paused to look at him, to check he was committed.

"Turn over," he said again, decisively, "Get your arse up for me."

She rolled over, watching him reach into the drawer, "What are you doing?"

He slapped her arse again, even harder. "I told you to get your arse up. Don't tease your affectionate, caring Alphonse and then act surprised when the beast emerges."

She pushed her arse as high as she could and he was quickly behind her and inside her but, as soon as he was deep, his rhythm slowed. She reached between her legs and touched his cock.

He slapped her hard again, "Yes, there's a cock ring. I want this to last, and I want to get thick and go deep, especially later in your beautiful arse. But I'm a reasonable beast, you do get some lube at least."

As she sipped tea and the scent of the tropical morning drifted in from the garden, she smiled to remember that the lube had been only partially successful — sitting was uncomfortable. But she smiled.

He'd seemed to get near his limit in her pussy, slapping her hard again when she stroked his balls. Then he pulled out and began licking her. She'd learned to love it with Jack, but nothing was quite like Alphonse, the way he would stretch her, the way his tongue seemed to go alarmingly deep, the way it would tease and caress her. The way his thumb on her clit would make her come while he was still licking her, still holding his tongue inside her.

But last night had not been like that. His tongue had been deep, but it had been brief; there had been little finger play, enough only to smear lube very deep and help her relax a little. "This is what I'm having now," he'd said, almost roughly, "I want to fuck your arse so hard!"

And he had. His hands had been vice-like on her hips, his thrusts had not been necessarily deeper, she always took all of his considerable length that way, but he'd pushed very hard, she could feel the bed bouncing beneath them — and she was loving it. She'd found her inner victim again. He'd found his dormant inner beast — and he seemed to be able to sustain it. He found a rhythm, a plateau and she felt him very excited, but as if he was standing back from an edge, able to choose his own moment to leap.

"Oh, keep, going," she'd cried, "fuck my arse harder, fuck my arse harder!" She sipped tea, had she really said that? Her body reminded her that she had, she smiled again, she'd begun touching herself: "Keep fucking, keep fucking, but I have to come," she'd gasped, and she had come then, loudly and violently, but his hardest thrusts were held back until she began to subside. Then he'd pushed very deep, she could feel a painful ache deep in her stomach — but she still had pushed back, trying to take more — and then he came, so long and loud and amazing.

They'd fallen face to face into each other's arms. She just caught a cloud of worry crossing his face, "I'm fine," she'd said, "in fact I'm wonderful. I wanted you like that, you knew, didn't you?"

Now she got his warm smile, "You have teased me about being cold and passionless too many times. I always knew the beast was there. It just seemed like he was really needed tonight."

"He was, my love," and she kissed him long and tenderly.

He moved away, saying, "I'm showering," to her puzzled face. He held out a hand to touch hers, "I'll be straight back, get a little sleep, then your loving, caring, passionless Alphonse will make love to you again. Things change in the morning; we should make the most of our last time."

She had slept a little, waking soon after midnight to feel his arms gently round her. She snuggled back into him to feel all his skin on hers, one hand on her belly, her body awake again. She wanted him to wake, but only slowly, so she turned and slid delicately down to take his slumbering cock in her mouth. It had been a joy as it woke gradually, she was able to enjoy it for a while in its almost-stiff state, running her tongue up and down its underside and then gently sucking on its head while her fingers supported it. It was a perfect thickness to suck — just too long to have thrust down your throat, but she'd been amazed by the thrill of being forced like that, and now, there it was growing again and filling her mouth.

He'd woken eventually, of course, and then she'd been able to relive the first hour, but more slowly and gently this time — yet just as deep everywhere, this was her Alphonse, as he had always made love to her before — and as she loved him making love to her. But the beast had been thrilling, could that happen again? But then his words came back to her — 'making the most of the last time'. How final was that meant to be?

29

Lou's obvious hangover did not make him a disruptive factor in the morning session, but Alphonse missed Lee's polite, well-directed interventions. He was always sharp enough to prod the architects out of their cosy, collusive complacency, his awareness of project details so thorough that he could set one up to challenge another. It had been an uncomfortable role for Bobby, since he'd provided the successful template — but Lee had been getting Luke and John to rein in some of their wilder, and always more extravagant, enhancements. Yet having an incisive intellect replaced by an obviously hungover neophyte had changed the balance in the room. Even Isobel now seemed to have set up some devil's pact with Daiyu and had become unusually quiet.

Thank God for Mei, he thought. Sometimes her questions jarred — and it wasn't poor English, these were genuinely aggressive questions — but they were always well-targeted. It was one of her questions to John in the late morning that prompted Lou's first intervention. It was brusque, but in Chinese, and she seemed, unusually for Mei, to cower a little.

"Could you share that with us, please?" Alphonse tried, with all the politeness he could summon.

Shen Liuwei kept his eyes on Mei as he responded, "Her question too rude."

"Could I respectfully suggest, Shen Liuwei," interjected Daiyu, "that Mei Tang has touched on an important area and it might repay us if we give some attention to it." Well done, Daiyu, thought Alphonse — he watched John, who didn't seem inclined to intervene.

Lou didn't react badly, "Yes," he said gruffly, now he looked at Alphonse, "but too rude."

That did have the effect of reducing Mei to silence for the rest of the morning — and Lou, for that matter, but Alphonse put that down more to disengagement than to embarrassment. The altercation also had the effect, it seemed, of making everyone else more amenable, so, by the time Claudia put the summary of outstanding issues together at the end of the morning, nothing seemed insurmountable.

He worried he might undermine Mei if he sat next to her at lunch, but he managed to whisper 'well done, please keep going' discreetly to her as they made their way to the dining room. He also wanted to head off any temptation to expose the photos. He hadn't detected any impact on Lou — but he'd been comatose at the time the photos were taken and he may not have been fully aware of what had happened, or even of their existence.

The normally ebullient Harry had been entirely silent all morning, staring predominantly at Isobel, who gave him not a moment's attention. She had been relatively quiet but seemed content with whatever arrangements she'd worked out in her hour with the architects.

It meant that most questions, after the effective silencing of Mei, were put by himself or Douglas. Alphonse had been worried when Will had excused himself from the morning session: "Douglas is very good, get a message to me if you're seriously concerned but I've got stuff I must get on with." And Douglas had been good, he just wasn't Lee.

Even Claudia had been unusually quiet and had given him only the odd, shy smile. Alphonse was trying not to think about the night, and the extraordinary first hour in particular. He'd given in to a side of himself that he normally kept happily buried — and done it to please a side of her that he knew existed, but had never got lost in. He did adore her, but hours like that only made the surrounding complications worse. They would talk about it sometime but, for the moment, his emotions were even more raw than parts of his body — and he still had to prepare for the evening and tomorrow; meetings with a tyrant — and a cuckold.

He never really thought of Peter that way, but the night's memories made the word pop into his head. Yet he'd seen Peter almost choreograph his previous wives into extraordinary situations, almost with relish, it seemed. But he was aware of how much more Claudia meant to him, how Alphonse himself had been required to almost stalk her through that extraordinary courtship, always aware that Peter's business interest in her was real but was used as a mask to conceal deeper feelings — feelings of loving someone that Alphonse had thought, in Peter, had become derelict — for the same distorted reasons that had blighted Alphonse's relationships in the years after Éric. But Peter nevertheless seemed to perversely push Claudia at him, knowing they were close and had been since they'd first met. Whether Peter was challenging her, or just ensuring that she was happy, he found hard to judge. Peter would always claim to be doing the latter.

But the fact was, he thought, as he tried to organise his thoughts during the architects' hour, his own feelings were getting more confused — and partings felt increasingly like wounds. Nevertheless, as he surveyed a coffee-table full of papers from the sofa in his sitting room, a glance to the bedroom had him smiling as he remembered the desperate and unprecedented 'fuck my arse harder, fuck my arse harder' cries from the previous night. And smiling again when he remembered her snuggling her naked body into his welcoming arms, each time they'd made love.

But the dangerous assumption was that her feelings exactly mirrored his; that they could continue to enjoy the easy, impossible love without consequences. He could always avoid the thought that other relationships were becoming harder for him because of his feelings for her. But she had to live permanently in another relationship — and Peter would arrive this evening and expect her in his arms, Alphonse was sure, and he reflected how easy it had been to keep Lee at a distance because Claudia was nearby.

He thought of saying 'the last time' last night to her. He'd meant 'for now', but he also knew that, at a deeper level, he was making an offer to free her, to allow her to focus on Peter and their relationship if she wanted to. But it had been a disingenuous offer. He doubted whether she would abandon him — or he her.

In the meantime, the day had to be got through — and the evening, where two bigger beasts would need to confront each other.

<h1 style="text-align:center">30</h1>

Shen Wengwei had arrived before dinner but had taken the meal in his villa with his son. Lou had grown more alert during the afternoon, but not notably more amenable, merely more obviously agitated. Alphonse had wondered how much that was due to his father's impending arrival or his growing suspicion of what had happened the previous evening — and how any evidence might be used. He'd stayed close to Harry in every break.

The combination of Claudia's summaries and Douglas' facile presentation of timings and budgets for all significant activities meant that they had a coherent framework for the programme. He'd felt comfortable enough by mid-afternoon to let the architects' teams go off to prepare what they would present in the big meeting the next day. He had offered his 'key issues' list to them, with a commitment to let them speak on what they saw as unreconciled when he closed tomorrow's meeting. He'd tried to leave unspoken the threat of allocating future projects elsewhere if they showed themselves to be uncooperative. It was also important not to attempt overreach, limiting John's portion in the future might be difficult if he wanted to sustain harmonious leadership of all factions.

But that was a hard topic to broach with Lou, now sat beside him in the reception area outside the meeting room where Shen Wengwei and Peter were talking. Peter had arrived during dinner, looking surprisingly hearty as he circulated quickly and greeted everyone, allowing himself only a little more time with Claudia for a chaste kiss and a few whispered words. For Alphonse there had been the firm handshake and the hand on the arm — the Peter gesture that always stopped short of a hug — and "I'm meeting him as soon as I've changed. Can you be ready to join us when we call you? He'll bring Lou in then." So, there had clearly been contact between them, and Alphonse had to accept the possibility that the week's preparation might suddenly be for naught: he was beset by memories of Peter's original antipathy, and by the curious, and unexplained, switch of the brothers — almost in mid-air, it felt like.

Had that not happened, he would now be sat with Lee beside him, talking animatedly, even joyfully, about a successful week — but now he had the sullen, pasty-faced man-child looking subdued and nervous, probably knowing even less about what to expect in the next hour than Alphonse did, in spite of him having spent the preceding hour with his father.

"Your father has a new interpreter?" It was a cheeky observation and Alphonse almost regretted it. The interpreter Alphonse remembered from Teluk had also been young and pretty, and of questionable value, her English hardly better than Wengwei's — doing business had relied principally then on Lee's interpretations.

"My father always has new interpreters," said Lou, not looking up from the coffee cup.

"How much of your group's business needs English? Yours is very good, by the way," that hadn't been mere flattery — and Lou looked as though a boost might help.

He nodded, still not looking up, and said, "Thank you, but not much, really; mostly just with you guys," then, after a pause, "What do you think they want to talk about?"

"With us? Or on their own now?"

Lou looked up, uncertain, "I don't know," he hesitated, "both, I suppose."

"What did your father say when you were together just now? Didn't he say what he wanted to discuss?"

Lou looked defensive, "Family stuff mostly. What does Dickinson want?"

That was a fair point, and Alphonse hadn't truly considered it, or asked for any guidance from Peter. It was Alphonse's project, he was clear about how it should proceed, the finance providers could ask questions and make suggestions, but they should leave the direction to him — and he realised that, even had Lee been sat beside him, he would have expected to have the final say in how it all evolved — and, although

Peter and Wengwei had every right to question and suggest, they would be unwise to intervene. But, as he looked at the hapless Lou, intervene they had. And Alphonse himself could be removed at any time — on any capricious whim. That would not be Peter's style, but his bigger decisions often seemed mercurial and instinctive — because they were usually about people and less susceptible, therefore, to logical analysis. He realised, after a long while, that Lou was looking at him, apparently expecting an answer. "I'm sorry, Lou, that was a good question, and it did make me think," he chuckled — and even got a half-smile from Lou. "I know what I want. I want this project to go ahead as we've been discussing — and I don't want Peter fucking it up!"

Now Lou even laughed, but then lapsed back and stared at his cup, "Not like my father, you mean?"

"Your father's put lots of money into this. I'm sure he doesn't want to waste it, does he?"

Lou looked up and shrugged, "As you might say, who the fuck knows?"

And Alphonse guffawed just as the meeting room door opened. The glamorous interpreter said, "Please to come in."

Wengwei greeted him warmly, "Hello, Alphonse, nice to see you again. You boys having fun?"

The laughter had obviously carried in, "We were just joking that neither of us knew what to expect now."

"Ah," said Wengwei, "like those poor gladiators in Rome, not know if lion or giant wait for them."

"Well, I think we have both."

And Wengwei laughed very loudly, Alphonse caught Peter chuckling and even Lou smiled. "Only question is, which is which?" and he laughed even more loudly at his own joke. Then he gestured animatedly to them, "Come, come, sit down, sit down."

Alphonse looked to Peter, who gave a small smile and an even smaller nod, all unhelpfully enigmatic, but he knew he had Peter's trust — although a brief and distracting memory of Claudia flashed through his mind. Trust was circumscribed.

They'd placed the interpreter at the head of the table, so he was sat opposite the Shens — and they looked even more alike than he'd remembered. Lee had obviously taken his mother's genes and another scurrilous thought went through Alphonse's mind. The interpreter looked not unlike Lee, indicating quite clearly, he thought, what Wengwei's tastes in women were.

"So, how you get on this week?" Wengwei was looking directly at him. Alphonse would have answered anyway but it was helpful to have direct encouragement.

He tried to be succinct but wanted to convey the enthusiasm he still felt.

Wengwei was nodding and, once Alphonse had summarised how he had organised the next day, he asked, again without looking to the interpreter for help, "And what problems you have this week?"

Lou began, "We haven't..."

Wengwei turned sharply to him and said something in Chinese. Even the interpreter looked shocked. Lou cowered and slumped. "Sorry Alphonse, boy must learn. You have problems?"

And Alphonse attempted to summarise what he expected the issues to be and tried to reassure them that there was enough contingency to cover most adversity.

"And you happy with architects?"

Alphonse chuckled, "I am very happy with all of them. They always want more, of course, and there are the usual tensions, but I think we're in control. But, may I ask, what do the lion and the giant want out of tomorrow?"

Wengwei laughed again, "Shall lion say? I lion. Peter obviously giant!"

Alphonse managed a genuine laugh, "Yes please, what does the lion want?"

Wengwei looked to Peter, who nodded slowly.

"I want project. Maybe go faster. We have money waiting. Must build brand quick. Other people also building. Better first than second. But also want help, Mister Alphonse please, help with property, not so good for us. Other son tell you, I think, and tell Mrs Dickinson. What you think?" Alphonse looked to Peter, "He knows, I tell him, what you think?"

Peter's look had been enigmatic, even with nearly twenty years of history, trying to guess Peter's thoughts was a fruitless and dangerous pursuit. "I need to be careful here, Shen Wengwei. I know our numbers look better, but I think you have a good portfolio. There's lots of luck and timing in all those decisions, even after you have spent months in meticulous research and planning." Wengwei looked sharply at the interpreter, who shrugged helplessly and looked embarrassed, "I'm sorry, I meant very careful planning and lots of research. It would take an enormous amount of time and this project already keeps me busy."

"You can't help at all?"

"I can't see me doing any more than giving some training and guidance. I couldn't make myself responsible."

"Who you train?" He turned to Lou, and looked with a little contempt, "This stupid boy? Can't keep his cock in his pants. You already train him on this. I hope he not useless."

"He's made a good start. It's a complex project. But you have someone who's very good on property…"

"Liqiang must work in Shanghai," was said almost savagely.

"No, I meant Mei Tang."

"Mei Tang?" now he looked shocked.

Alphonse just caught a surprised look on Peter's face but he wanted to focus on Wengwei. "She's very astute, she's clever — she solved our funding problem in the first place," here he did turn to Peter, "although Peter thought she showed too much imagination…"

"Too much, eh?" Wengwei was clearly pondering.

"She understands the market and, I can promise you, she's fearless about asking difficult questions."

"Rude," muttered Lou, but suffered another savage verbal attack from his father.

"So, you think she good?"

Alphonse looked to Peter, who was raising his eyebrows, "I think she's very good, but she is a great help on this project, she has the most experience now. I would hate to lose her."

"You have Harry," but here Wengwei looked at Lou.

"He's very capable, but he may be a little too diplomatic to challenge the architects and builders enough when it's necessary." Now Alphonse was in a bind, he felt he had a commitment to Mei, but he also needed her to keep the project under control. Douglas was a very useful addition to the team, but having a powerful Chinese voice was essential — and that would not be Harry. And judging from his father's attitude, nor would it be Lou. But Wengwei was plainly considering, it was time to take a chance, "If you could take a longer-term view…"

"I always take longer-term view," was said very sharply again, but he relaxed quickly, "sorry, please to go on."

"If she stays with us on this project, I will spend time with her, keep your property portfolio under review and train her as well as I can. I really think she could take it over in two or three years. Her English is perfect, that helps you stay close to your US and European properties."

"You think she is so good?"

"I do, and she works immensely hard. She seems to know everything about everything on this project — and she's not frightened of asking questions." Here he looked at Lou, remembering the morning's outburst.

Wengwei was nodding, the point seemed to have surprised and pleased him. "We think about it. Maybe two birds, one stone, yes?" He looked pleased with himself and looked to Peter.

Peter nodded but looked non-committal, "Perhaps you and I should review that tomorrow when we've seen how this project looks. Remember, if you want to go faster, it puts all resources under strain."

Wengwei waved that away good-naturedly, "You see, Alphonse, giant is coward, only lion have courage."

"Not in Wizard of Oz," said Lou. Wengwei looked puzzled, but Alphonse could barely stifle a snort of laughter. Peter smiled and the interpreter couldn't restrain a small giggle, covering her mouth demurely.

Wengwei cast a scornful look at his son again and said, "She explain me later. We finish now?"

"I think we've gone as far as we can tonight," said Peter, "I think we meet at nine in the morning, is that right?"

Alphonse nodded. Wengwei was standing now. Alphonse didn't envy the interpreter's next task — or the conversation Wengwei would doubtless have with his son in the morning. But he had found, in that moment, a little sneak of admiration for Lou.

***

"I should update you on a few things," said Peter, as they left the room, "Will you come to the villa for a drink?"

"Won't we disturb Claudia?"

Alphonse got merely an undecipherable look as a response.

***

But Claudia had been expecting them. She was wearing the hotel's cotton robe, but the evening make-up was still in place. "I thought you'd want to chat things over," she said when they entered. "I'll fix you drinks and then head for bed."

Peter embraced her lightly and brushed her lips, "I think you should listen in if you have the energy. This is getting very interesting. Especially with your creative organisational input this evening, young Alphonse." He didn't look especially approving — but they had usefully put off any serious decision-making until the closing review tomorrow. At least nothing had been sunk tonight.

She got them drinks and sat on the same sofa as Peter but a business-like distance from him.

"I had a phone call from Henderson while I was on my way here," he let the point sink in. Peter liked his little melodramas, thought Alphonse.

"It was interesting, and it became even more so when Alphonse made his creative offer to train Mei Tang as the property supremo for the Senlin Group..."

"That's clever," said Claudia, smiling at Alphonse, "she's very good."

"You see," said Alphonse, "then she could take over from her father in Shanghai eventually and his face is saved."

Peter shook his head and took a large swig of whisky, "She can't take over from her father."

"Why not? He's the head of the property division."

"No, he's not, that's the point."

"Well, who's the man in Shanghai, then?"

"On paper, he's her father — and she thinks he's her father." Peter looked closely at Alphonse, who was nodding as the point sank in.

"Who else knows?"

"Who else knows what?" asked Claudia helplessly.

Peter looked to Alphonse, who turned to Claudia, "Who else knows that Wengwei is her father," he said.

Peter nodded as Claudia gasped, then he spoke in a considered way, "Her mother knows, obviously, and Wengwei himself, of course — and the father knows. His preferment has something to do with that, I assume, certainly it's not his property acumen that keeps him where he is. I think you might achieve a lot with that creative little suggestion of yours if she's as good as you two think she is. But the family lawyer knows too, and hence Henderson, and hence, now, we three."

"Oh, God," groaned Alphonse.

Now Peter looked concerned, "What do you need to tell us?"

And Alphonse had to describe Isobel's picture — "But I have no idea how they staged it."

"They?"

"She had Mei and Lily to help her."

"Well, it won't help anyone to ponder what steps they took to get there."

"My impression was that Lou was comatose the entire time. I think we're safe from being accused of organising incest."

"I wasn't thinking of Lou."

"Oh, no, are you going to tell us something about Harry?"

Peter nodded, "But you're sure there's no romantic attachment between Mei and either of them?"

Alphonse laughed, "No, she's gay."

"Ah," said Claudia, "I thought so. She seems very close to Lily."

"Yes," said Alphonse, "I really don't know how they view that here, but it means we don't have to worry, as long as last night's secrets don't emerge. But what about Lee, though, did you get anything out of him on why they've changed?"

"Only bullshit. He needed a good businessman to run the old business, is his official line — at least he admitted that Lou wasn't growing into it — too easily distracted, is what he said, and his asides tonight seemed to back that up. Are you still worrying about your Chinese architect?"

"Yes. I don't know what role he plays in all this. I haven't picked any particularly homophobic distaste — none that rises above the parapet of his general disdain for us Westerners — or Christians, as you put it recently. But his work is good, I have to say, although I expect his number two to present tomorrow. I hope she does, for your sake. She's very good, and her English is excellent, and I think she's the main reason their work is so impressive. So, I don't suppose we'll ever find the predominant reason for the change — but we do have to get on with it anyway."

Peter began to look philosophical, "Maybe you've just described the human condition. We never pin down the predominant reason — for us there is only the trying, the rest is not our business."

"Eliot, I assume?"

"I'm impressed," said Claudia.

"Please don't be," said Alphonse, "it's the only poet he ever quotes."

Peter laughed, "Too well, my friend, you know me too well. But you must also know it's bedtime."

Alphonse stood. "I do know that, but I would like to say a big thank you. I know you're no friend of flying, but we've had your A-game this evening, thank you."

Peter stood, smiling, "Thank you, but with what you've concocted here, I've needed it. Is there anything else I should know?"

Alphonse focused rigidly on Peter, he dared not look at Claudia.

"I'm asking if Will has behaved himself with his old love. Martha asked me, very discreetly, to keep an eye on them." Plausible, thought Alphonse, but he didn't exclude the question having been posed as a trap, or exclude Peter reading something from his sluggish non-response.

"I think Will," said Claudia decisively, when Peter turned from Alphonse to look at her, "might be the only gentleman among you all."

"And we are in the presence, my love, of the only lady."
Alphonse wondered how ironic he was being, but it seemed completely loving and sincere — and he left as quickly as he could.

✳✳✳

To find Isobel waiting for him in his room.

31

He was surprised, of course, but not shocked, I didn't think. I'd made myself comfortable on the sofa, but I didn't have to wait as long as I'd expected. It was barely eleven.

"Raymond let me in." I was prepared to say more had he asked but he seemed strangely content with that.

I'd told Raymond truthfully what I wanted but he'd shown no doubt or curiosity anyway. I assume I'd been placed on some secret approved list of his. I hadn't wanted to keep calling until Alphonse returned — or leave a message that he could have ignored.

"I am, let me first assure you, here for you. I come with no requests for money or information — and I come harbouring no lustful designs on your body. Now, can I get you a drink? My suite mirrors this, so I guess I know where everything is."

Having looked hesitant at first — I never had even a fleeting impression he might ask me to leave — he settled in the armchair and asked, "Are you joining me? What would you like?"

"I always think bubbles are a good idea, and they have those sweet little half-bottles in the mini-bar. We

have no secrets from Raymond, do we?" He looked conspiratorially at me and smiled. "But room service would be unnecessarily public."

"Bubbles it is then, a good idea. I've left most of a glass of scotch in Peter's villa."

"Wise!" I busied myself getting bottle and glasses but then handed the bottle to him — let them never abandon that duty! I let him pour and we clinked glasses. "Why is she here, I hear you not asking." He chuckled. "I thought, my friend, that you've been coping magnificently this week, while dealing with two major sources of emotional turbulence."

He tried to look puzzled. What he didn't do was attempt to contradict, leaving me to feel that my conjectures were entirely accurate.

"I don't want you to talk about them, unless you want to, of course, but, at the very least, I wanted you to know that I'm here for you. Yes, I love the project and yes, I'll do unscrupulous things to make sure it goes our way — but I hope you'll be able to look past our commercial relationship and see that I'm a friend working for you. Cheers!"

"Cheers," he said, but his smile was a little melancholy.

I stood up, "I think you could do with a hug, my dear, dear man. I'm not Lee, and I'm not Claudia, but I'm a warm body who likes being close to you. Now please stand up and don't make me feel entirely stupid!"

He stood up, of course, as any gentleman should, but then I had a long enveloping hug. Yes, he had needed it, and he was very slow to release me. It was sexless, but it wasn't desperate, it just felt both needy and affectionate. When he finally sat down his eyes were brimming. He shrugged, then laughed at himself, "I guess you touched a nerve," and we raised our glasses again.

He cleared his throat and tried to look serious, "Without confirming either of the preposterous rumours you're disseminating, may I ask if they're widely believed and discussed?"

"First of all, bollocks, you've already confirmed them, so they aren't preposterous. You're just not that good." He smiled — but slumped back in the chair. "Secondly, in answer to your question, no they're not. I can't tell you whether people have suspicions — well, with one exception I'm coming on to — but no-one's talking about them, and I've got fairly close to most people this week."

Now he laughed, "Well, I have seen evidence of that. So, who's your exception?"

"Raymond, of course, but he knows I'm on your side."

He looked a little sceptical now, "How did you convince him of that?"

I just looked at him. He should work this out for himself. "How much do you trust Raymond?"

"Well, completely until this evening," but he was smiling, then the thought dawned, "You didn't?"

"Didn't what?" I can be coquettish — but now he looked sternly serious.

"You showed the photo. We'd agreed you wouldn't."

This was a silly reaction, but not unexpected. "I appreciate you have few grounds to see it this way, but I have inveigled my way in here because I think you could use my moral support. I know you'll tell me you're not on your own but you're probably wondering how guilty you are for losing Lee and I'm going to guess that you and Claudia are struggling with your feelings for each other — and desperate not to fuck each other's lives up. I happen to think the danger's not as great as you think, if I'm judging Peter Dickinson correctly. I know he loves her greatly, but I think he's a more genuinely wise and tolerant man than each of you probably realises."

Now he was staring into his glass, "You may well be right, but it would feel so wrong to go any further." Now he looked up at me, "Well, it feels wrong to go as far as we have gone this week." His look was a question.

"No, Raymond said nothing, all I got out of him was access to your room, but Peter Dickinson is at least as sensitive as I am, and it's been standing out clearly to me. These are the greatest skills our species has, reading other people's minds. I'll bet even the cavemen knew who really wanted to be clubbed."

He laughed quietly, "Are you good at sub-spotting?" Then a thought struck him, "Harry! You saw that at the first meeting. And Mei. Raymond has told me about that, of course. You are a very interesting lady."

"Now that's one thing I've never had the ambition to be called," but we were both finding it funny now. "But seriously. I do just want to help. Yes, I want to get my way with the architects, but I expect you only ever to be neutral there." Now I gave him my fierce look, "But no more stolen designs!"

He held up his hands, "No more stolen designs, I promise."

"Good! And Alphonse..." this was a little more delicate.

"Yes?" Obviously, he looked puzzled.

"Don't let yourself get lonely at night. Not while I'm here."

It seemed to make him ponder and, hey, with all this going on around me, I don't particularly like being lonely either.

32

There were two things I was forcing myself to remember at a number of points during this morning's meeting: when that monster dies, Lou will become a billionaire; and second, he and Harry had been viewing me as a sexual target the other evening. So, the little pangs of sympathy I felt when he suffered another offensive blast from his father — always in Chinese, of course, but with marvellously expressive body language — were immediately extinguished by those thoughts.

The worst came, funnily enough, when he tried to contradict a point that Mei was making. That was so verbally violent that Lou said nothing for the rest of the morning. Mei, however, flourished like a flower in morning sunshine as Shen Wengwei, with increasing frequency, asked her opinion on different aspects of the architects' presentations. She gave smart responses, but mostly supported them. I began to worry what the minx might have to say about my presentation when I pulled everything together but, apart from a sly, wicked smile the first time he asked her to comment, she was only positive — almost effusive, in fact, I needn't have worried. PD was splendidly complimentary when I finished my piece and Wengwei seemed to support him.

Lou was silent by now. Which is what Harry had been for the entire meeting.

As was 'the interpreter', I think you'll understand what the parentheses signify. Wengwei, bless him, never asked her for clarification on anything complex or poorly expressed — he would merely hold a hand up and shout 'Stop! No understand. Say simpler'. It worked; by the time I spoke, I'd already planned to dumb down my vocabulary — and I had plenty of pictures and sketches to talk to.

Luke and Bobby got some rough treatment — which will have helped Alphonse, I suspect; they had been trying to push boundaries. Yes, even Bobby. But Daiyu, whom John quickly introduced as his presenter, had a very easy ride — but that wasn't because she was a woman or a Chinese, in my view, she was simply better.

The numbers, for Douglas, were easy. None of the architects was, by now, standing up for their previously suggested extravagances. Well, the one small attempt that Luke made to reopen a discussion received a very short, but extremely polite, rebuff from PD. I had finished by then and I was studying the body language of him and Claudia. Now that's a relationship that intrigues me, especially now Alphonse has confirmed how he is with her.

She said very little in the meeting but made a few notes which she slid to Alphonse just before he closed the session; which he did, of course, consummately well, summarising what the big boys would discuss this afternoon. He managed, in the process, to mend some of the feelings hurt by the interventions, even finding a point to compliment Lou on. I wasn't sure whether that was just bullshit or an outrageous invention, but at least the little man perked up a bit.

As we went to lunch Claudia asked me if I'd have time for her that afternoon. I told her, of course I would — but asked if she wouldn't be in the big meeting: "No, they don't need me for that. I'm just here to manage the process."

"Well, you've been superb at that, I must say."

"Thank you," she said, and seemed quite touched.

That's OK, I don't do bullshit, so I can stand by everything I say. Then she went off to sit with PD and Shen Wengwei — and the interpreter. Look, I've made my point about her, I only need parentheses once.

Mei came up to me, beaming, "Have lunch, have lunch, I have to talk." She had obviously had a wonderful morning and I had been wondering how she'd become so emboldened. She dragged me to a quiet table — Lily had to go with Bobby and the other architects, so we were undisturbed.

"I got asked to breakfast today," — I hadn't seen her.

"Obviously, I have to ask with whom."

"Shen Wengwei asked to see me. His interpreter called early and asked me to be in his villa at eight."

She smiled shyly, I knew what was coming; I thought I'd make it easier for her, "You were fortunate that Lily was in your room, not the other way round."

She looked relieved and put her hand on mine, "Thank you for understanding, we haven't really talked about it. You don't mind?"

"This isn't what we're talking about, is it?" *She shook her head.* "Good. We'll talk about us later if you really have the need. But the two of you have my blessing, you might even make a relationship out of it." *I actually think Lily will always be too adventurous to settle — they used to use the word promiscuous when I was young; my God, those were dreary times!* "But in the meantime, the big man wanted to see you."

"Yes. He asked me about the project and my opinions on how it's going. So, I tell him, of course."

"Ha, of course you do."

"Well, he seemed very happy and said he been hearing very good things about me and how important I was to Alphonse, so he wants me to take a bigger role, to support Liuwei better — and make sure I learn as much as I can from Alphonse so I can prepare for a bigger job later. I was so excited. And he even gave me a big hug when I was leaving." *I must have had one of my suspicious looks on at this stage.* "No, no, it wasn't like that at all. It was like a hug I always wanted from my father — but he's a very cold man."

Well, that was interesting. But there was no doubt in my mind that Wengwei was picking the best brain to help safeguard his money. And the confidence boost will do her no harm, as long as she can do a better job of hiding the arrogance. We'll have time to work on that. It sounds like we have two years of working together to give me some opportunities. And she'll need me when Lily wanders. Don't get me wrong, that may work out, but I believe it's Mei who'll need to adapt more and loosen up a bit — enjoy the odd man occasionally, too.

33

Claudia was unsure exactly why she'd asked Isobel to come and see her, and it was simply easier to just blurt that out when she arrived.

"I was delighted you did. I've been dying to meet the lady of the blue bedroom — well, that's not strictly true, I was predisposed to envy for anyone whose man could lavish so much care on a project like that."

"It's a wonderful room," but Claudia's response, she knew, carried no conviction. Then Isobel surprised her.

"I'm sorry, I should have been more sensitive than to start with that."

"Why? It is truly wonderful."

"I already had an inkling that it wasn't quite the lamplit cave for you, no secret, bestial peace. I'm not prying, honestly, just guessing that, even for you, relationships aren't simple."

"Even for me is good," but Claudia didn't want to project self-pity.

"Look, we've been dancing around each other all week, with me admiring how you've organised everything, getting people working together…"

"We've all been doing that…"

But Isobel put up a hand, tilted her head, smiling, to one side, and said, "I know you've asked me here, and I don't know what you want to discuss — it could be lots of things — or maybe you have one reason — but hear me out a moment, please."

"I'm sorry, I'll shut up soon, but I have to comment on one thing there. We were puzzling last night about why the Lee/Lou switch had been made, and we couldn't think of a main reason, as you put it and I wondered if you might have gained a different perspective. Anyway… I interrupted you…"

"I just wanted to say that I can see the strain you're under. It's something I spoke to Alphonse about last night, he's creating these extra pressures for himself too. I don't have a particularly reassuring message for you, but what's plain to me must be very obvious to Peter. I've never met a more perceptive man."

Claudia found herself nodding ruefully.

"All I'm saying, my love, is that he must know how your feelings are; for him, as well as for Alphonse — and they're not simple, are they?"

Now Claudia was shaking her head silently.

"But I didn't come here to depress you. Look, I meet people who make much more complicated relationships work, I promise you. It does need openness though."

Now Claudia felt a bitter laugh stick in her throat, "I used to think that. Well, maybe I should have carried on believing. If you think you have openness, and you don't…" she sighed, "well, I've come out the wrong side of that one."

Isobel gestured cheekily around the villa, "Regrets?"

Now Claudia's laugh was genuine, "No, just painful memories, but regrets are the most stupid things, don't you think?"

"I completely agree — but I came here to talk, and I've no idea why, and on the Lee/Lou question, I have nothing to offer, I'm afraid. I don't think, on the face of it, that it helps us."

"Well, as I said when you came in, I'd lost any clear idea I had of what I wanted; the Lee/Lou switch was only one issue. There's been so much going on all week, and you and I seem to have been moving in non-concentric circles. I just wanted to chat, I suppose, about the surprising coincidences of our lives."

"Is Will on your list?"

"I suppose so. I think I'm allowed to say that Peter's on a spying mission from Martha to make sure you don't snaffle him again."

"Oh, I would love to, but that would never work," here Isobel's eyes narrowed, as if she was being careful about what to say, "I met him years ago when he was deeply in love with a friend of mine. I stayed close to them because I suspected it might not end well, and by then I cared a lot for him. I think I helped him through it — without realising just how much I'd fallen for him. I was committed to my no-relationship policy by then, so it seemed to work well for both of us — until he met that bloody woman and I realised I'd not been honest with myself. So, it's all very well you and I decrying a lack of honesty and openness in the important people in our lives, but we're seldom honest with ourselves… I'm babbling."

"No, you're not," Claudia said very forcefully, surprising herself and it made Isobel smile. "I'm sorry, you're not, you're making a lot of sense — which is what I expected, I suppose, and why I wanted some time with you. But I won't mention Will again."

"Oh, that's OK. I think he's more wonderful than ever, and I'm rather glad he's devoted to that wretched woman." She laughed.

"You'd like her a lot, really you would."

"Maybe, but I'm not expecting a commission to redecorate whatever they have in New York. I'm really just happy that we're in touch again — and that he's happy. I hope that doesn't sound too soppy."

"Not at all. But is he going to worry about you?"

"Because I'm not happy, you mean?" It could have sounded spiky, or challenging, or mournful, but it just sounded curious.

"I didn't mean that at all. I'm sorry if it came out that way. No, I just wonder if he might wonder about you. These things can be very distracting. We might almost have fallen into that with Alphonse this week."

"With Lee, you mean?"

Claudia felt pensive, wondering how much to say, but this charming, and very faintly dotty, woman felt like an agreeable confidante, "Yes. He'd never really recovered from a great love cheating on him many years ago, but I think he may have been edging towards trying a relationship again, but…" she shrugged, "who can say?"

"Would that have upset you?"

"I only worry for him in that respect, I like to think I wouldn't be upset — but maybe that's what you just said; an inability to be honest with ourselves. He does seem to attract needy ladies, though, and I try to have no views on that — but they sting a bit," but she found herself smiling, "But they never get serious, I don't think. There may have been some people worried that Lee could have been serious, though."

"You think that's why they made the change?"

"We've no clear idea how much of a role it played, but, like you said, he's a loss, although…" Isobel looked expectant, as if she were waiting for some confidence, "although they seem now to be pinning hopes on Mei…"

There was a narrow-eyed, suspicious look from Isobel, "How did that come about, by the way?"

"I think Alphonse spoke up very firmly in her favour. He sees her as having much more to contribute than Lou or Harry."

"So much so that Shen Wengwei asks her to breakfast?"

"She's told you then?"

"Yes, she was worried whether they'd even keep her, and now she's very excited — and we had become quite close."

"Had become? Is that a past tense?"

"Not really. I'll tell you a little about the last two weeks, but I'll also tell you that I think you have something to say to me. I have no idea what, but you seem unnecessarily edgy. Anyway, as I told Alphonse last night, I love this work, yes, I'm here for the business, yes, but I'm feeling part of something with this."

"Hence the help with the naughty photos? I've only heard of them, of course."

Isobel laughed, but didn't seem entirely relaxed, which was fair, thought Claudia, who was still struggling with how much to say.

"The photos were part revenge and part education, for the boys and the girls. I seem to treasure my didactic responsibilities. But it did occur to me that they might be useful, if only to help keep Mei on the project. But now it seems her star is in the ascendant. So, saying 'had become' with Mei was the right way to put it. We'd had a lovely week or so together but, since she's gay, we were only ever having an adventure. She'll be more at home with Lily, but I don't expect that will last — I think Lily will want more adventures than Mei — so I expect to look after Mei eventually the way I used to look after Will. At least that won't provoke future regrets. Now you're looking thoughtful. What is it?"

"I knew someone once who said, if I tell you a secret, then you're entitled to tell the next person."

"And this is a serious secret, not serious gossip."

"It's very serious, even Mei must never find out."

Isobel looked very puzzled, as though many ideas were racing through her mind, but only for a moment, "She said Shen Wengwei hugged her after they'd eaten breakfast," and she paused while Claudia looked expectantly at her. Isobel was nodding now, "Like a father, she said." They sat for a while in silence. Claudia knew that would be enough confirmation. "Who else knows?"

"Peter and Alphonse… and our spy, a man I find it impossible to talk about, but he does appear to have his uses. But the funny thing was, Alphonse was pushing the idea to Wengwei with no knowledge of the secret — but it wasn't a surprise to Peter why the old man was looking a little pleased and proud. Anyway, I'm glad that's out, I don't know why I felt I wanted to tell you."

Isobel shrugged, "I'm very glad you did — and I feel absolutely no need to tell anyone. It's obviously best for Mei if I don't, but I hope the old bastard tells her one day."

"Oh, I just wouldn't know what was for the best — and, fortunately, it's not down to us."

Isobel looked pensive, "You're right actually, not our business, but I am very happy for her. Although I rather wish she weren't coming with me now. I'm visiting the other two sites."

"The ones we're bulldozing?"

"Yes, but I have to get a sense of the locale…"

"That's been one of the most fascinating aspects of the week for me, listening to you talk about icons and vegetation and how you integrate those into your design ideas. It all made so much sense. Even the architects seemed impressed."

Isobel laughed lightly, "It won't have been new to them as a process, but I like to think I have an eye for picking compelling motifs — and I'm hoping, when I get back and ponder, to come up with one overwhelming and distinctive motif for each place," then she chuckled and shrugged, "not too hard with five resorts in different countries. I hope I can stay fresh and imaginative for the others."

"Will you want to do that?" she hesitated, "Oh, I'm sorry, I hope that didn't come across as I think you shouldn't, I think what you've done is wonderful. But I know your UK business is thriving. You must feel a pull to get back there."

"A little, and it wouldn't have been wrong anyway to think someone else should take over out here. Nevertheless, I'm tempted by the thought of setting up an office out here and finding some local talent to bring some fresh ideas to Psamathe and try some new things. I suppose I have connections now to get that off the ground."

"I'm sure you would have. I think that would be thrilling, if you could handle it personally."

Now it was Isobel who looked thoughtful — not sad, Claudia wouldn't have said — "I have friends and arrangements, mostly in London, but nothing that ties me down."

Now Claudia smiled, "I can put your own question to you now; regrets?"

Isobel laughed, "I did agree with you earlier: the most pointless things."

And Claudia realised that she liked her very much.

"I enjoyed this project right from the start, and I'll admit I was very disappointed when I didn't get the work on this place," and Isobel looked around and chuckled, "although it has an eerie familiarity for me, since that smooth bastard of yours just lifted my designs. I couldn't honestly say that he truly apologised — but I did get the commission for these five."

"That doesn't really sound like him."

Now she got a sly smile from Isobel, "I'm going to guess that your contact is more social than business." Claudia was a little puzzled. "Don't get me wrong, he was entirely straightforward and ethical — he had the contractual right to the designs — but he's actually quite a tough businessman. Unlike your dear Peter..." Now Claudia was even more mystified, "Oh, my dear, I'm sorry, that was a little joke I couldn't resist. The point is, he went to so much trouble over every detail of that bedroom for you. I stopped offering him choices because he always went for the most expensive thing."

"You're not making me feel any better."

Isobel reached out and touched her hand, "That wasn't my intention, but it also wasn't my intention to make you feel worse. Do you love him?"

"That's a terrible question, isn't it? If you don't say yes instantly; if you hesitate, or equivocate, you feel damned."

Isobel laughed, quite warmly, "And you're now doing both."

And Claudia laughed with her. "It's a funny love, but I do, yes."

"And he's devoted, isn't he?"

"I suppose so, and he's been through a lot with relationships… that's silly, isn't it?"

"Because we all have?"

Claudia nodded, "Yes, even our serene Will, apparently. I was a little surprised when he got together with Martha, there… now I'm hesitating again."

"You're quite close to her, aren't you? Was that business, or a man thing?"

Claudia chuckled, there seemed no point in secrets anymore, "Both, but we share a…"

"I'm quite happy about the word kink. It doesn't have any negative connotations for me whatsoever. And I know something of Will's preferences, so I've made my assumptions about Martha. And you?"

"Well, the man she and I sort of shared for a while got me into that, but Peter provided the real education."

"And now?"

"Now it still features, but it's all a bit perfunctory. Peter loves everyone else's kinks — he even enjoyed his wives', I think — but his own range is quite narrow, really."

"And Alphonse?"

"Well, it's funny you should ask. I love his body, I love his arms around me, but it's always quite sweet, a little careful — I sometimes tease him by calling him passionless — but I'd just assumed that was how he was. But he does have a more animal side apparently and I'm talking far too much and now I'm embarrassed," and they both fell, laughing, towards each other on the sofa. When the laughter subsided, Claudia said, "I'm saying this, making the assumption that your life is much richer than mine, and that nothing I say could possibly shock you. Is that very wrong of me?"

Isobel laughed again, "No, it's not wrong at all. I suppose I'm mostly top, and mostly straight, but I think I've given everything a chance. It made it quite easy to set up that little scenario the other night, but that was more fun than any Machiavellian connivance. I went past a boundary of mine, though, I don't think the boys were really that much into humiliation — and if people sub, they deserve to have their wishes respected. Still, I think, for poor Lou, it would only have been embarrassment to wake up with his hand on Harry's cock. My conscience isn't suffering too much. So, I do enjoy a rich life, but you're wrong to say it's much richer than yours."

"Well, it's not rich now."

"In spite of this week's adventures with Alphonse?"

Claudia wondered what she had revealed, then realised it was more than she had wanted to, "Well, the worry there was that it might have been a 'last time' thing. We're both finding it harder."

"And maybe Peter is too, then. It sounds like you're making it too difficult, honestly; I think it must be worth a little openness, all three of you look very capable to me — and it doesn't sound like anything should shock you."

"Well, you've made me think, thank you. I think I was wrapping a cocoon around myself."

"Maybe a different butterfly will emerge?"

"Oh, stupid analogies. I'm thinking more about making Peter and Alphonse more content."

"And my guess is, that's just about fucking typical…" and now they laughed even harder.

Claudia was wiping her eyes, "Thank you so much for coming in. I am so fucking glad I invited you. I really don't know why I did, but I feel much better…"

"And I think we stay in touch, don't we?"

"Oh, I very much think so." And Claudia felt intensely relieved as if some bridge had been crossed.

Isobel was standing up, "Hug? This means a lot to me too."

<h1 style="text-align:center">34</h1>

I'd meant it. I was attracted to the woman, in spite of my jokes about the blue bedroom. But we'd both spent lots of time on other people during the week, so an hour to ourselves was hardly an indulgence. And none of you out there is thinking that contriving the Lou and Harry scenario was all fun, are you?

But now I'm waiting for my feedback on the afternoon's big meeting from Mei. I need to be careful, of course, especially if she's still planning to visit the two bulldoze sites with me. That's going to be funny. I think she's grown a lot in these last two weeks; and learned a lot. I do have feelings for her, of course, but I'm not expecting the night-time cuddles. Well, we'll see. I'll find out more, no doubt, about her real feelings for Lily. That will be easy. What won't be easy is if she starts talking about the Shen Wengwei connection, or about her father.

She bounces in and hugs me. She even kisses me, or tries to. I'm not very responsive — she's caught me by surprise. "Are you still upset with me about Lily?"

"I'm not upset at all about Lily. I'm really very happy for you. I just don't want to get in the way of you moving on."

"So, you don't want me anymore?" She's pouting, child-like.

I put my arms around her and kiss her, "My darling girl, I think you're wonderful, and I'm very happy for you with the job, as it's now working out, and with Lily; but if you start pouting at me like that, our next piece of fun is with your bare arse across my knee."

She laughs and hugs me now, "You think it will work with Lily and me?"

She's not looking at me, her face is nuzzled into my neck. "You're having doubts already?" I ask.

She leans back and looks at me, her arms still around my waist, "So, you're having doubts."

"My beautiful child, I'm only worrying about what you think you want. I think you may want to settle into a bigger commitment too soon. You two could enjoy your lives a great deal, as long as you give each other plenty of freedom." She's thinking. "But that's worrying you, isn't it?"

She nods silently, "But you will sleep with me when we travel won't you?"

Bless you, Mei, you have a sweet way of being very selfish. "Of course I will, although I expect you'll be kissing fond farewells to Lily tonight, won't you?"

Her face falls, "Am I very bad?"

"Absolutely not. I'm just pointing out that you're not as ready for monogamy as you think you are — and you mustn't expect it from Lily either. That's the sort of selfishness that ruins relationships: it's alright if I sleep with B because my love for A isn't affected. Well, sometimes that's true — and sometimes it's even true that A is really accepting. But mostly, it goes wrong." And obviously I'm thinking about the conversation I've just been having with Claudia. *"But anyway, I shall be delighted to enjoy your body again next week, and try a few more toys from the box."*

"Even the strap-on," she murmurs.

"Well," I say, with mock crossness, *"you have to bring it back first!"*

Now she's laughing again, *"I will, and the clamps I've stolen."*

"Good, now sit down and tell me about the meeting. Does anything affect the project? Do I still have a job?"

She reaches across and hugs me as we sit down, *"Of course you do, they all think you're wonderful, even Shen Wengwei. He was so nice at breakfast, but he was terrible with Lou again in the meeting, he kept calling him Toto. It was a joke I didn't get, but I think Alphonse did; he tried not to laugh. Oh, he's coming with us tomorrow, to look at the sites, isn't that thrilling, did you know?"* I didn't, but I try not to look surprised, *"He's got to teach me, so I get more control over property. I don't know how that will work with Lou."*

"Is he coming with us?" This would get very difficult for some people, and not so easy for her as she thinks.

"No..." she paused, *"at least, I don't think so. No, he doesn't know about it."*

"You should tell him, you know. You don't need him as an enemy. So, don't call him Toto." I have no idea what that's about; perhaps Alphonse will tell me.

"You're right. Just like always. I'll talk to him, and I won't call him Toto." She giggles, *"I wish I knew what the joke was. Anyway, do you want me to say more about the meeting?"*

"That's why you're here, my little love."

And it seems like it's gone very well. If anything, Alphonse has been asked if he can go faster and it sounds like that's causing a little tension between Shen Wengwei and Peter; but I'd back smooth to beat rough on that one, especially with Alphonse in charge.

We talk a little about the Chinese architects, John and Daiyu, and their other projects — and I float my idea about starting a Far East office — and she seems absurdly thrilled by the prospect — *"That would be amazing, there's so much to do, and Lijun and Daiyu think you're wonderful."*

OK, maybe my life's opening up in unexpected ways.

35

Alphonse had been toying with the idea of visiting the other sites and, when it became apparent that Mei and Isobel were going there next, it seemed an obvious adjustment to his schedule. He wouldn't expect a happy reception: Raymond had told the local teams about the plans, but he'd felt that at least one resort head might be worth keeping — to be his local eyes and ears for the project — and to manage the resort when it was completed.

In the future, Mei would have to travel more to meet him, but he was very encouraged by how she'd started — and by the support she would clearly get from Shen Wengwei. He now expected Lou to fade into the background, but for the time being, he was still there and had to be appeased rather than provoked. He wasn't sure Mei would be up to that. And something else she wouldn't do would be to give him an easy ride.

He smiled to himself as he thought that and, with his recently acquired knowledge, maybe it was too easy to see her real father in her.

Shen Wengwei had been good in the afternoon session. He'd pushed on going faster but, when Peter challenged, he'd been content to do no more than ask 'that Alphonse and Mei examine the possibilities'. Peter had nodded, but only reluctantly, knowing, as he did, that Alphonse always followed up minuted actions thoroughly.

It would help to spend time on that with Mei.

But not tonight. Most of the architects had left. They'd had their green lights. Dinner might have its pitfalls but the atmosphere between Peter and Shen Wengwei had seemed surprisingly good, in spite of Lee's disappearance. It still troubled him, but there seemed nothing to stop him finding out more from Lee himself — but what painful impracticalities would that reveal. It was the nearest he'd been to falling for someone in a long time. He'd had no affair in years where he thought it could develop into something more than a temporary pleasure. Now Lee was gone, and he found himself not wanting to think about it — but he knew they would talk again.

In the meantime, there was Mei to train. It was day one of a new world for her and he hoped that her ferocious attention to everything he said would lessen in the coming weeks. Hopefully, her girlfriend would still be here this evening. He would have enough time with Mei over the next few days.

And time with Isobel, and he felt strangely comforted by that.

***

He realised why as he watched Peter and Claudia retire together after dinner. Mei, fortunately, still had her friend, Lily. Lou and Harry were heading for the bar, dragging a reluctant Douglas with them — Will had already left, no doubt having briefed the poor man to get to know the natives and practise his Mandarin. Shen Wengwei lapsed quickly into Chinese with his interpreter and ignored all others around him, merely shouting 'goodnight' over his shoulder as he left the room. Suddenly Alphonse was almost alone until a hand slid into his and Isobel said, "It's time for the other half bottle."

It was very easy to agree, "Yes, it's time for the other half bottle."

The hands disengaged, "I'd suggest the bar, but poor Douglas seems to have drawn the short straw there. He's under orders from Herr Wilhelm to improve his Mandarin and spy on the enemy. Oh, I'm not thinking of the Chinese as enemy, though. I have the impression that Will thinks anyone who spends money is potentially enemy."

"Did you get a chance to say goodbye? He was dashing off at the end of the meeting this afternoon."

"He got me at lunchtime, bless him. It's just lovely to be in touch again. I still love him, of course, but when you next meet her, you must tell her I'm not a threat."

"In spite of your apparent commitment to open lifestyles?"

She had a serious look when she lifted her face to him, "I know you know it's not that simple."

"I'm sorry," it made him think, "I hate being reduced to a simple label. I shouldn't apply silly phrases to other people."

"Where are we headed? It's my turn to entertain you."

"Then we're going to your room," and he realised he did want her company.

***

"I still want you to open the bottle."

"I'm on it, I'm on it — good heavens, woman, leave your control-freakery aside for a moment. You're not topping now!"

She laughed, "I apologise, good sir, and I thank you," he was pouring now. "I gather you're with us tomorrow."

"Yes, I should have said. It won't affect your plans, will it?"

"No, not at all. I have my little routine now. I think Mei has the itinerary worked out to my spec. I don't need her with me if you want to train her, the in-between days are free."

"That would be marvellous, thank you."

"You really think she can grow into it? Oh, something I should say to you."

He wondered what was coming, but surprises were no longer surprises from Isobel.

"I was with Claudia this afternoon," he felt a little tense, "well might you look worried, but this is something very specific that may influence the next few days. It was something I'd found strange anyway when Mei told me about breakfast with the big Shen. She said he'd hugged her like a father."

Alphonse tried to show no reaction.

"I'll give you that. You play poker better than Claudia. But I'm sworn to secrecy, I promise you. She'll find nothing out from me. So, back to my question, can she grow into it?"

He felt confident. He didn't know why he was hesitating, maybe because this woman was too close to too many confidences — and he wondered what she and Claudia had said; about him; about them; about anything. "Well, given that she now has support from on high, I think she'll do well. I suppose I'm most worried about what they do with Lou."

"Maybe I'll find out more about that from Daiyu."

Again, her surprises no longer surprised him, "You are an extraordinary woman."

"Thank you. That's at least better than interesting, which is what your beloved called me yesterday."

"My beloved?"

"Oh, Alphonse, my biggest challenge in this whole fucking thing is to get you to relax. I really am not the enemy. Claudia called me interesting. She meant it well, but it's not what a girl wants to hear."

"So, what does a girl want to hear?" He felt genuinely perplexed.

"Actually, in these current circumstances, only what I told you yesterday. I want to feel you know I'm with you on this one. I want us to build fabulous places together. That's all. Oh, my latest little plan…"

He groaned, but smiled, "Your latest plan?"

"I'm thinking of opening an office out here, if I can find more work and one or two good people. Please don't react straightaway, but the three of us can talk about it while we're travelling — and it gives me another reason to stay close to Daiyu."

"OK, I won't react straightaway."

She looked hard at him, "Don't be an arse, Alphonse, tell me it's a wonderful idea."

He laughed, "I think it's a brilliant idea!"

And she threw herself on to his lap, hugged his neck and kissed him. Then, almost as quickly, stood up and returned to her sofa, "Sorry about that, but you deserved it."

"Deserved it in a good way, or in a bad way."

"Both!" and she was raising her glass and beaming at him. "Cheers!"

"Cheers! Where would you want the office to be?"

"It's this afternoon's idea. You're the third person I've told — and the other two weren't such arseholes about telling me what a brilliant idea it was."

"I did tell you."

"Only eventually. Don't make me jump on your lap again. Anyway, I'm obviously excited about things, but I'm really here to make sure you are. I am worried about what you're having to deal with. Have you heard from Lee?"

"Only the letter when he left. I'll show it to you."

"Only if you want to."

"Why do I get the feeling we'll be sharing a few things like that?"

"That's all I wanted to hear."

"Have you got things to share? Shouldn't I be doing something for you?"

"I'm here, Alphonse, and I could use a change in my life. Oh, don't worry, I'm not running away from anything. I'll still keep London going; it'll make me delegate more, I have two good young people who need to grow. And on the emotional side, you've seen my last problem."

"Will?"

"Yes, and I didn't know how big a problem it was until this week. But I'm very happy for him — and, after a few days, I'm going to be glad of the reminder that I could still feel that way." And she drained her glass.

She seemed in control, although he felt a little nervous about her company now. But who else was there if he wanted to talk — and, working so far away, he knew that even he would sometimes want to talk to someone. So, he poured her more champagne, and was happy to see her lean back on the sofa, obviously relaxing, but studying him.

He topped his own glass up, emptying the small bottle, "You're making me nervous, looking at me that way. Is there some new revelation about to be unveiled?"

"No," she sipped champagne, "well, maybe it is a revelation, but it's a revelation for me as much as it will be for you."

He sipped his drink, waiting for her to say more, wondering what was coming.

"I'd like to spend the night naked in your arms."

He felt shocked but, because it was Isobel, strangely not surprised.

"But I do have a compromise offer, if you'll meet me half-way."

He was still nervous, "What would half-way be?"

"I spend half the night naked in your arms. That's my final offer."

"What are you expecting?"

"I was just hoping you might be open to the idea. I feel very close to you and, through this work together, I'll be staying close to you. I don't suppose we'll see each other often but, when we do, I like the thought of lying beside you, relaxing and chatting. It has more to do with closeness than sex."

"Is that a promise?" although he had no idea why he was worrying.

"No, of course it's not a promise. If that happens, it happens, but we're not going to fall in love with each other, are we?" She added quickly, "Don't answer that. I know the answer's no, and I wouldn't want it to be anything other than that, I'm just worried now that you might try to find something nice to say — and then feel guilty about it later. We're going to be friends, my man, and there will be nights, like tonight, is what I'm thinking, when we want each other's arms around us. You have done wonderfully well this week, in spite of all the emotional strain, and my thought is that wrapping your arms around my naked little body will help you. It will help me too, by the way, I'm doing this for myself as well. I've had a little too much of dealing with other people's needs this week too."

She stood up and held out a hand, "Come on. You'll find me surprisingly sensitive to your needs and wishes. At the moment, I think, I've got you as far as wanting me to stay and talk, and your mind's just opening up, I think, to how much more pleasant that would be if we lie together."

He unfurled himself from the chair and wrapped his arms around her, her head resting on his chest, "Wretched woman. I'm not used to being read so well."

"I'm going into the bedroom. I'm getting naked into bed — and I'm hoping you'll join me soon."

36

I still wasn't certain he'd come. He might have been gallant and stayed on the sofa, but I soon felt him sliding in behind me with his arms enveloping me. He cuddled quite close, but I admit I snuggled back to maximise our skin contact. "Just so you know," I said, "if this is what it is, I am perfectly content."

That was near enough true. It was my major need — and I was thinking it was probably his. Certainly, I wasn't being prodded.

"How close were you with Lee?"

He laughed, "Never this close, certainly. We touched hands once, I think. That's silly. I know, of course."

"It was plain there was something."

"You're more sensitive than most."

"I'm not going to deny that but seeing people falling in love is a very evident spectacle in their every interaction. I could see it with Mei and Lily — and I'm going to confess there to a little pang of jealousy, and the enhanced alertness that comes with that. It's a bloodhound with a very sensitive nose is our old friend jealousy. How much does it affect you with Claudia and Peter?"

He hugged me tight then, "Do I have to call it jealousy? I've shared her openly with another man, yet that didn't hurt. But that night she slept in my arms like this."

"And Peter?"

"That was before they were together. She was still with Jack then."

"Was he the other man?"

"No, no," he said quickly, "It was on Peter's boat in Miami, and it was a complete first for Claudia." He seemed to spend a moment with the memory. "Jack was still based in the Far East and they were trying to work out what being more open meant for them. I think she did remarkably well at understanding herself better, but she suspected he was getting darker and more secret."

"And was he?"

"Probably not, but Peter wanted her so much anyway... I can't really work it out," and, in that moment, I think he felt glad he was holding me.

Now, I'm nobody's distraction or substitute, but I was enjoying having his arms around me. It was worth the risk of turning round to face him. I put my hand up to his face, I was looking into his eyes. I kissed his lips very gently and felt his melting tenderly on to mine. I could feel his cock slowly responding. I pulled back a little, "You don't have to..." and he put a finger to my lips and then pulled me closer, squashing my boobs on to his chest.

"Aren't we just going to see what happens?"

I reached down and touched him, "Well, I'm glad he's available for the party. Is it best if I kiss him?" He touched me now, I was already wet, of course. "That would do it for me, if I can look in your eyes while you touch me."

He smiled, "Are we always going to talk this much?"

I laughed. I do talk when I'm nervous, and I was nervous. I wanted this to become something — for me and for him — "Just one more little question, please?"

The smile stayed still; the fingers were still moving. "I do have condoms."

I laughed — that's not so easy when your clit's feeling aroused — "That was the question. I've been safe for ages, but I think this week, for you…" It's funny, it's hard to talk about the third person in the situation we were in, "I'm just going to assume you've been with a very nice, clean lady and I am going to sit on your nice, naked cock in a little while," and the poor, softening organ began to respond again to my touch.

I was able to shut up then. It would have been several minutes anyway before I was able to speak. He has those lovely brown eyes and I got quite lost in them, looking up, kneeling between his knees, alternately playing with him and sucking him. He has a lovely cock; I still have a full hand around the lower shaft when my mouth is full. I will so sit down on him later, but for now I think we have this perfect. He seems to have all the control we need, but I'm skilled at gauging that anyway. If I go deep, his breathing gets ragged and I know to pull back — and then I get a bigger smile when I look up into his eyes again. I will sit on that face sometime soon but tonight I would come instantly. Not that we're here for protracted athletics. This is just us becoming lovers — and I want to come while looking into his eyes — and I want that now. I slide up and straddle him quickly. I'm ready to come, I hope he is, and dirty talk usually helps, "Come with me mister, or I'll be down there sucking your cock all night."

And, bless him, he's trying to slide his fingers between our bellies to tickle my clit, "No, no," I gasp, "not necessary, just fuck me, I'm coming. I'm coming..." and so was he.

We were soon back with his arms around me. I could feel him still dribbling on the back of my thigh. This was the time to stay shut up. There's no nice way of saying what an enormous thrill it is to feel the blobs and patches. You still get a little when the condom is cast aside, but I could feel his wet inside me and fresh dribbles on my leg. It was wonderful, and I was feeling charmingly sleepy.

"Were you taking the full offer, or the compromise?"

"Do you need to know now? Shouldn't we just see if our bodies like being together."

"OK, but I was just warning you. I am going to suck your cock again and you can't get rid of me until that happens."

It was a happy chuckle and we fell asleep quickly.

37

You cart around your school memories of atlases where the south of England has one page, as does South Asia and, however illogical, you equate the sizes. But it was a big page we had to travel the next day; two plane flights — one chartered for us — and two helicopter transfers, and it still took ten hours.

After the night we'd had, it would have been perfectly possible to enjoy the day with just Alphonse, but I used every opportunity to push the two of them together. That wasn't just to distract her; as soon as she'd got over leaving Lily, she was giving us suspicious looks. You see, it's true what I say, however hard you try to hide relationships, others, in this case even Mei, have fine antennae. So, if you're cheating on someone and they haven't noticed, I'm afraid they're just indifferent to you and it's too late anyway.
Not that Alphonse and I have a relationship, of course, and I'm almost resentful of Mei seeming suspicious. But anyway, he seems to be quite committed to explaining a lot to her. I get a number of careful, sly smiles from him through the day, though.

***

There's not much light left when we get there but, even walking into the huge reception area, it's easy to see why this is a candidate for demolition. The manager, a Filipino called Marvin, is the one we want to keep. I get that instantly. He's bright, friendly and smart and gets our bags dealt with unfussily. He has a lovely manner with the staff. He knows my itinerary for tomorrow and tells me the car will be here at ten.

He tells me the choices are excellent, he smiles at Mei, he knows it's her plan, but he has taken the liberty of adding a small formal garden, not in the tourist books, to my plan. It sounds like I might be spoiled tomorrow.

He hopes we'll have some appetite this evening, he's had chef prepare a small tasting menu to showcase what they can do locally. I'm already won over, Marvin, my man.

But the building is old, and the décor is tired, nothing sparkles, but the setting, when we meet on the terrace for a drink before dinner, is wonderful. Marvin hovers, but doesn't intrude. Alphonse calls him over and there's a conversation about Marvin's history and what he's been trying to do here that falls not far short of an interview. But Alphonse closes with, "Thank you so much, Marvin, I can see why Raymond thinks so highly of you, I hope you'll be with us to open the place up again."

For a second it seems like Marvin is almost as tall as Alphonse; he swells, he gleams, it almost overwhelms him, "I'll just make sure the chef is ready," and the poor, sweet man disappears quickly.

The sun has shimmered down now and left us a purply twilight. The warm air is gorgeous, the afternoon thunderstorm has rinsed it clean and it sings with the scents of alien blooms — time to study them tomorrow.

Hasty showers have revived us but, even though the food is delicate and inventive, I can tell we are flagging. Mei yawns first, we laugh at her, but copy the yawn and now we laugh at each other. "I think Marvin has a tour planned at nine," says Alphonse, and looks at me, "Do you want to join us, or are you lying in until your car comes?"

"No, I want to do the tour. I know the building will be completely different, but I want to see the grounds. I'm already won over by the terrace and beach. The guy knew what he was doing, but this place looks twenty years old. Not his fault, it was probably stunning then."

"Yes," said Alphonse, "sad story. He wouldn't have let it wallow, but one plane crash and a greedy family is all it takes. It's funny, I'm still convinced it's a good deal for us but there's part of me wants to see it through as a monument to his vision. I feel I'm walking in big footprints. Anyway, it's not that late but..."

And Mei yawns again, stands up, and says, "See you in the morning."

He waits until she's left the dining room, then takes my hand and smiles, "I thought she'd never leave." That's unlike him, "Seriously," he takes my hand now, "thank you so much for today, pushing us two at each other..."

"I would have been making silly smiles, I've warned you — and while I loved the odd furtive grin, I got from you — I was trying to discourage it. She's not the most sensitive little flower, but neither is she stupid."

"No, she's certainly not that, I really think she'll do well if Lou doesn't get too mixed up in this."

"It doesn't really sound like his father's encouraging him, does it?"

He shook his head slowly, "No, that was sad and embarrassing. Lou wouldn't be my favourite, but that all seemed to go too far. But I do have one other delicate little question..."

"Yeees," I said slowly.

"You are sure she's gay?"

I burst out laughing, not ever so ladylike, I'm afraid, "Alphonse, two things strike me immediately with that question..." now he looked puzzled, "you're telling me she's been coming on to you today?"

He looked a little uncomfortable, "It was just a funny feeling. Silly of me."

"No, but she does admire you greatly, and she knows you're the one who stood up for her — it's just a bit of hero worship."

"And the second thing?"

"You're gay, you say, and I completely accept that, but that's not going to stop me asking you to my room

tonight." Now I squeezed his hand, and I got a smile and a small nod of his head.

***

We hadn't been inventive or adventurous. I wanted to come, of course, and I certainly wanted him to come, but, as much as that, I wanted his skin and his arms around me and the pleasing scent of his well-shaped body.

I woke in the middle of the night, I've no idea what time, but his arm was around me, his chest was on my back, and there was a pleasing stiffening of his cock on my bum. I was tempted to slide my hand back there and encourage him, but I was enjoying the calm warmth of his embrace and his slow breathing. But something wasn't right, I was sure, but I didn't want to wake him. I eased myself slowly out of his arms, then froze when I saw the chair was occupied.

"Only me," whispered Mei quietly, "I wanted you. I didn't know."

So many thoughts were spinning around, I couldn't focus on one. I slid out of bed and pulled a robe around me. Alphonse carried on sleeping. I held out my hand to her, she seemed reluctant to be pulled from the chair but eventually she followed me into the sitting room. I shut the bedroom door behind me; if we kept to whispers…

"How did you…"

339

"Get in? Marvin thinks we're together, I thought Raymond would tell him, so it was easy to get another card," which she now waved at me. *"Is he why you sent me to Lily last night."*

Mei is, as you've seen, very self-centred, "Mei, my darling, you left two lonely people last night and we just found it much more pleasant to try a night in each other's arms."

"Did you fuck him? He's gay."

"You're gay, but yes, I fucked him, of course. He's a beautiful man, anyone would."

"Anyone?"

"Yes, Mei, even you. I haven't really given you a chance to appreciate a man by offering you only Lou and Harry."

"No, but I like Alphonse."

"He's very impressed by you, but you have a very difficult working relationship to build up with him."

"You too, but you fucked him; I could too."

"Doesn't he get a say?" we both spin round to see the naked man in the bedroom doorway. *"What are you doing, Mei?"* It's not put unkindly.

"I wanted her to cuddle me. So much is changing, so much is exciting, but I want someone's arms around me."

He spreads his arms, open-handed, in a helpless gesture towards me, "I guess we're all bringing our hidden needs to this little party. Mei, take your robe off and come here."

There's a brief look of fear on her face, she looks to me, I nod to her. She throws the robe aside and rushes to him and he holds her tenderly, looking over her shoulder at me with a helpless look on his face.

"I can see only one solution to this," I say, smiling at him. She looks round at me but snuggles even closer to his body. I'm guessing his cock is rising and she's intrigued. It's a few hours since he and I came, and I'm strangely enraptured by the sight of their two naked bodies embracing. I move towards them and stroke them, looking up at him, "Would you mind the top taking control for a while?"

"I think I'd like to know what's on the top's mind."

Mei is just holding him; she's had two weeks of my adventures and isn't going to be reluctant.

"The young lady is gay and, for the future health of what will be an important business relationship for both of you, you can be very glad about that. It shouldn't get complicated. But I don't want her closing herself off from experiences and adventures — and you have, I'm afraid, a lovely and responsive body, so there are things I'd like you to show her. Shall we go and lie down?"

I let them lie on the bed and cuddle while I arrange some subdued lighting — it's good, the hotel's not all bad — and the bed's a wonderful size for a threesome.

I lie down, and we have Mei between us. I reach across and touch him, I don't want her presented with an insurmountable challenge, but he rises quickly. He leans towards her and kisses her lightly on the lips. I let go of him and guide her hand towards him. Her reluctance is merely a show, she soon has a firm grip and is wanking vigorously. "I think that's quite hard, Mei," she slows, and he sighs, and is probably growing stiffer. They've stopped kissing now and he's smiling at her, and then, sometimes, at me. I lean across and kiss him.

"Our Mei," I'm looking directly into his eyes, she's now looking down, admiring her work "has wonderful oral skills, I can vouch for that, she licks me as well as anyone." If she's been used to men the size of Harry, however, the cock in her hand must be a surprise, but she seems focused and fascinated, "But she has a strange reluctance to orally engage the penis."

"No, I don't," she says quickly, disingenuously.

"Well, we'll have a chance to find out now, if Alphonse agrees..." he smiles and nods. "OK, let me take a moment to show you." He quickly adopts last night's position and I kneel between his legs. He has a lovely cock, and it probably helps that he's come already tonight. He's stiff now, and long. I can't see if she's surprised, I'm focused on his cock and his eyes.

I disengage a little, turn to her, to see her observing closely, so I begin this weird tutorial. I lick the underside of his head, run my tongue up and down, then slowly take the head in my mouth with minimal pressure. I look up and say, "If he's good, you can enjoy that for ages; you're controlling, not him. No hands on the head are acceptable unless it's what you want —

and I quite like it sometimes if the top is good. But here, change places for a while."

I think it's only a feigned reluctance. I snuggle under his arm and watch her. She's being a little tentative. "I said you were gripping too hard before, but you can lick a bit firmer now — I think he'll control himself well… that's it, now suck the head a bit firmer." He's gasping a little now and closing his eyes and smiling. I'm just starting to feel a little piqued when he turns his head and kisses me — it becomes quite passionate, but then we hear a 'hey!' and look down to see Mei, still holding his cock, but eyeing us as though she feels left out.

"We'll stop kissing but you carry on, you're learning down there. How's she doing?" I ask him.

"Well, it was getting very good until she let herself get distracted. Try a little more, Mei, take it deeper, if you can. You have a lovely mouth, but I would love it if it felt greedier."

Her hero had spoken, and first she sucks the head very hard and then, slowly, experiments to see how much she can take. He is quite long, and there's plenty more to take when she starts choking, but still tries to go back for more.

"Woah, woah," he says, "Come up now and kiss me."

I can tell she's tempted to sit on him; she looks at each of us — and we don't encourage her.

"That was lovely, my darling, but I think you've earned the right to be in the middle," he says. Now she looks puzzled. "Just let me get behind you and let Isobel kiss you."

"Ah!" she looks happy with that, squeezes between us and sticks her bum in the air.

He's very good with her. I'm kissing her and I've slid my fingers on to her clit — but I'm going to be careful with that — I don't want her coming quickly. There's more I want her to learn. But while I'm here I can play with his cock and his balls. I get a smile and a shake of the head from him — so, he's getting close, too.

Mei's obviously happy; her kisses are warm and fervent, broken by occasional gasps of 'touch me again'. No, dear, not yet, we must take your education on a stage.

"Alphonse," I say, very calmly, "would you say that was a pretty arse?"

"It's a very pretty arse!" It isn't, of course, but he's a gentleman.

Mei has realised what the next idea is and cries, "No!" a little horror-struck. I'm not sure where her hang-ups lie, but I'm reaching into the bedside drawer for the tube of lube.

I wave it around. "What do you think Alphonse? You'd love some arse, wouldn't you?"

I'm turning around now, I'm beside Mei, starting to edge my bum up. "I'd love all of that lovely, long cock all the way up my bum. It is the most gorgeous feeling!"

She looks over her shoulder, "You will be careful, won't you? You are very big."

Wittingly or not, if she can just remember that one line, she'll be able to enjoy a few little hetero adventures.

But now my job is to get her ready. Her face is down in the pillow, he and I are smiling conspiratorially. I squirt a big dollop between her cheeks. I love watching his cock going in and out, but he's being rather careful. Maybe that's not a bad way to start but, if he and I ever get round to this, I'm going to insist on everything. But for now, I'm playing with her, making sure the lube is well distributed. It's enormous fun for me, pushing one, then two, fingers into her arse and playing with his cock — but then he gasps and shakes his head. OK, Alphonse, top's honour, this is for you two — and there's no point in letting you come now — I want her to have a real cock up her bum. Obviously, a strap-on is more reliable, but there are few feelings as overwhelming as a big cock losing control in your arse. So, I pull my fingers out, I put my hands on her cheeks and start to stretch her. He is lovely and stiff and shiny — and there's quite a loud "Oh!" from Mei when he squeezes the head in. But it's not so loud, she can obviously cope, which is what I'd expected from the brief playtime she'd permitted.

Now I lie on my back beside her and she starts to kiss me. Initially it feels more like gratitude than passion, but, as I start to stroke her, and I can feel how much he is pushing, she is quickly overwhelmed. So is he, bless him, as I tickle his balls while I'm rubbing her clit. Ah, my dears, she's screeching, but obviously wants all of him. And he's looking at me, smiling and nodding, while he's pushing deeper and deeper and he frees one hand to rub my clit. Yes, I have found it a massive turn-on and I'm coming too; a little behind them, but every bit as loud and I find them laughing and smiling at me as I come down from my high.

Wow! Hadn't expected that.

It was sweet after that. We slept for a while, with Mei in the middle, but when I woke, they'd both gone.

I trust myself to deal with any emotional aftermath, of course, but there is a danger that Mei might have some issues. I hope not. I really do think she'll understand herself better now.

38

I needn't have worried. That was eighteen months ago and, apart from a few emotional outbursts — from each of us, it must be said — there were no other consequences.

But the outbursts have all been prompted by how we've all been working, not the relationships. I've never had work so intense.

Before I left the Philippines, Alphonse told me of a call he'd had from Peter. Was I really thinking of setting up a design business in Asia? Claudia had spoken to him on their way back. This is Peter's way, apparently; it's how Claudia started. He gives guarantees and covers any losses in the first three years. Alphonse and Mei were keen, they could see benefits to how they were managing property, but the most decisive step was talking to Daiyu about it. She thought it was an excellent idea and came straight out with the thought that she should join me. When we got round to discussing it, she wanted a break from Yang Lijun, our John, who'd been dallying with younger models anyway. So, it suited him too. He's our biggest client out there. We run Allen Chou Li out of Hong Kong.

I'd never have started so lavish, but Peter and Alphonse insisted and, to be fair, we've been busier than I could ever have imagined.

Li? Is Harry, the boy is a wonderful salesman — and has lots of contacts.

Mei had recommended him. I thought she'd just been trying to push him out of resorts and properties, but Daiyu (she's the Chou on our nameplate) spoke warmly of him. I had, as you can imagine, an interesting conversation with him — but I was very clear that our relationship would be entirely professional. The poor boy looked relieved, but I'd given him a clear briefing of what I expected from him and, within a year, Daiyu and I agreed to add his name on the door.

Yes, he had a little weep, and I got a very big hug. As Daiyu said, it's probably the first time in his life that he's been recognised for something he's done, rather than been given something because of some strange connection with the Shen family. That made me think, of course, of Mei's position, and I wondered if Harry had the same shady paternity. I mentioned it to Alphonse; he told me not to be ridiculous. Hmm.

Alphonse has been even busier than I — and he's still been dealing with his emotional issues, although they do seem to be resolving themselves.

He met up with Lee again. They danced around each other and decided they should meet. Claudia and I spoke about it at the time; we talk each month, mostly business. I guess she's safeguarding Peter's money, but she's very good on organisations; that's helped me beef up the London operation — being global gets you bigger clients and bigger projects — and she's helped me let go and trust people more. But she was worried about him, of course, and I was seeing more of him, since it was all unfolding out here.

He and Lee were together for a time, but I could tell it wasn't developing well, and we met up one late night in HK after he'd had a few days in Shanghai — "I don't think I'm cut out for monogamy, Sades," (yes, that's his pet name for me now), he'd said, "and Lee seems to set a great store by it. I think he's a wonderful man, he's very loving, kind, and sensitive — but a bit damaged, not really able to function independently. It's funny how that man's bastards are doing better than his legitimate children."

You see, this is when I knew he'd been bullshitting me about Harry. Never mind, no-one has to know. The Lee/Lou switch, though, was something we needed to know about. Irrelevant, you could say, because Mei is leading everything, with Lou assigned to 'special projects' but it was a big thing and could have been very disruptive, had Peter taken a different view. I couldn't talk to Alphonse about it, he was too wrapped up with Lee, but, funnily enough, Claudia — having discussed it with Peter, I assumed — and Daiyu — who would have spoken to Yang Lijun — had a similar perspective: yes, the old guy was homophobic, and hated having a gay son, but he didn't want his interest represented by someone who was too close to Alphonse. His predominant reason was how his business was going to be run, and everything else was just subservient to that.

Anyway, I think Alphonse is far enough past it now. I'll talk to him when he wakes up.

www.ingramcontent.com/pod-product-compliance
Lightning Source LLC
Chambersburg PA
CBHW032043050726
47590CB00001B/113